FILE UNDER:
MISSING

Also by Sarah Lacey
FILE UNDER: DECEASED

FILE UNDER:
MISSING

Sarah Lacey

St. Martin's Press
New York

Library of Congress Cataloging-in-Publication Data

Lacey, Sarah.
    File under—missing / Sarah Lacey.
        p.   cm.
    "A Thomas Dunne book."
    ISBN 0-312-10982-2
    1. Government investigators—England—Fiction.
    2. Women detectives—England—Fiction.   I. Title.
PR6062.A29F57   1994
823'.914—dc20   94-8222
                                                       CIP

First published in Great Britain by Hodder and Stoughton.

First U.S. Edition: August 1994
10   9   8   7   6   5   4   3   2   1

To Carole and Judith,
who believed it could be done

CHAPTER ONE

'Did I say dead? Lost means lost and euphemisms are a pain.' That was Dora's way of saying I'd misread what she'd been telling me. There are some days I just can't do right for doing wrong. I swear if the Good Samaritan had had my luck he never would have stopped on the road to Jericho.

My name is Leah Hunter, I'm twenty-five years old, brown hair, brown eyes, and single from choice. I was born and still live in Yorkshire, in a town that has notions of being better than its neighbours. It's a notion the local rugby team have trouble with, last season Bramfield ended up bottom of the table; that isn't something that worries me overmuch.

I suppose by now I should be used to making statements, but writing down every little thing can be very time-consuming, especially when you have to go right back to the beginning of things, like the day I let myself be coaxed into Dora's parlour for Sunday tea.

Dora is a nice lady, an ex-schoolteacher pushing seventy with a tabby-cat that gets spoiled rotten; right then it was picking its way around some figurines on the window sill. She got up from her chair and moved the fragile china out of harm's way, throwing me a look that was three parts defensive and one part calculating.

'Andy went out partying and didn't come home. I told Grace you might look into it sometime when you'd nothing better to do.' I opened my mouth but she wasn't finished yet. 'He's eighteen and an adult, which means Bramfield's finest don't have to strain themselves too much trying to find him, Grace got a lecture on how many sons leave home that way just to avoid saying goodbye to anxious mothers. Seems the most positive thing they've done is start a "Missing" file.'

She stopped looking at me and peered out through the window. I took that as a bad sign, Dora avoiding eye contact was Dora up to no good. Sure enough what she came up with next proved me right.

'I told her you could do better.'

I really appreciated her confidence. 'Thanks,' I said. 'It's nice to have a fan club but don't oversell me.'

'If you're too busy I'll tell her you just didn't want to get involved right now,' she said smartly.

Dora knows me too well, and that's a problem, she'd been a big help to me a few months back, and I was still looking for ways to do something in return. I tried for compromise.

'Let me have her number and I'll give her a call sometime,' I offered. 'Say as soon as I get the flat sorted out.' I should have known I wouldn't get out of it that easily.

Dora has an old-fashioned doorbell, the kind that has a bit of metal sticking out like a clockwork key; turning it gets a sound that's a straight cross between a rutting frog and a sick parrot. I knew from the look on her face who was cranking it right then.

'I asked Grace round to meet you,' she said heading for the hall. 'That way I didn't have to put you out.'

Nice.

If I'd had any foresight I'd have got up right then and made some excuse to go home, but I was hooked on Dora's home-made scones and what little sixth sense I had was taking a break.

Come to that, so was I. I'd taken a couple of weeks holiday to catch up on some things that needed doing to my attic home. I'm not all that domesticated and things tend to mount. Dora and I both live on Palmer's Run, she at the bottom and me at the top, and I rent her garage, which works out just fine for both of us . . . she gets a little extra pin-money and I avoid all the hassles of on-street parking.

She came back into the room with Grace and I swivelled my head round to say hello. Andy's mother had short hair that framed her face like a grey nimbus. Except for faint creases around her eyes and mouth her face had stayed relatively unlined; I never did ask how old she was but I'd guess around fifty, and unless you took a good look at her eyes you wouldn't have guessed what she'd been through. As I came to know her better I realised she had met what happened to her head on, coming through the initial grief and trauma to a place where the most important thing was her need to find answers. I'd half expected to be faced with a lot of tears and guilt but Grace didn't operate that way. I suppose it was recognising that, that made me see Dora was right in believing this wasn't a simple example of a son ducking away from a possessive mother.

I looked at the photograph she gave me. Andy had been gone almost three months and I wished I knew some easy way to find him. He didn't look all that different to any other well-adjusted male in his late teens except for his eyes, and they really got to me. I wished I had lashes that size. And then it came to me that if I hadn't known his sex I could just as easily have accepted the head and shoulders snap as a good-looking woman.

Grace seemed to know when the thought hit me. She said, 'Don't follow the line of thinking one bright CID Inspector came up with. Andy wasn't a closet gay, or any other kind come to that, although you might have it suggested to you by certain people with axes to grind.'

'What sort of axes?'

'The covering-up kind. Chopping away at other people lets you hide away from things you don't want to talk about. Andy knew gay men, and so do I. When you come right down to it, sexual preference shouldn't decide who your friends are, what matters is how they are as people.

9

That's the way I brought up both my sons, and I wouldn't want to do it any differently. Andy could handle having men find him attractive, we laughed about it sometimes, he used to say it gave him an insight into the hassle women get.'

'Learning to say no nicely.'

'Exactly.'

'Sometimes it doesn't pay to be nice.'

'Andy could handle that too.' She glanced at Dora. 'I don't expect miracles, Leah, but I've heard how good you are at finding out things other people don't want to see. I'd be grateful.'

'Grace . . . I snooped around once and got lucky, but that doesn't give any guarantee I would be again. I hope you understand that.' I had much too much sympathy for her to let her think I was some kind of genius who could ring a couple of doorbells and come up with the answer to what had happened to her son.

She shrugged.

'If you don't find answers it can't leave things worse than they are now, a blank wall is a blank wall.' She rummaged in a handbag that could have held a week's shopping and came out with one of those little shiny red notebooks. 'I wrote down some names and addresses of people he knew. They're mostly friends he's grown up with, and they might not be able to help much, but I thought it would be a place to start.'

I flipped through the pages. Grace's writing was as neat and organised as everything else about her; she'd annotated every name with a potted history of how long Andy had known that person, what they did, who they were. As far as I could tell the only thing missing was how often they changed their underwear, and I had a feeling she might even be able to come up with that if I asked.

I said, 'I can see he talked to you a lot about his friends but what about enemies, Grace, had he made any? Sometimes enemies talk more easily than friends.'

'He got into arguments like anybody else but he didn't

bear grudges. If he had enemies I don't know about them.'

I closed the book and balanced it on my hand.

'What do you think happened to Andy?'

'I think he's dead.'

The words seemed to hang in the air between us. She looked at me calmly as if she'd gone over and over things in her own mind until she could say them out loud without breaking up, but the way she said it hit me like cold air.

Maybe it wasn't me she needed, maybe it was someone like Tom. Tom Tinsley is a friend of mine with a private detective agency he started up after he left the police force. He knows all there is to know about tracking down missing people and a lot of other things too. I told her about him, but when I offered to introduce her, Grace looked disappointed; I wondered just how glowing a c.v. Dora had given me.

Dora herself didn't seem worried. She said, 'Why don't you leave Leah to think about it, see if she comes up with any new ideas.'

I drank the last of my tea and stood up. 'This party,' I said. 'Did he go with someone or solo?'

'He was supposed to be meeting up with Martin Lund when he got there, but it seems Martin decided not to go.'

It was the first time I'd caught a bitter note in her voice and I could understand the way she felt. If friend Martin hadn't dropped out Andy could still be around.

I caught myself there and stepped back from where the thought was heading. Apart from Grace's premonition I hadn't heard anything that should make me think he wasn't still around. The majority of missing people turn up sooner or later, and most of them within six months.

Over in her chair Dora was smiling with the same kind of satisfied look the cat had. She knew damn well I wouldn't turn Grace down flat, and she knew why. To begin with, I like poking around in other people's business, one of the perks of being a tax inspector is that it lets me do just that and pays well too. And right now it had another attraction; it got me out of all the things I'd taken time off to do – like repaint the flat and get the fluff out from under the bed.

I said, 'So where was this party held, and what was it, somebody's birthday, a Rave . . . ?'

'No, nothing like that. The party was at Dean Wilde's place, and as far as I know the people there were either business acquaintances or friends. Andy wouldn't have known many of them.'

'But he knew Dean Wilde?'

'Andy was Wilde's PA, but he wasn't working that night, he'd just gone to keep Martin company.'

'And Martin was going along because . . . ?'

'His father wangled him an invitation. Don't ask me why – Andy wasn't too clear about that and no one else wants to tell me.'

'Uh huh.' I found myself thinking maybe the police had been right after all, then I caught Dora's eye and knew I was going to have to find out for sure. I said my goodbyes nicely and left them to natter.

There are times when over-confidence can be a real hazard and if I'd known right then exactly what I was getting into I might not have felt so perky about it all. Mid-September is a good time of year, there's still enough of summer about so you can kid yourself winter isn't going to be a shit. I took my time walking home and thought how great it would be to play detective again. Maybe if I'd remembered how last time I did that it almost got me killed I'd have given Grace her little notebook back and waited for some other way to do Dora a favour. Sometimes I'm too absent-minded for my own good.

CHAPTER TWO

Most days I tend to get up early and take a gentle run; the distance varies depending on how lazy I feel and what the weather is up to, but it usually evens out somewhere between three and five miles, except for Saturday. Saturdays I trot down to the park and twice around the perimeter path, there's always a couple of dozen dedicated runners around and we say hello in passing and check each other's sweat. It's a ten-mile run and I can spend the rest of the day feeling virtuous.

Keeping fit doesn't run in the family; big sister Em goes in for the cuddly look. Maybe with a stockbroker husband and two moppet daughters she feels she doesn't have to try very hard, one day I'll get around to asking her – if I can manage to slot it in between her warnings about how unfeminine all my own activities are.

The day after I'd talked to Grace I rolled out of bed and did all the necessary things in the bathroom before I pulled on my sweats and went out on to the streets. It was an iffy kind of day weatherwise and I kept up a good pace, normally I'd have taken it easier but the early mist turned out to be the clinging kind that loads itself up with sulphur and grime before it hits your lungs.

As I strode out I worried at the problem Dora had given me. It would have been really nice to know what the police had on file about Andy Howe, but somehow I didn't think they'd care to tell me. That wasn't necessarily a discouragement, there are other ways of finding out things, the horse's mouth, for example – and in this case that meant Dean Wilde.

All that early morning pollution must have gone to my head, I was feeling quite pleased with myself when I got home.

I took a shower, zipped myself into black wool slacks and sweater and beat up a couple of eggs while I worked on some finer points of strategy. That's another good thing about exercise, I don't have to mess around with a piece of diet toast for breakfast.

Andy's employer had excited a lot of interested curiosity since he came to live in Bramfield around two years ago, bringing with him an entourage of people who dressed in the kind of clothes normally seen only on *The Clothes Show*. Ten years ago he'd been a big name in Rock and Pop with a group called Wilde Cards. While he'd been up there topping the charts he'd made a lot of money; enough to buy him an eight-bedroomed Georgian squat in five acres of land, with nice big wrought-iron gates to keep out the riff-raff and a wave machine in the swimming-pool. I couldn't wait to see it for myself.

I trotted down to Dora's and backed my car out of her garage. It's a nice little car, a black Morris Minor hybrid with a BMW engine under its bonnet and a close-ratio gearbox that lets it fly. I'd bought it as a put-me-on and now I didn't have the heart to trade it in, I'm a dope about that kind of thing.

The Wilde place was on the south side of town, tucked away off a narrow road that ran from the A61 to the A638. As manor houses go I suppose it was pretty small, but until Wilde had bought it, it had been part of Bramfield's heritage, left to the town by Sir Charles Braithwaite when he turned up his toes and stopped living there himself back in 1910. It had been a lot of things since then, including office accommodation, a mini museum, and a picnic place, all of which lost the council money on upkeep. A couple of years ago a bright new eagle eye in the town's legal department found a loophole in Sir Charles's will that let the town fathers take the money and run, and they hadn't wasted any time doing it.

I pulled up outside tall gates that still held the Braithwaite crest and tried to work out how to get in. I could see the house at the end of the drive looking swank with its big arched door and crenellated roof line; to build something in that kind of cream stone these days you'd need to own a bank. I got back in the car and hooted. Nothing happened so I hooted some more. This time a man in a black suit, white shirt, and the latest in Rottweiler protection came down the drive. He took a good look at the car and me and decided I was a tourist.

'It's private land now not a public facility,' he said, and reached through the bars to tap the notice that said NO ADMITTANCE EXCEPT ON BUSINESS. I gave him one of my special sweet smiles.

'That's OK, this is business. I want to see Mr Wilde.'

'You ring for an appointment?'

'No, I didn't think he'd mind seeing me, the name's Leah Hunter and the business is . . . personal.' I got a bit throaty on that last word and he looked at me in a new light. Maybe the reputation Wilde still had for collecting groupies hadn't been exaggerated.

'I'll check,' he said, opening up a box on his side of the gate. It held a telephone handset. I moved up to hear what he said and the dog propped its front feet halfway up the gate and let me see what good teeth it had. Its handler put the phone down.

'Nice little pup,' I said. 'What's his name?'

'You can drive on up.'

I hate it when people ignore what I say, it's so rude.

He called the dog back and opened up the gates. I got back in the car fast in case the Rottweiler hadn't heard I was off the menu. As I went by, I said, 'How do I get out?'

He said, 'How'd you get in?'

'I honked.'

'Right guess,' he said, and closed up again.

Wilde seemed to go for men in black suits; another let

me into the house, this time middle-aged and resigned looking, as if he wondered what he was doing there. He also spoke better English and bowed slightly when he said Mr Wilde was waiting for me in the study. He held a door open politely. It was the first time I'd met a real live butler and I itched to ask if he really liked the job.

The door closed silently behind me and I stood just inside the room and didn't see anybody. A disembodied voice said, 'Come on round and let's see what you've got on offer, darling.' Two fingers beckoned above the settee back. Nice. Why bother getting up if it isn't the Queen calling. I walked on round.

Wilde looked like an ad for what this year's sybarite should wear; paper-thin black leather pants, and a black silk shirt over a lean body that he obviously spent a lot of time on. If I'd known his tastes I'd have worn a different colour, I hated to blend in so well. His bottle-blond hair had the new wet-look, carelessly curled with a little hangover bit in the middle of his forehead. It was a look that might have suited his teenage son if he'd had one.

His eyes ran me over with the subtlety of a number eight bus. He said, 'So – you're a local bimbo. What's the act? Club singer?'

'Tax inspector.'

He stopped smiling and sat up straight. 'That a joke?' I handed him a business card. He read it and said, 'It's not me you want, darling, it's my accountant.'

'It isn't your finances I'm interested in, I want to talk about Andy Howe.'

His face took on a knowing grin. 'Oh yeah, and not about his tax return I bet. Andy seems to have been a bit of a goer. You'll have to keep off toy-boys, darling, they can't be trusted.'

I ran my eyes all the way down him and back up again, and decided that outside of his business affairs whatever brains he had stayed in his dance support. He didn't like being eyed up any more than I had and that was tough. 'If that's why you hired Andy it must have been a real shock

16

to find out he was straight,' I said sweetly. For a minute I thought he was going to have me thrown out of there, then the scowl eased off and he laughed.

'Got the wrong idea there, darling, I keep it strictly for the birds.' He came upright and his hands moved to the tight zipper. 'Want to check?'

'Only on what's happened to Andy Howe.'

He laughed again and went to a drinks table loaded with enough bottles to need a liquor licence. 'Want a drink?'

'No thanks, just information.'

'Don't fuck, don't drink, what's it like on Planet X?' He poured a glass of neat vodka and added ice and a slice of lemon.

'Alcohol bills are a lot smaller,' I said. 'Yours must be pretty high unless you're throwing another party.'

'So, what is it you want to know then?'

'We could start with what kind of jobs Andy did around here.'

'Personal assistant. Ran errands, answered the phone, ferried clients around. Nothing a PA isn't supposed to do. I run a legitimate music business here, there's nothing dodgy about it. I'm sorry he's gone, he was handy to have around. That's what I called him – Handy Andy. My little joke.' He drank, topped his glass up and got comfy on the settee again. That was black leather too. 'Sit down for God's sake.'

I leaned on the desk edge instead.

'So how long was he here, six months?'

'Started January, been gone close on three months. Didn't even bother to phone.'

'What made you hire him? I'd have thought female and attractive went with your idea of a PA.'

He raised his glass in mock salute. 'We all make mistakes, darling. I've got something more like that starting next week, have to deal with her next time you come. What else?'

I watched the vodka go down an inch and wondered if drink made him comatose or randy. Either way I needed to hurry things up a bit. I said, 'You didn't answer the last question; why hire Andy?'

'He was recommended. Jonty Lund's boy went to school with him.'

My ears pricked. 'Martin Lund?'

'That's the boy. My, but don't you know a lot of people, if I hadn't got your card I'd swear you were filth. I was doing him a favour, times are hard on the jobs front.'

'Nice thought, I'm sure Andy must have appreciated it. Do you know if he got especially friendly with any of your business associates?'

'Not that I noticed.' He held up the glass and clinked ice around. 'What's it got to do with the Inland Revenue anyway?'

'How did he spend his spare time?'

'I didn't ask.'

'What about the last day he was here, did he do anything unusual? Seem worried about anything?'

'Nope.' He held out the empty glass. 'Do me a favour, top it up.' I decided to be polite and oblige.

'So – what happened at the party then?' I said casually. His eyelids drooped a little.

'What party was that?'

'The one Andy didn't get home from. The shindig you threw for your business friends.' I lied a little. 'I hear it was quite a night.'

'Oh? Who told you that?' He took the fresh drink from me and contemplated it. 'You're not being straight with me, and I don't like that. I've had tax inspectors coming out of my armpits, and they don't ask the kind of questions you're asking. What's your real interest?'

'Personal. I promised Andy's mother I'd see what I could find out.' Sometimes telling the truth comes in handy, I wasn't sure if right then was one of those times, but I didn't see how it could hurt anything either.

'Mothers I respect,' he said. 'If she has money problems I'd like to help.'

'No money problems, she just wants her son back.'

'Can't help her then.' He swung his legs off the settee again. 'Goodbye, Ms Hunter, it's been nice talking, the door's right over here.' He held it open so I couldn't miss it. 'Next time make it a social call, it could be more fun. Never disappoint a lady, that's my motto.'

'Stick with the vodka,' I told him, 'it's a safer bet. I'm a real party pooper.'

He grabbed a handful of hair, hauling hard enough to hurt, his other hand with the glass in it went around and rammed me tight up against him. I didn't think his zipper would hold much longer it was under so much strain. His mouth tasted of alcohol with a little overhang of kippers; it was really nice to know what he'd had for breakfast.

I slammed down hard on his left instep and regretted I hadn't worn stilettos; his foot jerked sideways in reflex, letting me follow through in approved fashion with a knee that made contact where it really hurt. I hadn't intended putting so much enthusiasm into it but it was hard not to get carried away, especially when it felt like I was being scalped.

He let go the glass and it made a mess on the carpet, and then, since he seemed to need both hands for something more important, I moved away. He was a really nasty colour with breath coming out through his teeth in a high whistle. I guessed the butler might have more to clean up than just vodka.

'I warned you I was a party pooper,' I said gently and trotted down the checkerboard tiled hall to the front door. Behind me Wilde stopped whistling just long enough to say something very indelicate. I didn't let it worry me, he was under a lot of stress and I try to make allowances for such things.

I started up the car and drove back down to the gates. I could see the Rottweiler off to one side and I hoped the handler was around. I also hoped he didn't get any new instructions until Wilde had time to calm down a bit. I tooted the horn and he emerged from an undergrown gazebo near the gates and opened them up.

'Thanks,' I said as I drove past him. 'I've had a really nice visit.'

Chapter Three

Maybe when Dean Wilde had sobered up a bit he wouldn't hold too much of a grudge, that's what I was hoping anyway because it could be that I'd need to see him again. On the surface I hadn't learned much about anything except the size of Wilde's ego, but it really interested me that it had been the absent Martin's father who got Andy the PA job. Then again, that's how things work out in the male half of society – a friend of a friend who can offer a job, or make a loan, or knows a man who can.

I stopped off at a phone box and rang Grace. She'd provided me with a lot of information about Andy's friends, including Martin, but she'd missed out on Lund senior and I needed to know where I could find him. She wanted to know why I thought he could help.

I said, 'Well, that's how Andy got the job with Wilde in the first place, isn't it? Martin's father recommending him.'

She took a couple of seconds' thinking time. 'Dora told me you didn't waste time with things, you've been out to see Wilde already?'

I fed more money into the box and tried not to get impatient, it wasn't easy, I don't carry around a pocketful of loose change and I wanted to keep the conversation short.

'It seemed like a good place to start; he was full of praise for Andy and how good a PA he'd been. Did you get to meet him?'

'Once.'

I wondered if someone was with her, catching her side of the conversation and making her not want to talk right then. I asked her that too and this time the answer was quick.

'No.'

'Right,' I said. 'Well, if you can give me that address; I seem to be running out of change here.'

'Leah, I'm sorry,' she came back quickly, 'I didn't think. Look, reverse the charges next time, will you do that? You'll find Martin's father at Bloomers, but I already talked to him and he swears he doesn't have any idea what time Andy left the party that night.'

'OK, Grace, thanks,' I said, 'but maybe by now he's remembered something. I'll talk to you again later.' The liquid crystal display on the timer ticked over to zeros and I hung up and got back in the car.

Bramfield isn't a large town, some 60,000 souls in all, but with Leeds, Bradford and half a dozen smaller towns for close neighbours, it tends to import a lot of weekend trouble-makers. For some reason Bloomers nite-spot attracts more than its share. The bouncers there have to be seen to be believed.

Rumours get around; one such was that other things were on offer at Bloomers besides a flash disco and an over-priced bar, which is why the police give it a lot of their time and attention. Rumour also has it that sometimes you can get high just by breathing in the smoke. Up to now it's been a waste of police energy; that particular area of town is a rabbit warren of old buildings, all of which seem to interconnect, and when it comes to cat and mouse, the mouse wins every time.

I could see now how Martin's father and Wilde might be connected. Wednesdays and Saturdays the night-club put on live pop groups, and I made a guess the bookings went through Wilde.

I drove back into town and parked in the alley that runs between Bloomers and a kebab house, then I walked around to the front. When I went in the place smelled of stale beer with an overlay of sweat, and a woman was pushing a vacuum-cleaner around the foyer. I was looking for the office when a medium-tall male with a heavy Brummy accent asked what I was doing there. He didn't look particularly frightening in his granny glasses, but Red Riding Hood almost made a bad mistake for the same reason.

The nice smile I gave him didn't seem to have any effect, and when I told him I wanted to see Lund that didn't appear to impress him much either. 'No jobs,' he said. 'Out.'

'I have a job already,' I told him kindly. 'I'm a tax inspector.'

He'd been getting ready to give me a quick hustle to the door if I caused any problems, but it's amazing how the words 'tax inspector' tend to stop everyone in their tracks. It makes me think there's no one in the country not on the fiddle. 'Prove it,' he said.

'Prove I'm not,' I came back tartly. 'The name's Leah Hunter, so why don't you tell Mr Lund I'm here.'

He weighed things up and decided I wouldn't be that much of a threat to security if he left me there while he went off and asked what to do. After a bit he came back and jerked his head at me. I really loved his old-fashioned charm.

Martin's father obviously liked to impress, he had a blonde receptionist sitting in an outer office behind a gilt-edged white desk, and the raspberry-coloured carpet and raspberry-coloured chairs along one wall made her look like she was outside a beauty salon, but Lund destroyed the image. He wasn't exactly ugly, but neither would he make a *Cosmopolitan* centrefold. It was his nose that did it more than anything, and from the way he pushed up the hornrims with his middle finger I guessed he was a little nervous.

We went into the inner office and Granny Wolf positioned himself just inside the door. I turned my head and glanced at him. Lund said, 'It's all right, Tony, I'll see Miss Hunter out when we're through.'

Some nosy part of my brain made me wonder what it was that made it so important I had an escort. Most times I get left to find my own way out, it goes with the job.

I sat on the charcoal tweed chair Lund waved at, glad his personal taste ran more to grey and mahogany than raspberry meringue, and I told him why I was there.

Hearing that HM Taxes wasn't interested in him should have made him loosen up, but it didn't. He shoved a few things around on his desk while he thought about what to tell me and looked like a man with problems.

I said, 'You've met Grace Howe so you must know how she's feeling right now, especially with Martin the same age as Andy. I knew you'd want to give her all the help you can.'

He grabbed on to that, eager to come across as mister good guy. 'Anything I can do,' he said. 'Obviously, I'm trying to think of the best way to give assistance.'

He was still fiddling around with things; now it was his fountain pen that he was tapping on the blotter then turning over and over in his fingers. I wondered whether to tell him he shouldn't do things like that, it's a dead giveaway. I prodded a little.

'I've been out to Dean Wilde's place; I gather it was some party he threw. A shame neither of you saw Andy leave. You were at the party, weren't you?' He gave me a tight look and tried to work out if Wilde had told me that already. 'A pity Martin couldn't get there,' I added. 'He must have felt bad about that.'

'He wouldn't have reason to.'

'When his best friend goes missing? That's a lot of reason.'

'Missing? The last theory I heard was Andy wanted to cut Grace's apron-strings and moved on without telling her goodbye.'

I said, 'Sometimes the police come up with funny ideas; Grace said they'd mentioned that one to her too.

24

Personally, I can't see why he'd need to walk out of a good job to do that when all he'd need for independence is a place of his own. Grace thinks he's dead.'

The pen clicked a little faster. 'I'm sorry about that. If Andy's leaving home has made things hard financially maybe I could . . . '

'Could what? Funny, Dean Wilde said roughly the same thing. What's the going price for an eighteen-year-old?'

Lund didn't appreciate that and I didn't really care, his busy fingers said he was a man with something to hide, and if I had to be pushy to get that something out in the open then I'd be pushy. He put the pen down carefully and straightened it up with the left-hand edge of the blotter.

He said, 'I don't know where Andy is right now, I didn't see him leave, neither did I talk to him. If he had problems that night I wasn't the one he confided in.'

'But he did confide in somebody?'

'Did he? I really have no idea about that.' Lund stood up, his eyes an odd shade of hazel, his gaze remote; a middle-aged man with a hooked nose and a lot of worries that he wasn't going to share. He said, 'That's as much time as I can give you, I'd like to help but I can't.'

'You can tell me why you recommended Andy for the job,' I said without moving.

He swung his hands impatiently. 'I might have been trying to do something good for a likeable young man, what the hell would be wrong with that?'

'I wouldn't know, Mr Lund,' I said, 'suppose you tell me.' Instead he walked across to the door and held it open. People just didn't seem to appreciate my friendly face that day.

'I'll see you out, Miss Hunter.'

'That's really nice of you,' I said as I walked past him. 'I'd just hate to get lost.' He didn't react to that at all, that's the trouble with sarcasm, it's wasted on some people.

When I got outside I prowled around a little wondering where he parked his car, then I found a white Merc tucked up close to the back wall of the club and decided it had to be his. I moved the hybrid to a side-street across the main road and settled down to watch. If Lund was into something he shouldn't be, chances were he wouldn't be in it alone, and although it irked that I couldn't make a guess right then what that something might be, I guessed it involved Wilde. And if my visit had disturbed him as much as I believed it had, I thought he'd want to pass on his worries. Instinct said he wouldn't want to do that on the telephone, which meant there was a good chance he'd be taking a little drive before long.

Ten minutes later the Mercedes nosed out on to the road and proved me right. I let a couple of cars go by and then moved after him, expecting to be led back to Wilde's place, but when he headed south along the bypass and took the turning for the A636, I realised he wasn't going there after all. I stayed back and kept some traffic between us until he made a sharp left on to the wide drive leading up to Lakeside, then I let him get round the curve before I went up after him.

Lakeside is five miles out of town and calls itself a country club, which sounds much more up-market than a leisure centre. It's a swanky place with tennis and squash courts, and an all-weather heated swimming-pool with a Fun-Splash, built in and around a late-Victorian red-brick building that's all gothic arches and ornamental stonework trimming. The local wealth queue up to dine and dance in its high-priced restaurant, and when they've licked their plates clean they go upstairs and spend some more in the casino.

Lund parked around the back and went in through a side entrance, I found a handy space and went in after him. It crossed my mind that if he turned around and saw me I'd have a real problem explaining why I was there; luckily when the lift doors closed on him his mind was on other things. The motor whine stopped while I was on the last flight of stairs.

I speeded up and took a peek through a pair of swing

doors that looked like white chocolate, with a port-hole at head height on each. On the other side of them a semi-circular foyer led to the casino. There was a lot of chromium plating around and a half-dozen giant parlour palms set off Lloyd Loom chairs. Chrome-framed cinema stills of Humphrey Bogart and Edward G. Robinson shared wall space with 1920s pin-ups and Prohibition posters. I thought what a neat scene setting it was for Bramfield high-rollers. The doors into the casino itself were open and I could see the sheet-covered tables.

Lund stood with his back to me, and I knew even from that distance that the air was pretty charged. I didn't like the look on the face of the man he was talking to, it was a smooth face that would have sat well with the others on the foyer wall, and right then it held a chill and subtle menace. Maybe like Bogey he packed a rod under the snazzy wide-lapelled suit.

I pushed a little on one of the doors and eased it open. Two things were for sure, he wasn't pleased to see Lund, and from where I was standing I couldn't hear a word they said.

CHAPTER FOUR

There have been certain times in my life when the ability to lip-read would have come in useful, and right then was one of them. I gave up on watching Lund and Mr Smoothy and went back downstairs, out the side door, and around to the front where a plush reception area with ankle-deep carpet led to inner delights. I didn't exactly look like I owned enough money to join, but what the heck, who says a millionaire has to look rich? Anyway, I didn't want to join, I just wanted some information.

The letters LCC, monogrammed on the receptionist's white silk blouse, matched her emerald-green skirt, and she had a scrubbed fresh look about her that I guessed was Lakeside's daytime image. No doubt night-time activities demanded something quite different.

She gave me a friendly smile and said, 'Hi! Are you a member or just thinking about joining?'

Sometimes I lie so easily I'm ashamed. I said, 'Well, you know, I'm thinking about joining but I'd really like to take a look around the place first. I don't suppose I could just wander?'

She shook her head. 'Insurance – you know? Members and members' guests only, but don't worry about it, I'll find someone to give you a quick tour.' She didn't warn me I'd feel overdressed.

The someone was called Gary and looked as healthy and scrubbed as she did, but his bulges were in different places and they all showed. Maybe it had something to do with

28

the green singlet and white shorts. The thought flipped through my mind that working out with him could be a lot of fun.

As I trotted round with him he tried to sell me on what a great place it was, obediently I admired the pool, and the squash courts, and the high-tech gymnasium that made the one I work out in look like a throw-out.

From a window in the members' bar I saw Lund get into his Merc. I turned to Gary and gave him my best smile.

'I'd love to take a look inside the casino,' I said. 'As a member I'd be able to use it, wouldn't I?'

'Membership covers everything on offer, but the casino is closed during the day so I'd need to get Mr Cresswell's say-so before I take you inside.'

'He's the manager?'

'Owner.'

I spread my arms. 'Everything?'

'The lot.'

'I'm impressed,' I said.

We rode up in the lift Lund had used, and I stepped out into the foyer and got a closer look at the old stills. This time the casino doors were closed, but it didn't matter that much because Cresswell's name was in neat gold letters on a door to the right. When Mr Smoothy opened it Gary didn't exactly touch his forehead to the carpet, but his voice did it for him.

I tried not to feel embarrassed. Like Gary said, I was just a prospective member who'd like to see the casino, but in case that idea got the thumbs down I crowded up to take a look in Cresswell's office. It doesn't pay to waste opportunities.

Like him, it was smooth, all walnut and expensive, with a big brown leather couch in case he felt tired. In the deep window recess, an Edwardian marble clock with a sweet Westminster chime struck two-thirty, and my stomach realised just how hungry it was. Cresswell looked me up and down, said, 'Next time maybe,' and closed the door in our faces.

29

'Nice man,' I commented moving back to the lift. This time Gary looked embarrassed.

'He isn't usually that way with clients.'

'You mean he keeps it for the staff?'

He didn't answer me.

We rode down in awkward silence and he escorted me back to the reception desk and apologised again. 'Don't worry about it,' I told him. 'Having a lousy boss isn't your fault, but I think I'll skip the membership.'

I thought I knew why Cresswell had been so short on courtesy. Lund must have done a good job describing the nosy female who'd upset his morning schedule. I went back to the car-park, retrieved the hybrid, and joined the mid-afternoon traffic back to town. All the way there my stomach kept up a monotonous conversation of its own.

I took the road up past the library and the half-built multi-storey car-park the council seemed to have lost interest in, and parked near Greasy Joe's. It may not be ritzy, and I wouldn't take my mother there, but if you can stand grimy windows and polystyrene cups the food's OK. I pigged out on fried egg and tomatoes with a pile of crispy chips that would have satisfied a navvy. I didn't feel that guilty about it, usually my diet is strictly healthy, and I work on the principle that occasional wickedness stops life being too boring. The place was fairly empty; a couple of schoolboys playing hookey tried to look laid-back with Coke and crisps, and an itinerant with a piece of rope round his coat reeked gently in the far corner. I sat under the extractor fan and kept out of his air stream.

On my way back to Palmer's Run I dropped by Grace's, but inconsiderately she was out, which meant I'd have to talk to her about Lund some other time. I drove on home and tried to come up with some good reason for Lund to worry about me asking questions about Andy. Obviously he knew something he wouldn't like me to find out, but as yet I didn't have enough information to make a guess what that something might be. Telepathy would help.

Around six-thirty, I changed into black leggings and a

long sweater. Monday evenings I practise throwing people around at the Martial Arts Centre. Karate is a useful knowledge to have at one's fingertips and I like to know I can look after myself without a man around. Jack both owns and runs the place, and he and I are old friends; he looks lean and mean, but he's a real pussy-cat until someone tries to give him any hassle. When that happens he's a different kind of animal altogether, and anyone who underestimates him is making a bad error of judgement.

Jack teaches all comers from five to eighty how to deal with bullies, and I have to admit it's addictive. Dora might be coming up seventy but since she enrolled for a course in self-defence around three months ago she's picked up a lot of extra confidence.

That Monday I had a good reason for getting there early; Jack is a mine of useful information, there isn't much going down around Bramfield that he doesn't get a whisper about, and if Lund, Wilde and Cresswell were tied into anything together, chances were he'd have heard about it. I got dressed up in my neat little pyjama suit with its snazzy black sash, stowed my going-home gear in a locker, and barefooted it down the corridor. The last session was still winding up and I went into Jack's office and amused myself watching the big boys play. He has one of those clever two-way mirrors in there that let him see without being seen.

After a couple of minutes they all bowed to one another nicely and trooped off to the men's room. I let them get by, then padded out to where Jack was changing mats over. Physically he's around five feet ten, with a squarish face, round eyes and high cheek-bones that give him a thrown-together-in-a-hurry look.

'Been gettin' an eyeful then?' he said. 'Seen anything you fancy?'

'Only you, Jack, only you.' I grabbed one of the mats and pulled it around.

'You know your trouble,' he said, 'all promise and no pay. I'm ready when you are.'

31

I grinned at him. 'I have this rule about married men.'

He dropped the last mat into place and leered in a friendly way. 'Well, if you haven't come to have your wicked way, what you after then?'

'Gossip.'

'I should have guessed. Somebody done a runner on his taxes then?'

'This is private,' I said, 'not HM. A friend of Dora's is missing a son.'

'That so? Nice lady that Dora, what you want to know then?'

I told him, and he sat down cross-legged, folding up on one leg like a graceful stork, and looked at me.

'Monkey face,' he said, ''aven't you learned nothing from last time? What you trying to do round here, start a one-woman vigilante squad?'

I dropped down opposite.

'Sometimes a person can get pushed into doing things; a friend is a friend, and from what I've learned about him, Andy seems to have been a really nice person.'

'Have been? Found his bones then?'

'His mother has this feeling.'

'Not good. I heard a whisper somebody had gone missing but I wasn't paying much attention.'

'What do you know about Lund?'

'Lund's a wage-earner, he just sings along. Speaking of which, it wouldn't hurt to chat up Richie Venn.'

'Do I know him?'

'Maybe not. He's had business with Wilde and it's left him out of pocket. I hear he's not too happy about it. Might have a word on Andy, worth a try. Park Terrace, middle block, number three. Meantime . . . ' He put both hands behind his ears and wagged them.

'Thanks, Jack, I owe you.' I frowned a bit. 'What makes you say Lund's a wage-earner? I thought he owned Bloomers.'

'Nah. It's Cresswell's place, Lund's just a front man.'

'You sure about that?'

'Wouldn't say it if I wasn't. How's the boyfriend?'

'What boyfriend?'

I got up and started on a few leg stretches. It's annoying how nosy people get about my private life, anybody would think there was something odd about being solo and happy. With a sister who makes it her life's work to find me a husband, I could do without Jack adding to the angst.

He grinned. 'Still that good eh? Glad about that, he can keep an eye out.'

'You know what Jack? You're sexist.'

'Part of me natural charm. You seeing him tonight? 'Cos if you are you want to put him in the picture.'

I gave up on the stretches. 'A picture is what I don't have, and a minder is what I don't want.'

He unwound himself in much the same way as he had settled, coming up on one long leg. 'Who said anything about wanting, Leah love? Like my ma used to say, wanting's one thing, need is different.'

'I don't *need* looking after.'

'Yeh. Well, put the kettle on while I sort this lot out and we'll have a cuppa before the Valkyries turn up.'

I padded off obediently, not everyone gets access to his Lapsang Souchong.

A couple of hours later, when I came out into the car-park Jack shares with the next door pub, my mind was on Richie Venn and the business deal he'd had with Wilde that had turned sour. I didn't think it would have anything to do with Andy, but I stowed my kit in the car boot and headed for Park Terrace anyway. I can't stand unanswered questions. I was also really curious to learn why someone who did business with Wilde lived in that part of town.

Despite its name, Park Terrace is nowhere near the park, and it's no terrace either, it's a name the planning department thoughtfully gave to three blocks of council maisonettes, grey concrete, stacked two by two six-storeys high.

Richie's flat was on the second floor of the centre block, and he showed a lot of caution in the way he kept his door on a chain. The eye that looked out at me might explain why, it was an artwork in dark blue, green, and grey streaked with yellow. If that was the kind of thing that happened to him round there he was right to be cautious.

I said, 'Jack told me I should talk to you, he says you know Dean Wilde.'

'So?'

'So I'm looking for someone who worked for him a few months ago. An eighteen-year-old called Andy Howe. Do you know him?'

'Why would you want him?'

I smiled nicely at the eye and went through it all again. Near the end he took the chain off and let me in. Close up he looked like an ad from a mugger's handbook, his bottom lip was thick and puffy and I could see where a split was healing. From the way he moved I guessed there were bruises in other places too. I followed him into the kitchen and saw that I'd interrupted his supper, although he didn't seem all that put out about it. He poured me a cup of coffee from a filter jug and I sat on a spare chair and waited for him to finish eating. He had some kind of mushy stew, and from the way he winced when it went down I guessed it was a painful process.

He ate without talking but his eyes weighed me up from time to time. I squinted around the way people do when they're in someone else's place, sort of half curious, half guilty. The table had white metal legs and a red Formica top that matched the padded plastic seats on the chair bottoms, and like me he wasn't over keen on washing-up. I admired the stack of pots in the sink and eventually he finished eating and poured more coffee.

I said, 'What about Andy? I don't want to add to your problems but anything you can tell me would be a help.' He kept up the silence and I tried to work out what he'd look like when the bruises and swelling were gone. He had good shoulders and lean hips, maybe late twenties and no wimp. I wondered how many had jumped him. When he caught the way I was looking he tried a grin and it hurt enough to make him swear.

His voice was too thick to get an idea of what it sounded like normally, but I'd have guessed it wasn't northern. He said, 'Like the man in the book you could say I fell among thieves. If Jacko hadn't come by I wouldn't be around.'

'Muggers?'

'In a manner of speaking. Over-zealous bouncers according to the police, not much point me saying it was laid on; not with a half-bottle of whisky down my throat and a pocket full of grass.'

'So what's their story?'

'I'd been caught dealing.'

'But you weren't?'

'A few years back I tried the stuff, it sort of oils the wheels in the music business. Dealing's different. Dealing's shit. So guess who looks like getting done for possession?'

'But it wasn't yours.'

'Try telling the fuzz it was a gift from Wilde when I wasn't looking. They wouldn't believe that, not with all the contributions he makes, being a civic-minded citizen. That's why he hired Andy to look after his public image. A good kid, but I don't know what happened to him. I was at the party where he went missing; I hadn't found out about the way Wilde had been busy robbing us blind then, we were still thick. Last I saw of Andy he was talking to a bloke called Lund.'

'Bloomers?'

'Right.' He touched his face and I thought about Granny Wolf. His next words confirmed the thought. 'That's where I got fixed up with this. Lund's a toe-rag, I'd keep away if I were you.'

'Do you want to tell me what Wilde was up to?'

'Told you. Robbing me blind. Always read the small print; it's easy to forget that. I'd signed everything over without knowing it, copyright, music rights, every bleeding thing.'

In the back of my head I was trying to come up with someone in the rock-pop world who probably looked a little like Beau Bridges, and the name was almost there. I put him into black leather and loaded it with silver studs, and then it came. The name behind Black Brood's success, Rick Vicars, the lead singer with the voice like well-tuned gravel. I said the name out loud.

'And we had the best manager in the business,' he said. 'Least that's what we thought. You know how much he's creamed off? Around one and a half million.'

I thought about all those zeros. 'What happened to the other two,' I said. 'The same thing?'

'They had *accidents*,' he put a lot of stress on the word. 'That's what I thought at the time and that's what the coroner said, but you know what? I'm starting to wonder. Des OD'd, Len got smashed up on his bike, I mean, he rode it like crazy so it could have happened that way. I'm taking Wilde to court, doing it the legal way, but I'll be doing it from a distance after this; the way I see it if Andy's moved on he's done the right thing.'

'Did anything happen at the party? Any trouble that Andy might have been involved in?'

'Shouldn't think so, trouble-makers wake up with sore heads. Wilde gets funny about people spoiling his party.' He fingered his jaw.

'Bouncers?'

'They're the boys.'

'Might Andy . . . ?'

'No, not Andy, told you – nice kid! Didn't do drugs, didn't drink much, only bit of aggro I saw was him pulling a randy old sod off of a waitress. Don't know what it was about though, you'd have to ask her.'

'Where would I find her?'

'Hang on.' He went and got a Yellow Pages and started leafing through Caterers. 'That's the firm,' he said, sliding it across the table with his finger on a name. 'Can't help you much with the waitress though. Thinnish, youngish, reddish hair, that's about all I remember.'

'What happened to the man?'

'Don't know. Wilde went over and calmed things down.'

'What about Andy, did you see him again, later?'

He looked at me thoughtfully. 'No. No, I don't think I did. Though I wasn't around myself much after that.'

'You went home?'

'Not exactly. I saw something I fancied. When I came back downstairs Andy wasn't around.'

'What time was that?'

'Around midnight.'

'I don't suppose you'd remember the guest list?'

'Not right now I wouldn't.' He reached down a bottle of soluble pain-killers and put four in his mouth. I got up to go. He said, 'Sorry I can't tell you much about Andy, but take my advice, keep away from his boss.'

I said, 'Thanks, Richie, I appreciate your help. If there's anything I can do . . . '

'Just hope I stay healthy long enough to collect,' he said and let me out of the door. When it closed I heard the chain slide home. Richie Venn, alias Rick Vicars, was a worried man.

CHAPTER FIVE

When I went to bed I had a lot on my mind, too much perhaps because I didn't sleep well, and by six-thirty the next morning I was out on the streets, sampling Bramfield's early morning air. The sky was still that nice dark-blue velvet that nobody's managed to synthesise yet but the eastern edge of it was bleaching out. I stepped out briskly to beat the chill and a pale patchy-thin mist moved with me, smelling of wet brown leaves.

Halfway along Carter Lane a nondescript dog with a friendly face came out of a back gate and ran with me for a while; then he got tired of the exercise and went home, leaving a hot, steaming pile behind to show he'd been around.

By the time I got back to my attic home the sky had lightened up and – save for the awkward one or two that didn't know when to quit – the street-lamps had gone out. I took a shower, and read the *Independent* while I ate breakfast. Then I rang Grace and asked how much she knew about Lund and his activities. She took some thinking time again. I was starting to worry about Grace not being straight up with me.

I said, 'Grace, every time I bring up Lund's name you seem to back off a little, why is that?' I doodled on the message pad and waited. Eventually she said maybe she'd been a bit precipitate and we should leave it for the police to find Andy after all.

Great! So now I could get on with the decorating, no

more excuses.

'Has Lund been around to see you?'

'Leah, I really don't like the man. Martin's all right, but I just can't take to his father and I don't want to have him cause you any trouble. He called round yesterday about seven, wanted to give me a cheque to make up for Andy's wages and said he and Wilde felt bad about him dropping out. I told him he had it all wrong, Andy wouldn't do that.'

'How did he react?'

'Said maybe I didn't know my son as well as I thought, and how he and Wilde were upset about you going around asking questions.'

'Too bad. I think they have things to hide. Did you take the cheque?'

'I did not.'

'I'm glad about that. Did Andy ever mention Robert Cresswell, or Lakeside Country Club?'

'Only that Wilde supplied Lakeside with bouncers.'

'Bouncers? You're sure about that?'

'I'm sure it's what Andy told me.'

'Thanks, Grace,' I said. 'I'll let you know how things go.'

When I'd hung up I wandered back to the kitchen and had a third cup of coffee while I thought about what to do next. I'd read someplace that drinking more than five cups a day of the stuff is a really unhealthy thing to do; changing to decaff would be a good move. Cutting down would be even better. Tomorrow. Maybe. Today there were more pressing things, like trying to work out what kind of scam Wilde and his friends had going, and why Lund was so jumpy about it all. The problem was that while digging into that side of things might be fun, it wasn't necessarily going to get me any nearer to finding Andy, and that's what Dora had asked me to do.

I had to take her word for it that things had been going right for him at home, having her back Grace's view didn't mean it had to be true; both opinions were subjective and Andy might not have seen things the same way, maybe he *had* cut and run. When you get right down to it families are claustrophobic affairs and a lot of people duck out of that kind of set-up. But then I came up against one hard fact I couldn't turn away from – Dora was a pretty astute lady; which made me inclined to take her word for the way things had been.

So – since I hadn't any facts, I'd have to start with suppositions. Let's say Andy'd found out something he wasn't supposed to know about Wilde's business, something that could cause a lot of trouble if it got to the wrong ears. What would Wilde have done about that? Richie Venn's technicoloured eye showed one sweet way the music man dealt with boat-rockers, maybe Andy had got the same only worse.

I needed to find out more about that damned party; but first I leafed through the little red notebook and copied out some names and addresses. Talking to friends of Andy could help . . . if he'd had worries he didn't want to load on to Grace he might have dumped them someplace else, and it seemed sensible to cover that kind of possibility first.

It turned out to be a good way to waste time.

I'd set out with three names and they all told me the same thing, Andy was a great person. When I asked about Wilde I didn't get any unusual reactions; yes, Andy had talked about his job, yes he'd seemed happy with it. Worries? None that he'd passed on. And there was one other thing they all agreed about; Andy wasn't the dropping-out kind.

The catering firm that Richie had told me about handled a lot of outside functions: wedding receptions, business conferences, even tot parties for the gilt-edged nappy brigade. They also had a calorie-careless restaurant that I stepped into for a bite to eat, because the daytime waitresses made themselves a little extra money by doubling up for night-time functions. I hung back in the funnel-shaped entrance, from which vantage point I could see the whole restaurant, and pretended to give my full attention to a neat display of handmade chocolates. The tables were pretty full and the waitresses were doing a good job weaving and swerving and not dropping a thing. Maybe it was my lucky day. I trotted down two steps, passing the dragon lady who decides if you sit with the *hoi polloi* or in the money-belt. She ran her eyes over me. I was definitely *hoi polloi*.

'Just one? There's a nice little table over here? She headed for a distant corner. I headed the other way.

'This one here will do me fine,' I said over my shoulder.

'It's reserved.'

'It doesn't say so.' I moved a little closer. 'Nope. I'll take this one.' With a friendly smile I parked my bum and waited for her next move, she iced me with a long-nosed look and gave in.

The waitress was a skinny little thing who looked as if it would do her good to sample a few of the dishes she served. I gave her my order and then showed her Andy's photograph. 'Oh, yes,' she said. 'I remember him. He was really nice, not like a lot of that crowd, some of the weirdos there seemed to think we were on the menu too, if you know what I mean.'

I thought I did.

'But Andy,' I said, still holding the picture. 'He wasn't like that.'

'Oh, no, I told you, he was great; this fat slob had me backed in a corner and Andy comes charging up and hauls him off. Got a right mouthful for doing it, too. Then his boss came over and smoothed things down.'

'Do you know the fat man's name?'

'No, and I don't want to, if I never see him again it'll be too soon, he was a real lech.' I sympathised with her, I've met a lot of people like that. The dragon lady was mouthing something unintelligible in our direction. My waitress caught a panic bug. 'O-oh, look, I'll have to go now.'

'Just one more question,' I said, grabbing the little white pinny. 'Did you see him leave? Andy I mean.'

'No. No, I didn't. Sorry.' She gave a quick twist and was gone. I consoled myself with the thought that there was always another day. When she came back with her loaded tray she handed me a scrap of paper. 'I don't know his name,' she said, 'but that's his car. He left at the same time as us. We had a taxi home and he followed it, though it wasn't him driving. I was dead scared until I got in.'

'Then what happened? Did he come after you.'

'My boyfriend came out when he heard the car doors banging. He saw him off.'

'Lucky he was around.'

'Yes, that's what I thought too.' She poured out the Perrier for me and trotted off. I toasted the dragon lady and got to work on the fricassee. She still hadn't forgiven me, I could see it in her snarl.

Walking back to the hybrid I felt pleasantly well fed, and it was really nice to have had things work out the way I'd hoped for once. I day-dreamed about what a big help it would be to know what the police had on file about Andy, and how it would be an even bigger help to know who owned the registration number the waitress had given me.

If I were Philip Marlowe I'd have a co-operative friend in the local cop-shop who'd tap into the police computer and help me out, but dreaming never gets me any place, or at least, not very often. This time though it might – just supposing I could catch Detective Sergeant Dave Nicholls in an unwary moment.

I'd met up with Nicholls at the beginning of the summer when everything, including his pheromones, seemed to be burgeoning into rampant life. Gran used to say, 'Nature is a wonderful beast if you don't let it run away with you.' Ho-hum. I wished she was still around so I could tell her how sometimes that can be nice too.

I left the car where it was and walked across town to Market Street, where the local police share house with the Regional Crime Squad, of which Nicholls was a part. Then I cooled my heels waiting at the front desk and thought about how I hate asking for favours because they get called in at the most inconvenient times, and along with thinking that I tried to come up with a smart way to ease into things because it isn't easy to out-fox a fox. Even a detective sergeant with a less suspicious mind than Nicholls would wonder why an off-duty tax inspector wanted to know about somebody's car registration plate, and Nicholls knew me well enough to guess I was up to something he would think of as no good.

I appreciated his coming problem, but life is tough.

When he finally put in an appearance and I told him what I wanted, his face registered disbelief.

'I'm doing a favour for a friend,' I said defensively. That bit was true! 'It's just a man this girl met at a party and she didn't get his name.' That was truthful too. I did my best to look virtuous, but it didn't work, his face took on a pull-the-other-it's-got-bells-on look.

'Huh! I always wondered what this place was,' he said sarcastically, 'and now I know. It's a marriage bureau. Forget it, Leah, I'm not running a number-checking service for Miss Lonely Hearts, you'll have to come up with something better than that.'

'Thanks,' I said bitterly. 'I'll remember that next time you come knocking on my door.'

'And don't try the hurt feelings business. I know you too well, you're up to something, I recognise the look. If you want something specific, ask for it, but leave out the fantasies.'

It was really nice to know he trusted me like that. I put my hand over the place my heart should be; he knew it well. 'Everything I told you is the exact truth.'

'Except for the bits you missed out.'

I sighed and moved in a little closer. 'I make good cocoa.'

'I remember.'

I straightened the knot on his tie and patted it gently. 'I thought you might,' I said, and turned around. He let me get halfway through the door before he gave in. Sort of.

'Fill in the missing bits and I'll think about it.'

I bet he was a really stubborn kid. If I ever got to meet his mother I'd remember to ask.

I sighed.

'Judas! Sometimes you're really hard to talk to. It's about a favour I owe Dora – you do remember Dora? And it's also about a very good friend of hers who's missing a son the local constabulary don't seem interested enough to find. Dora thought I could do better, if I can't I'll get Tom to have a look at it, I hear he's really good at picking up balls CID have left lying around.' I said that very gently because Nicholls just hates to be reminded his friends in blue have any shortcomings.

'How old is the son?' he said shortly.

'Eighteen.'

'Maybe he doesn't want to be found.'

'Maybe. Dora thinks differently, so does his mum.'

'And the registration number?'

'Last person to see him at a party.'

He got out his little black book and wrote down the number and Andy's name. 'I'll dig a little, but I'm not promising anything.'

'No – of course not. What time are you coming round?' He got a look in his nice blue eyes I remembered well. I slapped him down gently. 'The only reason I ask is so I can put the coffee on.'

'Not cocoa?' He sounded regretful.

'The world's a cruel place,' I said, 'the way friends can't trust each other any more. You just reminded me about that.'

'I'll try to get there around seven, maybe we can go out and get something to eat.'

'Why not?' I said. 'The Pizza Hut are offering a two-for-the-price-of-one special.' He got a hurt look but I didn't let it worry me, it was the kind of guilt I could live with.

CHAPTER SIX

Big sister Emily complains a lot about my terrible lack of a social life, but what she really means is that I don't get all dressed up and go out with the girls. She's wrong, of course, sometimes – like at Christmas – I do just that, but most of the time I have other interests to pursue. Tuesdays and Thursdays I work out at the health club and usually catch up with all the female gossip I need while I'm there.

That Tuesday I went down early so I could get home and clear the washing-up before Nicholls got there; not that I'm ashamed of my sluttish ways, it's just that I hate the martyred look he puts on when he has to rinse a mug. When I got to the club the work-out room was empty and the chrome and leather Nautilus machines had a bored look. That didn't worry me overmuch, it meant I hadn't any competition when Jeff Holt wandered in with his muscles rippling in all the right places. Jeff runs the place, and newcomers walking in and getting an eyeful of all that machismo tend to sign up on the spot. He gave me one of his long, slow smiles and watched me working up a sweat.

I said, 'So what happened to all the customers?'

'Quiet time, you're early.' He leaned against a high bench and crossed his ankles. 'Maybe you should add a bit of weight, it's looking too easy.'

I said tartly, 'I'm keeping fit, damn it, not training for Bramfield's Miss Biceps.'

'Bramfield's Miss Biceps,' he said thoughtfully rolling it over on his tongue. 'That could be a good idea.'

I sat up and looked at him. 'You're not serious.'

'Is that so? Rent's up, membership's down, and the friendly listening bank's got ear-muffs on. A body show could be just what we need.'

I shrugged and got back to work. 'Well, good luck, just don't ask me to get in on it. Where'll you stage it?'

'Bloomers maybe.'

I sat up again. 'It isn't the kind of place to have a healthy image.'

'Maybe not but the boss's son works out here when he's home, little things like that help.'

'If you mean Lund, he just manages the place,' I said. 'Martin pulls iron here?'

'Yep.'

I moved on to the next machine.

'Regular?'

'Once or twice a week when he's home.'

'On his own or with friends?'

Jeff shrugged. 'Varies.'

'What's he like?'

'Still gets acne.'

'Is that the most positive thing he has going?'

He switched ankles and studied his trainers. 'Why the sudden interest, you know something I don't?'

'Did he ever come with a friend called Andy? Good looking, long eyelashes . . . about the same age.'

'Andy Howe, right? Nice fella, shame he dropped out of sight.'

'How'd you hear about it? Martin?'

'Yep.'

I gave my muscles a rest. 'Tell me more.'

'Nothing to tell, he came in alone and said Andy quit his job and left Bramfield. When I asked why, he said he supposed Andy'd just got fed up with things.'

'He didn't seem worried?'

'Hard to tell, bit quiet, didn't stay around long I remember, not unusual that though, not exactly the life and soul at the best of times.'

'Did you get anyone coming around asking questions? The police, for example.'

'Nope, why would they, quitting a job isn't illegal yet, is it? Come on, Leah, give, why all the interest?'

'Andy's mother would like to know where her son is, and so would I. Call it curiosity.'

I waited for him to tell me it had killed a lot of cats, but he didn't, instead he straightened up and flexed a few muscles while I watched and covertly admired the ripple effect. 'Well,' he said, when he was through entertaining me with his stretch routine, 'thanks for the contest idea, it could be a winner.'

'That's OK,' I said, 'just remember when the money rolls in to contribute to my favourite charity. Me.' He grinned and left me to get on with my own business.

On the way home I detoured past Richie Venn's place but he didn't answer the door, and when I stuck my ear to the crack I couldn't hear any noises from inside. The landing window had been whole yesterday, but today a pungent smell breezed in through a broken pane and hung around the stairwell noxiously. It's amazing how fast things can deteriorate. The smell seemed to be part chemical, part organic. I took a look out through the gap and found the breeze was blowing straight in from the sewage works about a half mile away. It was something Bramfield didn't list among its tourist attractions, and I guessed it was one more reason why Richie would be glad to leave Park Terrace. It was a long step down from Dean Wilde's butlered black leather to this place, and if Richie was to be believed a lot of his money had gone to pay for the music man's rich living. I wondered how many other musicians had come out of contracts with him and discovered they were losers.

It seemed to me Martin Lund's old man hadn't done Andy any favours getting him a job with someone like that.

I retraced my steps and went and sat in the car for a couple of minutes' thinking time. Across the road a single-storey infants' school had been built from the same kind of grey concrete slabs as the maisonettes; I thought about how it was a neat way to get the kids used to living on the downside of life. Then the smell of chemically treated effluence crawled into the car with me and I started up the engine and went home.

Nicholls rang just before seven and said something had come up and he'd be late. 'How late?' I said suspiciously.

'An hour?'

'Hah!'

He came at nine-thirty. By then I'd changed a clingy little plum-coloured dress for jeans and a scowl. 'I hope you didn't come empty-handed,' I said, 'because if you give me some stupid excuse about not having time to look up that registration number you're wasting your time around here.'

'I didn't come empty-handed,' he said brightly and held up a red, white and blue bucket of Kentucky Fried. Great! Just what a starving girl needed!

'Let me guess: you got buffalo wings?'

'No, I didn't.'

'Salted beaks?'

He looked hurt again. It really cut me up. I backed away from the door and thumbed him in, by then my stomach didn't care what food it got just so long as it ate.

He came past and headed for the kitchen. 'I looked up the file on Andy Howe,' he said over his shoulder, 'there isn't much in it.'

Hah! I hadn't expected there would be, an information-packed file would suggest efficiency.

I set the coffee-maker going and wished I wasn't such a cynic. 'Never mind,' I said frostily, 'at least there's a file, that's something I suppose, even if some bright ass marked it "no further action to be taken".' A quick peek at his face said I was right, a bright ass had done just that. 'It's nice the way your simple friends always look for simple answers, like the one about how Andy just left home because he felt like it.'

'You don't know for sure he didn't.'

'And you don't know for sure he did.'

We glared at each other across the table, then he yanked the lid off the bucket.

'Have some chicken.'

There's nothing like food for easing arguments.

After a while he stopped chewing long enough to tell me CID were going to dig around in things a little more. I licked my greasy fingers and didn't say a thing about it being too little too late, I reminded him about the registration number instead.

'Won't help you any,' he said smugly, 'it belongs to one of Anderson's rental cars.'

I eyed him. 'I don't suppose you took the time to ask who had it the day Andy disappeared.'

Virtue rode his head like a halo. 'You suppose wrong, it was one of six cars on hire to Dean Wilde. It's a regular arrangement when he throws a party.' He smiled at me like I ought to pat him on the head for bursting the only balloon I had.

Shit. I didn't need to ask who'd made the booking, naturally it would have been the PA's job. It was so comforting to know I'd wasted all that time. Nicholls took the last piece of chicken and said: 'I thought you'd be pleased.'

I cleaned the grease off my fingers and thought about how it'd be better to humour him since I might need a few other things looked up from time to time.

'I'm pleased,' I lied.

'You don't look it.'

'So? I forgot to tell my face, it happens that way sometimes.' The smile I gave him stretched out over my teeth like old leather. Maybe I ought to pat him on the head after all – if I could just lay my hands on a hatchet.

He hung around the place with a hopeful air and watched *Newsnight* flopped out on the settee while I settled for the rug, but after that I sent him away. I wasn't in any mood that night for dalliance.

49

I slept badly, Andy wouldn't stay out of my dreams, he was a shadow almost but not quite in sight, vanishing when I turned my head. It was a relief to wake up when morning came and haul myself out from under the duvet. I felt as sluggish and heavy as if I'd been up all night. How did I get into these things? Damn it, I'd taken time off to clean my nest not run around playing hide-and-seek. I took a hot shower, dried off and pulled on a clean pair of jeans. If slapping a paint brush around was starting to seem all that attractive an idea I must be really pissed off.

A thick mist had cooked up during the night and now hung heavily outside the window; I wondered if the sun would come out and burn it back or if this were the start of winter. Then I wondered if every thought I had that day was going to be depressing; you know how it is, some days you wake and think you can move mountains and other days a pebble is a ton too heavy to lift. I slumped on the settee and tried to work up a little enthusiasm for going out and playing detective again.

It wasn't easy.

Around nine the mist thinned out and lost a lot of its wetness. I pushed open the sash window and stuck my head out. I believe a lot of people do that kind of thing on misty autumn mornings . . . throw open the window and take in lungfuls of clean, fresh, invigorating air, rich with mellow fruitfulness.

I breathed in a ripe mix of sulphur, carbon monoxide, and next-door's compost heap, and a chill nip that brought winter that much closer. I ducked back inside like a real philistine and thought about how things never seem to work out the way they should. Take that registration number. I'd really expected it to lead me down a helpful path instead of leaving me in the middle of nowhere.

Maybe with a whole night to think about it the waif-like waitress Andy had played gallant young hero for would have remembered something new, something she hadn't been able to come up with while the dragon lady's eye was on her yesterday.

I dropped by Benson's Restaurant to find out. The place was a lot less crowded mid-morning, there were plenty of empty tables and the dragon lady was missing. I stood around for a while and watched the cake trolley unload. Bramfield ladies aren't all that hot on staying slim. My waitress seemed to have been demoted to the *hoi polloi* area which suited me fine, people get served faster if they're crammed up near the kitchen doors and fortunately I've never been claustrophobic. I sat down and said, 'Hi.' She didn't look all that glad to see me but tax inspectors get used to that kind of thing.

I watched her unload her tray two tables down and thought about how the chocolate éclairs looked really yummy, then I thought about how I hadn't gone out running that morning. Sin compounds sin and that's a fact.

She propped the empty tray on a chair and stood looking at me with her pencil poised over the little order pad.

'Coffee and an éclair,' I said. 'By the way, what's your name?'

'Annie. Why?'

'Because I hate having to say "hey you". I was hoping you might have remembered something else since yesterday.'

'Pot or cup?'

'Pot. You can guess how Andy's mother feels not knowing what's happened to him, it'd really ease her mind if I could find out.' I pasted on the look Em gives me when she's playing big sister. 'It seems to me you owe him a little help.'

She pinked up.

'I know, and, look, I'd help if I could but I don't know how I can, didn't the number help?'

I shook my head. 'Hired car.'

'Oh.'

'Working here you must see half of Bramfield come in to eat, and I expect you've got to know a lot of them by name, were any of them at the party? If I could get hold of a couple of names I'd have another starting point.'

Annie's face filled up with bad news.

'But they weren't local people he'd invited, well, not anybody I knew anyway, so I can't help out with that.' She sounded genuinely unhappy about her lack of knowledge. 'I mean, I'd like to because of Andy and everything, but I can't, can I, not when I don't know.'

'No,' I said, feeling depressed, 'no, of course you can't, don't worry about it.'

She said, 'What about the coffee and éclair then, do you want to change your mind?' What she really meant was, if I'd only come for information and I hadn't got any, did I still want to waste money.

'Make it two éclairs,' I said.

There's nothing to beat a good sugar binge when things go wrong.

CHAPTER SEVEN

It was the middle of the week already and I'd got exactly
nowhere, a real private eye getting paid as a day-man
would have to do a whole lot better than that – look at the
size of Magnum's car. I brooded a bit on that and decided
Tom Selleck had one big advantage, he always knew the
plot – I had to work it out for myself. The thought wasn't
exactly helpful, I still didn't know where to start, what I
needed was a Teach-Yourself book on basic detection. I'd
found out a lot of things that I didn't know what to do
with, like how Dean Wilde had unpleasant friends and a
dishonest streak, but I couldn't see how either piece of
knowledge was going to help any.

I wondered if Andy had kept a diary. It's something not
many males do, I suppose it's bound up with a common
dislike of sharing their innermost thoughts with a sheet of
paper. I read that revelation a while back in a piece entitled
Psychology and the New Man, and there's maybe a grain
of truth in it . . . or perhaps it's a case of when a bottle's
empty it's empty, and you can't get nothing out.

Grace didn't seem all that surprised when I turned up on
her doorstep and asked to look through Andy's things,
neither did she make a fuss, just took me matter-of-factly
to his room and left me alone to get on with it. It was a
typically male room, no frills or frippery, just basics. Not
much of the wall surface was visible under the collection of
photographs, posters, badges and other bits of flotsam
Andy had collected during his growing-up years and not

got around to dumping. I moved around slowly, getting some idea of the things and people he'd liked, or admired, until I found myself staring at Richie Venn in his Rick Vicars persona, bare-chested under the open silver-studded jacket, mean and moody over a black bass guitar. It must have been quite something for Andy to meet up with him face to face at Wilde's party.

Rooting through someone else's things is dispiriting, the room had a waiting feel about it, like it was a dog that had somehow misplaced its owner. I really hoped he'd turn up alive and well somewhere. I wondered if Grace had been in the habit of picking up after him, if not, Andy was a whole lot tidier than me, his sweaters were folded, his drawers tidy, nothing fell out of the wardrobe when I opened it. I worked my way around the room methodically and didn't miss a thing, if I hoped there might be something here to point me in the right direction there was no sense in not being thorough about it.

I found a pile of back copies of 'Q', and the *New Musical Express*, and leafed through them. They were packed with snippets about comings and goings and gigs and concerts, and slotted in between all that were news items about wheeling and dealing, with people as the base product to be sold instead of some commodity. I'd left all that Rock and Pop scene behind a long time ago, it was all hype; the right sound, the right image at the right time, and all packaged up and marketed like some glossy book. There was a time when I'd head-banged along with everyone else but I hate to be manipulated. I set the magazines back where I'd found them and turned to the only stone left unturned, a two-drawer desk under the window.

It was old, and scuffed in places under the polish, and the top held marks and stains that were a legacy of school homework. I felt bad about intruding in it but it had to be done.

The top drawer held recycled writing paper and envelopes, neatly stacked; letters from friends answered and to be answered. I read the letters like a real snoop and felt like

Peter Pry, and when I closed the drawer I hadn't learned anything useful, but I did better in the second drawer. The diary lay at the back under a slim account book, and under both was a building society pass-book. I wished I hadn't found that, it was something I thought Andy would have taken with him if he'd intended to leave home, and I wondered if Grace knew it was there. I checked for big withdrawals and found there'd been none since Christmas, so, would he still have access without a pass-book? Maybe, if he'd memorised the account number. I copied it down and put the book back where I'd found it. When I turned to the diary, most pages were blank, with here and there initials followed by a location like a bowling alley, or cinema. On half a dozen of the dates the initials were followed by the word, *birthday*. Near the end of May things changed a little and initials started to crowd up, but now they were circled and followed by question marks. Interesting. Some were followed by dates and numbers.

I closed the drawer and took the diary back downstairs with me. It was now just after midday and Grace was in the kitchen stirring a pan; when I walked in she was insistent I stay and eat with her. 'It's home-made soup, there's plenty of salad, and it'll be nice not to eat alone,' she said, clinching the matter. I thanked her and showed her the diary.

'I'd like to borrow this if it's all right with you, there are some dates and numbers in it I'd like to check out.'

She flushed a little. 'I've never looked in his diary, we respected each other's privacy in things like that.'

'There's nothing private in it, Grace, not in that sense, just memos to remind him what he had to do.' I held it out. 'Take a look.'

She shook her head. 'Bring it back when you're through with it,' she said, and stirred a little harder. I tucked the diary in my shoulder-bag and hoped it would give me a thread to follow. The trouble is I'm always expecting fact to follow fiction and it doesn't often work out that way.

The rich, warm herby smell as she ladled soup made me

suddenly ravenous. I broke a bread-roll in half. 'Leah,' she said, 'what I don't want is for you to get yourself into trouble on my account, I made a mistake piling worries on to Dora.'

'Hey, I pile things on to Dora all the time, and she piles things on to me, that's what friends are for.'

I thought about telling her how CID might be looking into things again and then thought better of it. Who knew what went on in their overtaxed brains. Maybe they'd resent having a detective sergeant from Regional Crime hinting about how they might have missed something; maybe they'd resent it enough to forget he'd mentioned it at all.

The soup was really good, and it seemed to please Grace when I told her so. We ate and chit-chatted amicably about this and that, and I dug a little more information out about Andy and his brother John, who'd joined a firm of surveyors in Edinburgh. When we'd finished eating I offered to wash up but Grace said I had more important things to do than that. I felt gratified; it was the way I'd always felt about that particular chore myself. She walked me out to the car and watched as I started it up. Her arms were folded across her chest and her face was calm but her fingers moved restlessly. There was something else she wanted to tell me but she didn't know how. I wound down the window and said, 'What's bothering you, Grace?' She smiled faintly.

'A guilty conscience, that's the long and short of it, I wish you'd leave it alone, Leah, I really do.'

'Maybe if you said exactly why you wanted me to do that I would,' I said. 'Or is it that you think telling me would have the opposite effect?' The way her face tightened up I knew I'd guessed right, I always was a smarty pants. 'It's Lund, isn't it? Just what did he say when he came to see you?'

'Dora was right about one thing,' Grace said, 'you do get right to the point, and it was more what he left out than what he put in, like how much he admired what you were

56

doing, and what a shame it would be if other people didn't see it that way and got nasty about you poking into their affairs. I told him you weren't interested in anything, except where Andy was, and he said he understood that and he'd feel just the way I did if Martin left home without even a word. It was right after that little bit of shared wisdom that I showed him the door, but I've been worrying ever since.'

'Then don't. I have good friends who look out for me, I'll be fine.' That much was true, the first part anyway, the white lie came next and I didn't feel any guilt about it. 'I'm not about to do anything that will get me in trouble with the wrong people,' I said. 'Trust me. Lund's all hot air.' I didn't add that he'd no need to be anything else with Granny Wolf to watch his back.

'I hope you're right,' she said not sounding one bit convinced. I pulled out from the kerb and waved as I went.

When I checked the rearview mirror at the T-junction, Grace was still standing there. The sight wasn't comforting, I hoped she wasn't holding back on a piece of information I really ought to know . . . mistakes like that can get people killed. I don't know why I had that thought, it came up from nowhere on big goose feet and I really loved the way it made my damn hairs stand up and be counted.

Anderson's Car Rental takes up a corner site at the north end of Paulgate, where a short new spur runs off up to the ring road. Aside from the rental business they run a fleet of wedding and funeral cars, and over the last few years have done very nicely thank you. The business had come a long way from the two petrol pumps and one taxi that had been there when I was small, thanks mostly to old Dan Anderson's grandson, who'd gone into the business at sixteen and persuaded the old man to put some pep into it. Neil was four or five years older than me, and it was him that I asked for when I walked into the office. I hadn't been in there before and I took an instant dislike to the manager, a colourless man in his mid-forties with straw-textured hair and distant, pale amber eyes.

'He's busy,' he said, 'perhaps I can help.'

I didn't think so. 'Tell him it's Leah Hunter,' I said, pushing out a lot of confidence. 'I think he'll see me.' I hoped Neil would remember the name, it'd been a couple of years since I went out night-clubbing on a regular basis. He eyed me up, I hate that.

'I really don't think . . . '

'Just do it,' I snapped impolitely, 'unless you want me to go through and do it myself.' He dithered a second or two, then stiff-necked it through an inner door whose brass plate read *Private*.

I waited around and hoped he wasn't just hiding away some place without passing on the message, it's a terrible thing to have so little trust in people. By and by, Neil came out with the manager smoothing along behind him.

'Leah!'

'Neil.' We pumped hands. I'd forgotten how enthusiastic he was with such things.

'It's been a long time, I thought you'd been whisked to the altar. You *were* going steady, weren't you?'

I shoved the memory of Will back into the dustbin where it belonged, it had been in there since the day I found out he was married. Cramming the lid back on the hurt that came up with it was a little harder. Will hadn't even had the guts to tell me, I'd had to learn it on the grapevine. I didn't let Neil know any of that.

I grinned at him. 'Hey, what gave you that idea? I'm a dedicated career girl, remember?' He didn't, it showed in his dark grey eyes but he didn't pursue it either.

'So is this social or business? I hope it's social, I could do with a break.'

I felt a little guilty. 'A bit of both.'

'Intriguing. Come tell.'

I caught the tail end of a scowl from straw-hair as I went through the forbidden door, maybe he was jealous.

Neil didn't go for opulence and that pleased me. He had a no-fuss office with a busy desk, and a grey and white colour scheme unrelieved save for bright splashes of colour from two Chagall prints on the wall. 'Nice,' I said. 'Not the kind of place to feel lazy in.'

'That's the way I like it, if I made it too comfortable I'd probably go to sleep on the job.' I doubted that somehow. He moved a couple of tweed-covered chairs, angling them so we could sit and talk. 'So, what's this career of yours, something I should know about?'

'Not unless you try to cheat on your taxes,' I said.

'Oh?' His face took on that wary look a lot of people get when the word taxes comes up. He looked disappointed. 'Is that the business part of why you're here then?'

'No, I'm not that sneaky, and right now I'm on holiday. What I want is a bit of help and I was hoping you might supply it. You hired out some cars to Dean Wilde a couple of months ago when he threw a party, I think you've done the same thing for him before? Don't you need to know who's going to drive the cars, I thought you had to check driving licences, endorsements, that kind of thing?'

'Is this curiosity or something else?'

'Something else.' I told him about Andy and how I needed to find the fat man. I hoped I wasn't making a mistake in doing that. Neil's face stayed flat, he would have made a good poker player.

'I don't quite see where you fit in,' he said when he'd thought about it for a while. 'Andy is a friend of yours, is he?'

I sighed. Why was nothing ever easy? 'Not exactly,' I admitted, and backtracked a little so I could tell him about Grace. I should have done that at the beginning, it seemed to bring him on my side. He left me alone for a while and I had a closer look at the Chagall prints, when he came back he had a couple of files in his hand. He dropped them on his desk and leaned against it. His mood had changed from sunny to angry.

'We've had someone else asking about the same cars,' he said. 'The police wanted to know who'd been driving them too.'

'Oh? Did you tell them?'

I'd kill Nicholls if he said yes.

'It seems not,' he said shortly, and from the way he said it I guessed that straw-hair might be in trouble. 'I can't help you, Leah. The way that kind of booking works is for Wilde – or whoever – to say how many cars they need, and for each driver's documents to be checked when he picks up a car. If that happened this time records weren't kept, or if they were, they've gone missing. Somebody's going home tonight sore-tailed.'

'Shit,' I said softly, but he heard it.

'I'm sorry.'

'Not your fault, you can't be the boss and the dogsbody too.'

'It wouldn't be the first time.'

I stuck my hand out. 'Well, thanks for trying, I'll just have to find some other way.' This time he just gripped without pumping, I was glad about that.

CHAPTER EIGHT

When one door opens another slams shut in your face. Some old sayings have a lot of truth in them, I felt like I was playing with Chinese boxes, whichever lid I opened the space inside was empty; but the answer had to be in one of them if I could just stop lifting the wrong lid. The solution must be to try harder, but whipping up enthusiasm for that wasn't easy, I felt bunched up with tension and it needed a physical way to get out.

Mid-afternoon when I left the hybrid in the car-park behind the ice-cream van and set up an easy pace round the perimeter path in the park I was the only runner in sight. On the hard courts two women put minimum effort into a desultory game of tennis and behind them half a dozen undedicated pitch-and-putters ambled around the hummocky course. Up on the hill a couple of dogs were getting together and I eyed them in a voyeuristic kind of way and thought about how dogs never had to worry about which was on top.

Guilty about snooping on their precious moment, I picked up some speed and left all the heavy breathing behind.

The weather had brightened since morning and the air felt cleaner, a little optimism inched in, maybe things weren't as bad as I'd thought. After one circuit I dropped down to a gentle jog, letting sweat evaporate, and thinking about how now I'd have to go on home and shower. But the exercise had done me good, I felt relaxed, my muscles warm and unknotted again. My brain had loosened up a bit too, enough to remind me that Lund had known Grace would pass on his message; he'd gone out there thinking he'd found the weakest spot to apply pressure, knowing Grace wasn't the kind to make trouble for other people, but when you came right down to it the discouragement had been meant for me. I wished he'd been a little more specific about who these people were I might upset; it seemed a shame the way he'd picked up a habit of leaving out the most important things.

I got a can of Seven-Up from a bored-looking woman at the kiosk near the bowling greens and sat by the pond to meditate on my sins. Ducks glided around and made brief forays to the concrete banks with an airless panache. They were fat, well-fed ducks, plumped up with bread and cakes. Sometimes in winter the pond froze over and they'd stand around disconsolately like feathered ghosts. I wondered why they stayed around at times like that instead of winging off somewhere and decided it must be because of the easy pickings. Ducks are a lot like people.

I was home soaking delightfully in a hot bath, sipping coffee and eating chocolate biscuits, when the telephone chirruped. Nice! Sometimes I think the damn thing knows when it's inconvenient. I wet-footed across the carpet; maybe it was a double-glazing salesman, or a heavy breather; or maybe it was Annie who'd remembered some names.

It wasn't any of those, it was Neil Anderson.

He said, 'Hi, is that you, Leah? I was hoping you'd be home. Didn't catch you at a bad time, did I?' There was a little drippy trail down the hall from the bathroom, I eyed it, if it left clean patches I might have to get around to washing the whole darned carpet.

I said, 'You found the lost sheets?'

'No, I didn't, wish I had, can I buy you dinner to make up? Tonight maybe?'

I hedged a little. 'Well, I don't know, things are pretty

busy right now what with one thing and another. Maybe some other time.'

'I booked us a table at Lakeside,' he said doggedly, 'I hear the food there is worth talking about.' My ears pricked up, maybe he was playing my tune after all. It would be a real shame to leave him feeling guilty.

'I hear they have a casino in that place.'

He laughed. 'We can try that too if you like. Pick you up around seven?' Masterful. I don't really go for that kind of thing but sometimes you have to examine options. I took a second to think about how it'd give me a chance to snoop around Lakeside again, and how if I stayed home I'd have to buy in a take-away or cook up something from the freezer.

'Seven will be fine,' I told him, 'but just so there's no misunderstanding we share the bill.' He hemmed and hawed a bit at that but finally agreed. I liked Neil fine, but I'd need to know him a lot better before I let him put me on his debtors' list.

Things happen when you use a certain brand of bath tonic . . . or so they say. I added another generous dollop of the stuff to the bath water, tempting both fate and the truthfulness of advertising.

Neil drove up Palmer's Run a minute before seven in a Porsche as sleek as a black panther, all polish and pulsing power. I was glad I'd got dressed up. The black velvet and lycra came demurely to just above my knees, stretchy enough to step out in but skinny enough to look good, and his eyes appreciated that. I wished Nicholls was around to see me drive off in style, but that's the way of things, he's never there when you want him to be.

By Bramfield standards the Lakeside restaurant was posh, with a *maître* who came forward in quick little steps and ushered us to a table with the kind of deference that said it wasn't Neil's first visit. The linen tablecloths gleamed white and the silver-plated flatware had a nice shine. I ordered melon and strawberries with a ginger dressing, with Dover sole and a green salad to follow. Neil chose a seafood platter and followed up with a steak Béarnaise.

'This is nice,' I said, looking around at all the well-heeled people and wishing I could check their tax returns. 'The *maître* didn't act like you were a stranger, d'you come here a lot?'

'Not a lot,' Neil said easily. 'I bring clients to wine and dine occasionally if they do a lot of business with me, it pays to let people know they're appreciated.'

'Anderson's has certainly come a long way since your grandad's day,' I acknowledged. 'He must be really pleased with you.'

'He was, up until he died eighteen months ago.'

I felt tactless and awkward the way one always does when attacked by a bad case of foot-in-mouth disease. I said, 'I'm really sorry, Neil, I didn't know about that.'

'No reason why you should, it isn't the kind of thing that makes the nine o'clock news.' He was right but I still felt bad about it. He gave me an easy smile. 'Look, it's OK, Leah, really, don't worry about it.'

The first course came with a flourish of starched white cuffs and we chatted and ate companionably. I tried not to think about how much it was going to cost me, everything has to be paid for and in return I was going to get a look at the casino and maybe another sneak glance at Cresswell's domain. I gave a little thought to why I wanted to do either of those things, I certainly didn't intend leaving any of my hard-earned money at the tables, and I wasn't expecting to find Andy tied to a chair in Cresswell's office. I settled for being able to satisfy a nosy interest in the size of the casino operation and the kind of people who could afford to shed enough cash to let Cresswell run it, because with Neil at my elbow I'd have to pass up on any chance to poke into places I'd no right to be.

While we ate I had time to study him; his dark blond hair had got bleached during the summer and he still had the kind of tan you can't get from a sun-bed; coupled with grey eyes, a strong chin and good teeth, the effect was pretty devastating. He caught me looking at him and grinned. By and by, the talk came around to Andy and why I'd taken on the business of finding him. I tried to explain about Dora and the obligation I felt and he looked like he understood, although he chipped in a sharp comment that she shouldn't have asked. I resisted the impulse to tell him I was a big girl and didn't need to be looked out for. Men like to hang on to their dreams of female fragility and the middle of a dinner date isn't always the best time to disillusion them.

'You could ask Dean Wilde what went on at the party,' he said. 'It seems to me he'd be as keen as anyone else to know what happened to his PA, especially if one of his guests were involved.'

'Asking Wilde about his party guests wouldn't be a good idea, he's feeling a little sore at me right now.'

'Oh?' Neil registered a new growth of interest. 'Why's that?'

I shrugged. 'I already went to his stately home to ask about Andy, but he'd been hitting the vodka bottle and we had a little disagreement about what he should do with his hands. I ended up using some forceful discouragement and I don't think he'll have forgiven me yet. Of course, if you want to help you could do a little digging yourself,' I added off-handedly. 'All you'd need to do is tell him how you've lost the records, it wouldn't even mean telling a lie.'

It took him a while to consider that, I could see him walking around it in his mind. 'Explain how it would help,' he said finally. 'I mean, let's say you had a name, what would you do about it?'

'Ask him the same questions I've been asking everyone else. Someone had to see Andy leave, and somebody has to know if he left alone. What I'm really hoping is that the waitress Andy played white knight to remembers some other titbit that will help.'

'Well, whoever this guy is he won't be local, that's for sure,' Neil said, sounding like he was trying to head me off. 'Wilde uses hire cars for ferrying guests back to their hotels, so this man's home could be at the other end of the country; how far would you travel to talk to him?'

'If it's too far I'll pass on his name to the police and let them do the talking. It doesn't matter who asks the questions as long as they get asked.'

'You said the police weren't taking an interest.'

'They weren't, but if something came up to make them feel inquisitive, and I could give them a name to go on, then maybe I could dust my hands and back off with an easy conscience.'

'I think that might be a good idea anyway, Leah, to back off. You could walk into things that don't involve Andy.' There was a flat note in his voice and I looked at him curiously.

'Like what?'

'I wouldn't know, but I'm sure Wilde has a lot of business dealings he wouldn't want the world to know about. Anyway, I get the impression you'd be glad to walk away from the whole affair if you could. Am I right, is that what you'd like to do?'

I looked at him and didn't answer. He was asking a fair question, did I want to walk away and leave finding Andy to somebody else? I hate it when I'm expected to answer that kind of thing. I picked up the menu and carefully read the list of desserts. 'I think I'm going to have the Bombe Surprise,' I said, 'how about you?'

'Shut up, Neil, you're becoming a bore,' he said, and signalled for the waiter.

'I didn't mean . . . '

'Of course you did, Leah, and you were justified, we've talked about missing persons enough for one night, it's time to change the subject.' He leaned his elbows on the table and said confidentially; 'Now, what's a nice girl like you doing in a place like this eating out with a grease-monkey.'

'Having a real good time,' I said, and we both laughed and moved on to other topics. Around nine o'clock we went upstairs to the casino. The bouncer on the door put

Granny Wolf to shame, but he nodded Neil through without a quibble, which was nice because the couple coming along behind had to hang around while the male half hunted for his membership card. The long brightly lit room was hung with three crystal chandeliers and looked like a glossy scene from *Dynasty*. I'd had no idea so many glitterati lived around Bramfield. Neil weaved his way around the tables, stopping every so often to say hello to somebody or to watch the play. As a matter of professional interest I tried to work out how much Cresswell must be taking in, but gave up on it after five minutes. Why waste time doing that when I could take a peek in his file when I got back to work. We stood around the roulette wheel for a while and watched the bouncing ball; I placed a few mental bets and lost every time. Neil said, 'If you want some chips I'll play along with you for a while.'

'The only chips I'm familiar with come in paper bags with salt and vinegar,' I said brightly. 'But you go ahead if you like.' I caught a familiar face. 'O-oh, speak of the devil.' Neil followed my eyes and raised his hand.

Wilde began to walk across the room towards us and I wondered if he remembered me too or if it was only Neil he'd recognised. The woman with him put my little black dress to shame, but her eyes were on Neil, not me, and they had the same look a chocoholic gets in a sweet shop, When they got level she draped herself around him and gave him a very friendly kiss. 'Neil, mmm, what fun to find you here.' I got a whiff of alcohol laid over heavy scent.

Wilde took her arm none too gently and moved her away. 'Let the man breathe,' he said. She swayed, looking like an out-of-season Christmas tree in her green satin catsuit and gold high heels. The chains around her neck and the bangles on her wrists followed up the gold motif. I blinked a little and wondered which Bramfield scissor-man kept the tawny mane in shape. She was smiling at me but it didn't seem all that friendly a smile and I stayed out of range. A back-hander from one of her bauble-bedecked hands would really cut me up.

Wilde said, 'Strange company you keep, Neil. Take a friend's warning, don't get in a clinch, she has lethal knees.'

'It was a little harder than I intended,' I admitted, 'I got carried away.'

'Try it again and you will be,' he promised and turned his eyes back to Neil. 'I'll be needing half a dozen cars again soon, usual arrangements.'

'Fine, glad to have the trade.' Neil hung a careless arm round my shoulders. 'Leah's really a pussy-cat, I've known her for years, you just got off on the wrong foot.'

'You do surprise me,' Wilde said on a sour note, eyeing me for a second time without warmth. 'I'll remember to get cat food in next time. Stay healthy.' He fast-stepped away taking the Christmas tree with him.

A while later I was watching a high-roller get lucky with his dice when I got that prickly feeling that comes when someone stares at you. I swivelled casually and took a look around the room. Wilde was near the door having a tête-à-tête with Cresswell, both were looking in my direction and I knew they weren't forming an admiration society. I gave Wilde a little wave . . . what the hell, he didn't like me anyway.

Around eleven, Neil drove me home and gave me a brotherly goodnight kiss before he drove away. I wondered if he was going back to the roulette wheel, I also wondered if he was a good enough friend to get the names I wanted from Wilde.

I climbed the stairs, made some more coffee and thought again about how I drank too much of it, but the thought was so well used that it didn't make any headway and I watched the end of a late TV movie while I sat and drank the stuff. When I got bored with reading sub-titles I took a quick shower and washed the smell of cigarette smoke out of my hair.

For some stupid reason when I rolled into bed I thought tomorrow would be a better day.

CHAPTER NINE

I woke bright and early, full of good resolutions. I'd slept for only six hours but it had been a good deep sleep and I felt refreshed and ready to go. Yesterday's laggard didn't get a look in, I was out on the streets with only the milkman, postman and a tired-looking paper-boy to swap good-mornings with. Over the power-station cooling towers the sun was waking up too and a fast-brightening sky promised a better day. I was glad about that, I hate it when the weather turns sulky, today the air went into my lungs like cool satin. A spent tom dragged himself home, fur spiky, tail limp, I guessed when he got in he'd hit the basket and stay there most of the day. I crossed Copperpot Drive and headed for the foot-bridge over the bypass, turning north at the other side of it and coming back to Palmer's Run with the incoming traffic over the road bridge. Having a low boredom threshold it's nice to vary the route I take.

Back home I collected a bottle of milk from the front step and picked up two more for Marcie, who lives on the middle floor. Marcie's a single parent with an active two-year-old; she's also a brilliant illustrator who supports herself by freelancing. We get on fine. I stuck my ear to her door and checked she was up before pounding on it, no sense having friendship come to grief over mistimed help-fulness. I heard Radio One playing low and guessed it was safe to knock.

When the latch clicked back I chirped, 'Hi, Marcie, I

brought up your ... ' The rest of it sort of trailed off. Marcie's yellow towelling robe looked a little skimpy on the hunk. I thrust the milk at him and backed off; he looked tousled and he needed a shower. 'I'm just the upstairs neighbour,' I said, 'saving Marcie a trail.' I backed away and started on up the next flight.

'Hey,' he called, 'the name's Greg and don't get the wrong idea.'

'None of my business,' I said, 'and I'm no prude. Tell Marcie hello for me.' I picked up a little speed and heard the door click shut behind me. If Marcie had found someone to get close to that was good, I was happy for her. I'd never asked about Ben's father and she'd never told me, I suppose I'd always pegged him up as another freeloader like Will. Maybe with Greg she'd be lucky, if that's the way she wanted it to go.

I took a shower and pulled on clean jeans and a lemon top then breakfasted on hot cheese toast and orange juice. While I'd been running I'd also been thinking. What was needed was for errand boy Lund to take a message back to his friends making my place in the scheme of things clear. Right then I didn't give a bogey what kind of scam Wilde and Cresswell had going, all I wanted to know about was Andy. How silly of me to think once I'd established that little fact they'd fall over themselves to help out.

Day-dreams are such fun!

I dumped the mug and plate in the sink, virtuously shoved a load of washing into the machine and set it going, and tripped downstairs and out the front door. The timing was perfect, Nicholls was just getting out of his car and he didn't look as though his day had started out as good as mine.

I said kindly, 'You look lousy.'

'Thanks.' He slammed the door and came round. 'I need you to identify someone.'

'Who?'

'If I knew that, she wouldn't need identifying.'

'She?' The back of my neck got prickly. 'What she?'

'A hit-and-run she. Happened sometime last night but she wasn't found until this morning.'

'So why are you on it?' I said suspiciously. 'Since when did Regional Crime get interested in local traffic accidents?'

'Since I was short-sighted enough to ask for anything concerning you to be referred through to me. I thought doing that might keep you out of trouble.' He held open the passenger door and waited for me to get in. I let that little revelation about his busybody nature pass and thought about the women I knew. Dora leapt to mind and my stomach flipped, then I relaxed a little, it couldn't be she, Nicholls knew her well enough not to need me to say who she was. I said, 'Is this a hospital visit or a . . . '

'She's dead,' he cut in flatly.

I walked around him and got in the car.

Nicholls has a lot of faults, and one of them is the way he can be tight-lipped. I hate it when I can't get anything out of him. Going to identify a body that he believed belonged to someone I knew, wasn't something I enjoyed the thought of, and he wouldn't give out any hints to help me along, no age, no hair colour, no nothing. Not even why he thought I knew her. I ran through names and faces once more and couldn't come up with anyone who wouldn't have been missed if she hadn't gone home last night – no one that is except Grace. I squinted sideways at him; I didn't want to do this.

I said, 'It's about time you filled me in on what's happening because I don't appreciate all this secrecy. How come my name came up? Nicholls, answer me, I don't have to go to the damn morgue with you, there's nothing in any law book that says I do.' He braked, leaned over and opened the door, then sat back in his seat. 'So what's that supposed to prove,' I snapped.

'Should be obvious, the door's open, you don't want to help, don't help.' He didn't look at me when he said it.

Shit! Nicholls had learned a lot since I'd first met him, he knew damn well I couldn't walk away without knowing what it was all about. I slammed the door and said tersely: 'Drive, but don't damn well expect me to confide in you any more.'

'I don't,' he said, 'and you know why? Because you never do confide in me, if you did you'd spend less time visiting the morgue.'

That was really nice of him, I appreciated it enough to ignore him the rest of the way.

Walking into the single-storey brick building gave me a nasty feeling; last time Nicholls had dragged me in there it had been to look at a body with a neatly holed head where a bullet had performed a final rite of passage. Nothing, I told myself, could be that bad again. It's amazing how wrong I can sometimes be.

There was a graze on her otherwise smooth forehead, a raw red patch that spoiled her pale skin, but Annie wasn't worrying about that. Her face looked up at me impassively, not uneasy, not accusing, not anything. The mortuary attendant had been moving his jaw rhythmically ever since we went in, giving out little bursts of spearmint that hung on the air and mixed with ether spirit and carbolic. He'd seen just about every way of dying there is and come to terms with it in his own way, now he quit chewing long enough to say: 'Neck broken. That's what killed her.' The words came out flat and emotionless, and he gave the side of her head a little shove so it moved and lolled over drunkenly. I backed off and made good time through the swing doors and across the corridor to the washroom. I wished I'd eaten a more meagre breakfast. When the heaving subsided I splashed cold water on my face and took a drink from under the tap.

Annie hadn't deserved to die like that and I didn't want to let the thought that I might have had anything to do with it enter my mind, but it was too late to block the thought out, it was already in there, and telling myself how hit-and-run accidents happen all the time didn't help at all.

Nicholls was hanging around in the corridor. He looked apologetic. 'I didn't know he was going to do that,' he said, 'I'm sorry.' I shook my head and went past him, making for the outside door and some fresh air. 'I'm sorry,' he said again. I leaned against a low brick wall in the car-park and took in some lungfuls of air, I didn't close my eyes because I knew if I did I'd see Annie's face.

The light breeze on my skin eased some of the clamminess. I shook my head again. 'It's your job,' I acknowledged. 'I'd have been all right if he hadn't . . . if he . . . ' I heaved unproductively, and leaned forward, hands on knees, taking some more deep breaths. He waited until I'd got things under control, and then put an arm around my shoulders as we walked back to his car, it felt comforting and I didn't shrug it away. There was a flat, half-bottle of Scotch in his glove compartment with about a third of its contents gone. He took the top off and handed it to me wordlessly. I scuffed at the neck and took a good long swallow. It burned a little on the way down but it pepped me up and eased my stomach.

I said thanks and handed it back. He screwed on the top, looked at the new level and raised his eyebrows a little, but he didn't complain – sometimes you wouldn't guess what a mean streak he has. 'So,' he said, staring through the windscreen at nothing in particular, ' – why did she have your telephone number in her pocket?'

'I gave it to her.'

'Keep going, there has to be more than that.' His voice had the kind of weary harshness that comes with near anger; he'd misread the simple answer and thought I was going to act clever and come up with something flip, but I wasn't, right then I couldn't think of anything but the way Annie's head had rolled. Maybe it's true about the way everything happens for a purpose but right then I couldn't see it.

I said, 'Her name was Annie and she waitressed at Wilde's party, the one Andy Howe never came home from. I asked her to try to remember who else'd been there so I could ask around a little.'

'That's all?'

I ignored the disbelief, maybe he was entitled to it.

'That's all. Nothing else, why would you think there was? Annie died in a road accident, you said so yourself, in which case it couldn't have involved anything I said to her.' A thought I would rather not have had intruded. I stared at him. 'It was a straightforward accident, wasn't it, you can say that for certain? She wasn't deliberately run down?' He looked uncomfortable.

'I don't know,' he said, 'but the telephone number was all she had, no handbag, no purse, and before you ask me, Leah, I don't know why it is you always stir up a hornets' nest when you ask simple questions either, but you do, it's a fact of life.'

I didn't even try for a smart answer to that; for maybe the only time in his life I let him have the last word. He drove me to the police station and I made a statement, and when we were through he took me home.

It was still only noon when I climbed back up the three flights of stairs to my attic, but it felt like twice that amount of time had gone by since I got up. I had an oddly disembodied kind of feeling as my mind worked to distance itself from what had happened. Setting up the coffee-machine was automatic, so was stripping off my clothes and standing under the shower long enough to get near waterlogged. Maybe I was trying to wash guilt away.

When I stepped under the shower-head the backs of my eyes were hot and throbbing. I held my face up to the spray and told myself I didn't need to hold back; it was all right for me to cry, nobody had to act brave all the time.

My grandmother had passed on that welcome bit of wisdom a long time ago. Crying wasn't something I did much of in my teens, for one thing it let people know I'd been hurt, that something had made it through the neat wall of defence I already had in place, and I didn't want anyone to know that, especially not, at that time, my mother. But with Gran it was different; with her I could cry. I don't know why I thought of her again right then but it was balm to me, because when the heat in my eyes spilled over and mingled with the shower water I knew I had her blessing to let it happen. I needn't always be tough, it was all right to cry . . .

Chapter Ten

I warmed some lentil soup, defrosted a bread-roll and forced myself to eat, knowing if I didn't make myself do that I'd spend the rest of the day with a churning stomach and feel like hell. The first few mouthfuls weren't easy but after that the knots in my diaphragm straightened out and I started to feel better.

Annie was heavy on my mind, and the thought that I might have unwittingly contributed to her death was something I found hard to handle; I didn't want to believe it had anything to do with me but I had to face the possibility that it had. The temptation to just curl away in a corner was hard to resist, but nothing I did or didn't do from now on could make things worse for Annie, and there were things I still hadn't done, like talk to Martin and hear why he'd stayed home that night. Lund had probably tried to stop me doing that already by telling his son what to say if I turned up on the doorstep, but eighteen-year-olds don't normally like to be told what to do, and I hoped Martin was that way.

Talking to him was something I'd skirted around without fully understanding why, but it's true that shock does sometimes quicken up a brain. What had bothered me was the way Grace put so much importance on his absence that night. Logically I couldn't see it mattered. The party had been at Andy's workplace, not some obscure dive where he didn't know anybody, and he'd probably done most of the organising; damn it, Andy would have known as much about the guest list as anybody, so why did it matter if Martin backed out?

There had to be something else, something I didn't know about and it was time I dug down instead of pussy-footing. Mothers don't usually think the worst when a young adult drops out of sight, they tend to keep on expecting them to walk back in the door any minute, and I knew that for a fact. Great-aunt Ruth's middle son went missing in Korea, but she kept on believing he'd come back right up to the time she died. I didn't look forward to asking why Grace felt differently about things, but it had to be done.

I stacked the dishes in the sink and worried about how hard it was to whip up enough enthusiasm to go out there and ask more questions. Maybe this time Nicholls' advice to leave things alone was good; playing detective was zilch, I should leave all that stuff to Magnum, Rockford, and the police. God, I was so stupid, tripping along gaily getting Annie killed and collecting enough guilt to drown myself in.

All the while I was thinking that, some part of me stubbornly kept on getting ready to go out. I've always hated to give up on things just because they get difficult, I suppose I'm scared of turning into one of those people who spend their lives ducking away from hard decisions. Which was probably why I drove into town right then instead of staying home.

Occasionally a problem carries the key to its own solution. Until then, Andy's disappearance had been kept hidden away in the dark and out of public view, and that had suited Wilde and his friends very well. It was now time for all that to change and for the bright spotlight of publicity to shine, and I knew just the man for the job.

Darius Dixon and I are old friends, although it hadn't always been so, once I'd bloodied his nose to show I was tough enough to play commandos. I was around eight at the time and it had come as something of a surprise to him that girls could fight dirty too. After that I got treated as one of the boys until puberty spoilt things. We'd dated a few times but it had never progressed to the real girl-boy stuff, we knew each other too well for all that.

At eighteen he'd got a job as trainee reporter on the *Bramfield Echo*, because like me he really loved to poke his nose into interesting things. Over the last two years he'd played with the idea of taking up job offers on a couple of the national dailies, but so far the lure of London hadn't grabbed him all that hard; sometimes it's fun being a big fish in a small pond.

I wasn't a stranger at the newspaper office, I'd called in to see him there a couple of times before. At the first visit I'd been expecting to find high technology, busy telephones and lots of activity, but it had turned out to be about as exciting as a tax office on Bank Holiday Monday. Television raises a lot of false hopes.

I hadn't seen Darius for a year or so and he'd put on a little weight, not much, but enough to take away the too-busy-to-eat look he'd always had before. It suited him and he looked pleased when I told him so. We spent some time catching up on this and that and then I got down to what I'd come to tell him; I saw lights wink on behind his eyes as he scented something good and smelly hiding in the compost heap.

When he got busy making notes I knew he wasn't going to let me down; I felt really pleased about that. The way I saw things I'd come up with a sweet way to cause maximum aggravation for Dean Wilde and his friends without putting myself up as an Aunt Sally, and that had to be good. I trotted out of the *Echo*'s big glass doors knowing Darius would be bothering them with some difficult questions.

Unwanted publicity occasionally moves mountains . . . ask any Cabinet Minister . . . and with Darius acting as stringer for two of the nationals, and given the extra little fillip of a tie-in with an ex-pop star like Wilde, there was an even chance of Andy's story being taken up by the dailies. It might be a few years since Wilde had strutted his stuff, but he was still well enough remembered to create a bit of interest, especially in the middle of a news famine when there was nothing much happening at home and everybody was getting bored with wars in hard-to-pronounce places.

I had an extra reason to go talk to Grace again now, I couldn't risk her opening up her newspaper and finding Andy's face looking out at her. I hoped she wouldn't mind me passing on his photograph like that, but it seemed to me the more people we had out looking for him, the more chance there was that he'd be found. I felt really pleased to have done something positive; self-satisfaction is a sin I suffer from a lot!

Darius had said he'd try to find time to dig through the masses of back files in the *Echo*'s cuttings room to see if there was anything there that might be helpful, and I'd grabbed at the offer, guessing it had been made out of spontaneous gratitude since the lead story before I dropped in had been a skating hamster. Darius must have seen some disbelief on my face when he told me about that, because he'd dug into the chaos on his desk and come up with a black and white print captioned: LOCAL ATHLETE MAKES GOOD – HARRY THE HAMSTER SKATES TO STARDOM.

'Things are that slow?' I said.

'They were a while ago but not any more.' He'd jiggled the notes he'd made and looked happy.

It's really nice to help people, especially when it can be done without any sweat.

I trotted round to the car-park at the back of the building where I'd left the hybrid and waited for a while. A couple of minutes later Darius slammed into his Escort and did a tyre-squealing exit. Very flash. He gave me a little wave as he went to show he knew I was there, checking up on him.

I felt a little more cheerful; like all good reporters he would check his story at source and I hoped Wilde enjoyed the experience. I also hoped Darius would remember not to tell him how helpful I'd been in spreading the news.

It was a little after three when I got to Grace's. She let me in, led me through to the kitchen, and put the kettle on without asking why I was there. 'Well, it seems Dora was right about one thing,' she said when she had the gas flame at the right height, 'you certainly do know how to put a squib under people. I had a visit from Bramfield CID today wanting to know all the things they didn't want to hear about before.' While she was telling me that she banged cups around like she really wanted to smash them, and I didn't need a degree in psychology to tell me she was as tense as a drum-skin and angry with it.

'I think we could maybe look on that as making headway,' I said cautiously, 'having CID show an interest has to be good, they can ask a lot more questions than I could get away with, and they tend to get really nasty if they don't get answers.'

'Hah!'

'What did you tell them?'

'Same as I told them before, the difference is this time they appeared to listen.'

'Grace,' I said, 'you already put five teaspoons in.'

She stared down at the pot then tipped the whole lot out and started again. 'I asked why the sudden change of mind, I said why hadn't they taken all this interest when it first happened. Nearly three months, I said to them, nearly three months they could have been looking, and now they come round with some feeble excuse about how it might be involved with another case and they have to look at it again. Can't even come right out with it now, and admit they were wrong!'

'What time did they come?'

'Just before one.'

Which meant Nicholls hadn't wasted much time, I could see his hand in it quite clearly.

The teapot shook as Grace filled the cups. She said bitterly, 'Why couldn't they just believe me in the first place, I told them all along Andy wouldn't just leave home, but did they listen? No they did NOT!' Slamming down

80

the teapot so its lid rattled.

She sat down at the table and looked at me. I said, 'I know this is probably a bad time, Grace, but I need to clarify something about Martin, I don't understand where he fits in. I kind of got the impression Andy wanted him along for company, but that wasn't it, was it?'

'Maybe not, but if he'd been there, they'd have come home together,' she said doggedly.

'That's all?'

'Isn't it enough?'

'I just get the feeling you're still holding something back.' She stared at her hands and didn't answer. I said, 'It'd really help if you told me what happened that day, before he went back to Wilde's?'

'I go over and over it in my mind, Leah, twisting and turning and thinking how I should have tried to keep him home. He came back mid-afternoon when I was cutting the lawn, it was hot and I must have made it look hard work because he took the mower from me and finished it off. Then we sat outside and had lemonade and chocolate biscuits the way we did when he was small, and we set the world to rights a little, and he said how he might look around for another job, go into banking maybe if he could find an opening because he didn't like the way Wilde did business. After that he went up to his room. We had a light supper at six-thirty and a little after eight he went back to Wilde's.'

'How did he get there?'

There was a long silence and she kept on staring down at her hands. Then the words came out, desolate with misery.

'I gave him a lift.'

A little finger of ice ran down my back; sometimes people seem to be given just too much to carry. Enough that she'd had three months not knowing where her son was, without having an added burden of guilt piled on for that last ride. Maybe that was why she was heaping blame on Martin, because she couldn't bear to carry it all herself. I reached across and gave her hand a squeeze.

81

'Grace,' I said, 'it wasn't your fault, there was no way you could have known.'

She went quiet at that and I sat back and gave her some time. The tea she'd brewed was stronger than I liked but I got it down in quick gulps and tried to look as if I was appreciative, although right then I don't think she'd have noticed if I'd waved my hand and turned it into wine. After several minutes had gone by, I said gently, 'Grace . . . ? There's something I need to tell you, I gave Andy's photo to a reporter friend of mine on the *Echo*. The whole story will be in the paper Friday. I wanted you to know so it wouldn't be a shock when you saw it.' Her head came up and a bit of the dullness went out of her face. I said, 'Darius would like to talk to you about it, I said I'd ask if he could come round?'

'You think it might help?'

'I don't think it can do any harm, except maybe to Wilde and Lund, and I can't say I'd shed any tears for them. Darius is a nice person, Grace, some reporters are regardless of all the horror stories. I promise he won't give you a hard time, he wants to do a follow-up for next week, that way the story stays fresh in everyone's mind. Look, Grace, I'm no expert, I can't say all this will work miracles but it seemed like a good idea.'

'Tell him I'm grateful, and I'll answer any questions he wants to ask. I just wish . . . ' A silence came and grew.

'What?' I said. 'You wish what?'

She ran a shaky finger round the rim of her cup, then gulped the lukewarm liquid too hard and too fast so that she choked a little. Coughing made her pink up.

There are times when it's hard to know what's best, and sitting there opposite Grace was one of those times. When the spasm subsided I tried to push out a positive attitude and hoped it was the right thing to do, because sometimes raising hopes makes things harder in the end. I tried not to think too much about that, and finally I had to leave her to work things out on her own.

I took the bypass home thinking that way I'd miss the

rush-hour bottleneck in town, but I should have known better. Halfway along, an articulated truck had broken down and blocked one lane of traffic. I inched along and fumed while two lanes frog-hopped into one. I still hadn't asked Grace why she was so sure Andy was dead; maybe I never would, maybe I thought I already knew.

I got back to the flat around six and did a quick turn-around, grabbing a fast cheese sandwich and a bottle of Purdy's before I hauled out my work-out kit from the drier and headed for the health club. I'd been too lax on routine already that week and it had got me nowhere, plus which I felt corked tight enough to explode. I put as much energy as I could into the exercise routine and worked up a good sweat; I also got rid of a lot of the pent-up emotion that I'd been carrying around all day.

When I was through I showered and got back into the near respectable jeans and sweatshirt I'd arrived in. By then I was close to ravenous so I took myself out for a solitary meal at the Dolce Vita, a pleasant and friendly Italian restaurant squashed in between a building society and a bargain divan centre.

For once I felt lonely at my little corner table and wished Nicholls would walk in and join me, it would be really nice to have someone to pick a fight with, but he's mostly not around when I want him and always there when I don't.

The lasagne when it came was excellent, piping hot, with the pasta just at the right point between chewy and soft; my stomach welcomed it in with little growls of approval and I followed up with home-made lemon sorbet and espresso coffee, then paid the bill and drove back to Dora's. She opened her sitting-room curtains and waved at me as I locked up the garage; I waved back and felt good with myself for the first time that day, it's really nice to know someone watches out for you.

When I came out of Dora's gate and trotted along for home I didn't see anybody hanging around, but on a quiet residential street it's easy enough to hide and I'd only gone a few yards when my ears picked up soft footfalls coming up behind me.

It's weird how these primitive signals still work but the hairs on my neck rose like a dog's hackles. Being mugged is no fun, I knew that from experience, and with the memory rising clear in my head I didn't see why I should take chances on having it happen again. I swung round reflexively and saw a puggy-looking man with a mean face, the street-light shone right on him and I knew from the way he let his arms swing that I was a target. When he made up his mind and came in fast I straightened an arm and let him have the heel of my hand in his face.

It felt like I'd just stopped a bus. Puggy staggered back and shook his head, spraying a little blood around from his nose, then he came on again but this time there was something in his hand to tip things his way. The light caught a long, flat blade and shone silver.

Nice! I wished Jack were around to tell me what to do next. I went into a crouch, the weight on the balls of my feet and shifted in little cat steps, my eyes on the shiny steel. Behind him another shadow moved and I thought: Oh great, he remembered to bring a friend! Panic raised up a fine film of sweat, I could feel it trickle on my skin. He wasn't going to rush things, he made a couple of feints and swung gently from side to side, looking like he was set to enjoy himself, then the shadow moved silently up into the light and took a swipe at him. Glass broke and chattered on the pavement. Puggy's knees went out at right angles and his eyes rolled back. Dora looked down at him with interest and said, 'I hope I haven't killed him.'

I hoped so too. Squatting, I grabbed a wrist and found the sleep state was only temporary. I said, 'You haven't killed him, Dora, but I'd be really grateful if you'd go back indoors and ring Bramfield's finest.' She went off reluctantly, Dora hates to miss half the fun. While she was gone I took off his tooled leather belt with its bull's-head buckle and rolled him over, it wasn't easy getting the leather to hold his hands behind his back, but I managed it about the same time as he began to shift around.

84

I straddled him and got a comfortable seat. Puggy wasn't going anywhere but a police cell.

A car came up the street and its headlights picked out the two of us playing bondage. It pulled up and reversed a bit and a male voice asked nervously if everything was all right.

'Everything's fine,' I said brightly. 'We're just having a little fun.' I hoped it wasn't someone I knew. He drove on up Palmer's Run and Puggy heaved a bit and tried to buck me off but unfortunately for him Dora came back right then and added her weight to the argument. I guess we must have looked really funny out there on the street. I told Puggy if he didn't keep still I'd ruin another milk bottle, after that he was good. The thin wail of a police siren keened over the chimneys and got louder, and I thought about how I now owed Dora another favour.

CHAPTER ELEVEN

I've always been ambivalent about age but grey hair does have certain advantages, and with Dora keen to demonstrate how she felled a mugger with a single blow the attention I got from the two patrol officers was minimal. I was glad about that, with any luck Nicholls might not get to hear about it at all.

I watched Dora's admiring chronicler set it all down neatly in his notebook and kept myself meekly in the background, which given my nature was a hard thing to do. When she got to the end and offered to run through it all again if he'd missed anything, he said, no thanks, he had it all, and what a very brave lady she was; sometimes such discernment takes me by surprise.

He started walking back to his panda car where Puggy was parked on the back seat, and Dora said, 'Don't I have to come down to the police station then?'

I swallowed a peck of disbelief, she actually sounded disappointed he was leaving without her. Maybe I could let her stand in for me some time, I seemed to get taken down there a lot.

'Drop by tomorrow sometime, love, and sign a statement, that's about all that's needed. You too, Miss, if you don't mind,' he said, 'it's always useful to have a witness.' I noted the sharp drop in admiration when he got to me, after all I'd just been standing around watching while Dora did all the dangerous stuff. 'Sure thing,' I said sweetly. 'I'll be in just as soon as I can find a spare minute.'

Puggy scowled through the rear window as they drove away. I waved to him nicely, it seemed a kind gesture but I don't think he appreciated it, maybe he was emotionally stunted, maybe he'd had a terrible childhood. I gave that a little thought and tried to work up some sympathy for the dick-head but I never find such things easy.

I went back to Dora's house and we sat around for a while and drank cocoa, and talked about what fun it was to live in such interesting times. When her adrenalin seemed to have dropped back to normal I lifted the fat tabby-cat off my lap and said goodnight, it had been a long and wearisome day and I was bushed.

Back home I brewed up a darkly potent shot of caffeine, and thought about how if I was a real investigator I'd come home from the mean streets and swallow something a lot stronger than that, something that lived in a bottle and kicked like a mule. And I felt sad and shed some tears, and wished I'd learned how to say no to friends, because if I hadn't overlooked that vital step in my development I wouldn't be nose-deep in problems, and I wouldn't have had to go down to the morgue that morning to look at Annie. Knowing that little detail didn't solve anything, and it didn't help much either, come to that neither did sitting like a dejected buddha in front of a late-night TV re-run and feeling sorry for myself.

I flopped into bed around two a.m. and rolled out again about six-thirty. The few hours in between were not something I wanted to repeat and I felt neither refreshed nor rested. I hate it when I have bad dreams. Outside the night chill was still lingering and there was a brisk intermittent breeze that whooshed between gaps in the buildings and played tag with bits of rubbish on the pavement. An empty crisp packet bowled along with me for a while until it got tangled up in a hedge bottom. I didn't pay a lot of attention to the route I was taking, it was enough that for thirty minutes one foot followed another and I ended up home again.

I showered, breakfasted on a bowl of muesli and a crisp

apple, and at eight trotted back out again to get a copy of the local paper. Darius had performed wonders in the time available. Andy's photograph had been enlarged and centred under the banner headline:

DISAPPEARANCE MYSTIFIES POLICE
CAN YOU HELP TO FIND ANDY?

A couple of inches below and to the left of the photograph an old publicity shot of Dean Wilde that Darius had dug up from somewhere took up two column widths and around five column inches; level with it on the right-hand side of the page sat a view of the mini-mansion where Wilde now lived. I thought it made a much better lead story than a skating hamster but I didn't think Wilde would share my view. I had a really bad conscience about that!

At eight-thirty I rang Darius, I always like to let people know when I appreciate what they've done for me. 'Hi,' I said. 'I read your piece in the *Echo* and I think it's great.'

'Leah! Yeah ... reads OK, doesn't it, fills up the page nicely.' He sounded pleased with himself, and why not.

'What about Wilde, did you make it in to see him?'

'After he'd sent his pet Rottweiler down to scare me off. Intimidating beast, that. I told its handler, fine, if Wilde didn't want to talk to me I could write a good, interesting piece from hearsay.'

'Changed his mind fast, huh?'

'Yup.'

I said, 'I see he handed out the line about how Andy wanted to get away from home; thanks for not making too much out of that.'

'He didn't come across as a honest broker, if he had I'd have slanted things differently; I'd say getting truth out of Wilde is as easy as milking a bull. Did you mention to Andy's mother that I'd like to talk to her?'

'She'll see you any time, Darius, she's eager to help. Did you pick up anything new?'

'Nothing I can verbalise, just a hunch that digging around might turn up something he wouldn't want known. I'll keep you posted.'

'Do that,' I said. 'Maybe we can swap rumours.'

He jumped on that. 'What rumours?'

'Uh-huh, your turn first, you already got one good story, don't expect me to run around and do all the hard work while you sit on your butt and write about it.'

He said, 'Friday's usually a slack day, I might get time to look through those cuttings you wanted.' I made encouraging noises at that, it was nice to hear he didn't intend to be a laggard. Then he tossed in: 'And maybe later I'll drop in at Bloomers, have a go at Lund.'

I thought about Granny Wolf. 'Take a bodyguard,' I advised unkindly, 'the bouncer there makes Wilde's dog look like a pussy-cat.' That couldn't be the best news he'd ever heard but forewarned is forearmed.

We said our goodbyes and I grabbed a spare sweatshirt and headed down to Dora's. Much as I like her I hoped that that morning I could get the hybrid out without her noticing I was around, I didn't have time to get involved in any chit-chat about doing my civic duty at the police station – signing my name on another bit of paper wasn't all that high on my priority list of things to be done.

Dora's drive has a gentle slope and the up-and-over door is well oiled for silence. I felt really sneaky wheeling out the car without starting up its engine, but sometimes these things have to be done. When I tiptoed back to lower the door there wasn't any sign she'd heard a thing. I drove around a couple of back-streets on to Thornberry Road and headed north until I turned on to the bypass; half a mile further I came off on the M62 slip road and went east.

Jeff had told me Martin was back on campus, and with term not due to start for another two or three weeks I wondered why he'd gone back so early. Of course, it could be that he disliked his old man as much as I did, but at Martin's age sons are still usually trying to get along. My own guess was that he'd been sent back so he didn't give out any wrong answers when questions were asked, although I could be wrong about that, it's easy to get paranoid. I'd got the address of his student flat from Andy's desk, and I hoped he hadn't moved on since last year, otherwise I'd be playing hunt-the-thimble around Hull.

With term not started there were plenty of spaces in the university car-park, I tucked neatly into a sheltered corner and headed across the campus. There were more students than I'd expected, wandering around from A to B and knowing how to get there. I intercepted two who were wrapped up in and around each other and asked for the Simpson block; they looked at me with that dewy-eyed pity reserved for near wrinklies and pointed it out.

Feeling old was a new experience.

Most of the buildings were red-brick, those that weren't were concrete-faced, but there were little oases of trees that took away the bare look. I found a five-storey accommodation block that said Simpson outside, and went in through the swing doors and up two flights of beigy-brown, resin covered stairs to a blue door hung with the number B8. When I knocked the sound echoed around emptily and I hoped somebody was home. I stuck my ear to the door and thought I heard a shuffle. I knocked again, and Martin came to the door.

He had white-blond hair, bleached so pale that it was almost the hair of an albino, and gelled to a prickly spiky finish. He didn't seem happy, the bright-eyed bushy-tailed look I'd seen on his fellow students was missing. As Jeff had said, he looked like somebody with a lot on his mind.

I said, 'Hi, Martin, you don't know me but I've heard a lot about you from Jeff Holt, down at the health club, and I'm a friend of Grace Howe. I'm trying to find out what happened to Andy. Grace is really low right now, but I expect you'd know about that, I mean, being a friend of his you must be feeling pretty bad about it all yourself?'

He shrugged in a ragged, lopsided kind of movement, and shifted his feet. 'Don't know much about it.'

'Maybe I could come inside so we can talk,' I suggested.

Until then his eyes had been fixed at a point somewhere

near my chin, but when I said that they lifted and looked directly at me, pale hazel and cloudy looking. 'Talk about what?' he said, 'I wasn't there, I don't know what went on. If I had . . . I mean known . . . I'd have . . . ' The thought, whatever it was, trailed off and died.

'I'd still like to talk.'

He waved a vague hand behind him. 'It's a mess back there, you know? Sorry.'

'Can't be much worse than my place,' I said. 'Hey, I was born messy, don't worry about it.' His feet shifted again but he didn't give ground. 'Five minutes,' I coaxed, 'just five minutes, that can't hurt.'

'I don't know . . . I mean . . . Look, he'll turn up, I'm sure, you know, he'll turn up . . . ' He began to back away and I knew the next thing would be he'd shut the door on me and I'd have wasted my time again. Like any doorstep salesman I moved after him so he couldn't do that without slamming my foot.

'How about we go to the cafeteria and talk,' I said, 'I really need to fill up my stomach a little before I turn around and go home.'

His eyes were back on my chin as he considered whether he could do that or not. I wondered why he needed that much thinking time; maybe he was on something that slowed him down, Finally he moved out on to the landing and slammed the door shut behind him.

'I guess it can't hurt,' he said unenthusiastically.

We chatted our way across campus. Or, at least, I chatted, Martin kept his hands in his pockets and his head tilted down far enough so he wouldn't have to look at anybody we happened to meet.

By the time we clumped down the basement steps to the coffee bar I'd just about exhausted all the small-talk I had. 'My shout,' I said brightly as we went in. 'How'd you like it, black or white?'

'Black.'

He wandered to a table near a fire door and sat down. Great! This was turning into a really fun-time experience. I grabbed a tray, ran coffee into a couple of neat plastic cups that squashed around when I lifted them, and picked up a couple of donuts.

'I think I know what the problem is,' I said as I set the tray on the table and put a coffee in front of him. 'Your father told you not to talk to anyone about Andy, didn't he?' I sat down. 'I can appreciate that, but whatever happened it can't be blamed on you. I mean, all right if you'd been there he might not have taken off like that, but chances are he would have left home eventually anyway, it's just the way he did it that's worrying. Had he talked his plans over with you?'

That was a lot for him to work on but this time it didn't seem to take him as long. He said tonelessly, 'I wasn't at the party, I wouldn't know why he cut out.'

'That's what you believe he did? You and he had been friends a long time from what I hear, right from junior school, you'd have got to know him pretty well in all that time. Did he talk much about home, how things were between him and his mother? Were they that bad he'd have gone off without a word?'

'What he did, isn't it?' he mumbled.

'You don't sound too sure.'

He stared intently at the table. We were back to non-communication again.

I shoved a donut across to him and started dunking the other; he watched me acting like I hadn't been well brought up and followed my lead. I gave him thirty seconds' eating time, he didn't need more than that, the donuts had been economically sized to give good profit margins.

'It must be really heavy on your mind,' I said, 'thinking how if you'd gone that night he'd have got home safely. I guess you feel you let him down.'

He got pinched looking round his nostrils.

'Shit,' he said. 'Oh *shit*!' He said it really quietly like he was talking to himself. I watched his Adam's apple bob a couple of times and felt like Torquemada.

'Martin . . . tell me about it?'

He jerked up on his feet like somebody had pulled his strings and started moving out from the table.

Sometimes ideas come without any prompting, the one that swung into my brain right then turned everything I'd believed on its head. Suppose I'd been asking the wrong questions, suppose things weren't as simple as I'd thought and it wasn't just a case of Martin not turning up after all. Suppose he'd been there, at the party, all along and that's what was being covered up. I said flatly, 'Your father lied, didn't he? You weren't at home that night, you were at Wilde's. That's the truth, isn't it, Martin? That's what really happened.'

He didn't say anything, he didn't need to, he just stopped moving for a second and looked at me, and I read all the answer I needed in his face.

'*Why*, Martin?' He was no slouch when it came to moving and he was through the door before I'd got out from the table. The six heads that were in the place busy troughing swung round and watched us go; it was something to brighten a dull morning.

He headed across campus for the main road, finding a gap in the traffic that almost got him hedgehogged. By the time I'd made it after him he'd lost himself in a maze of residential streets.

I ran around for a while trying to pick up his trail, but in the end I gáve up and went back to the hybrid with as many unanswered questions as I'd come with; the only difference was they weren't the same questions.

CHAPTER TWELVE

Nicholls eyed me like I was nothing but trouble. There was a table and four chairs in the small interview room but he didn't sit down and neither did I. He had a file of papers in his right hand and from the angle he was at, a chip two feet high on his shoulder. I sighed a bit and thought how just a simple little thing like signing a piece of paper caused me strife. 'Hey,' I said, 'I was about to be mugged, I didn't ask the fat ale-can to sneak up on me.'

'According to the ale-can he didn't do a thing wrong,' Nicholls snapped. 'His story is, he was walking peacefully along minding his business when some crazy woman swung round and punched him in the face. Not content with that little act of assault she then threatened to "kick his balls off".'

'Oh, come on!'

I shouldn't have wasted breath, he carried straight on without skipping a beat. It's sad the way he gets carried away in his work sometimes.

' . . . Then some other female comes up while he's still staggering and smashes a milk bottle over his head. Sound familiar? He says he might sue.'

'Let him!' I ground out. 'I suppose he said the knife he had was for cleaning his nails.'

'Something like that.'

'Huh!' I got a good scowl going and thought about why doing what I'm asked to do never seems to work out right. I'd got back from Hull around one and grabbed a burger and chips at McDonald's before I went to sign my statement like a good little citizen. I hadn't expected to find Nicholls hanging around but he tends to pop up at the most inconvenient times. It's an open secret among Bramfield's finest that he and I have something going, so every time my name comes up some helpful busybody trots along and tells Nicholls what I've been up to. Gossip can be a terrible thing. I know now why the police informer system works so well, it's because they get such a lot of experience snitching among themselves.

I said, 'Look, this is nothing to do with you, it's a little local skirmish, nothing for Regional Crime to stripe their pants about. If it had been any other female but me you wouldn't even have got to hear about it.'

'Maybe, maybe not.'

'So where's the statement, let me sign it and get away, I've things to do. Can I help it if I look like a mugger's dream?'

'That's what you think it was then?'

'What else?'

'You tell me, you're the expert.' He lounged against the wall to the left of the door like he had for ever to spare. That was nice for him, he got paid to take his time, mine always seemed to be on the house.

'If trouble follows me around,' I said, 'is that my fault?'

'Usually it is, yes,' he came back unkindly. 'Are you still poking around the Andy Howe business?'

'Have you found who ran Annie down yesterday?' We faced each other out for a minute or so until he opened the door and started out of the room. 'Hey,' I said. 'What about this witness statement?'

'None of my business,' he said cheerfully. 'You need to see Sergeant Nolan, it's uniform's affair, not mine.'

Sometimes I wonder what it is I see in him! I stamped around the place until I found the sergeant, checked through what I was being asked to sign, and scribbled a signature at the bottom, it didn't take long. Nolan said kindly they'd tell me when I was needed in court, and I thanked him nicely and thought about how that was some more of my time I could waste. Nicholls just happened to be hanging around the front desk when I went out and gave me a friendly wave. He looked smug. I stopped by and leaned on the counter and asked if he'd seen the local paper yet. He said no, and I tut-tutted and told him what a shame it was he didn't keep up with the news.

Trotting back to the car I felt a vague regret that Nicholls wasn't part of the regular CID; if he had been I might have been tempted to tell him all the things I'd learned lately. I thought about Martin Lund and the way he kept his head down like he'd never be able to meet anyone in the eye again.

I wished I could come up with a good reason for the lie behind it all, it wasn't something anyone could have hoped would stay undiscovered; especially when Martin had problems going along with the story. I needed to talk to Lund senior again but I didn't fancy sneaking past Granny Wolf; outside of work he might be a really nice person, kind to dogs and old ladies, but I wasn't either of those and by now I'd be on his list of people most likely to get thrown out. I'd have to come up with something more subtle. Life is full of problems.

I eased out into the traffic and headed for the architectural splendour of Park Terrace. On a dull day it looked even worse and the litter had multiplied; there's something about scrunched Cola tins and old chip papers that's really disheartening. An old Capri with three bricks holding up its off-side front hub was parked outside the third block of maisonettes, and a droopingly pregnant woman with a pushchaired toddler and whining three-year-old was dragging her shopping home. It looked real hard work. I locked the car and hoped it didn't lose a wheel while I was gone.

There was a pungent fusty smell in the concrete stairwell, the kind of thing that drifts out of men's lavatories on a warm day and I tried not to think too much about it. Someone had taped a piece of cardboard over the broken window. I looked at the drawing it held with interest and thought how nice it was there were so many artistic morons around.

I banged on Richie Venn's door. He was the one man I knew who didn't owe Wilde any favours, all he owed was a sore head and an empty bank account; with any luck he might see helping me as a down payment on that. I banged a little harder and the door across the landing shot open.

'No use bloody bangin', 'e's gone, in't 'e.'

The girl looked around sixteen, in army drabs with panda eyes and side-shaved head. 'Gone?' I said.

'As in 'e don't live there no more, cleared out Wednesday.'

'Wednesday?'

'You a bloody parrot? Look, 'e's gone, an' don't fuckin' bang that door no more, you 'ear?'

'What time . . . ?'

'I dunno, elevenish, look, piss off you'll wake 'im up.'

'Who?'

'The fuckin' kid.' She was too late. A wail started.

'Aw, *fuck*!'

'He's yours?'

'No, I bloody borrowed it, din't I! 'Course it's mine, got to mind it while me mum's at work, don't I? So piss off!' The door slammed. I knocked on it gently; we'd been having such a nice conversation. It snapped open. 'What?'

'Do you know where Richie went?'

'Didn't ask, did I.' I put out a hand and kept the door open. 'You wanna be careful,' she said, 'there'll be my fella round in a bit.' Somewhere behind her the wail picked up steam.

'Look, did you see the removal van? Do you know which town it was from?'

'Might 'ave, depends wacha want to know for, run out on you 'as 'e then?'

I started a denial and gulped it down, sometimes lies work a lot better than truth.

'Always happens, doesn't it, we pick the wrong man and end up stuck with your problem,' I nodded inside to where the siren noise was still picking up decibels. 'Knowing where Richie's gone would be a help.'

'Yeah, well . . . ' She struggled a bit and decided we were maybe sisters under the skin. 'Down south, Walthamstow I think it were.'

'What about the removal firm?'

'Liver somethin' or other . . . look, I got to go shut it up, all right?'

'All right,' I said, and took my hand away. 'And thanks, sorry about . . . ' But she'd already closed the door. Life has a lot more losers than winners, and that's a fact. I took the stairs down slowly, out of sorts with myself. I wasn't getting anywhere, the more I poked around the less I seemed to know. Dora had been wrong about me . . . I wasn't all that good at finding things out, not unless I knew where to look; maybe I was going in too many directions, what did I have that was really worth keeping? Martin? Yes, because there must be some good reason for not letting on he'd been at Wilde's, and the most probable was that he'd seen or heard something that put him at risk – if that was the why of it I could understand Lund lying the way he had, the urge to protect one's bloodline can be strong.

The fat man I could scrub. He'd had a dispute with Andy, yes, but he'd left when Annie left and followed her home; he was beginning to smell more and more like a common-or-garden lech. He'd also had a driver, which probably meant he'd been too smashed to drive himself. Forget him. If need be I could always pick up on that angle later.

I could also stop picking names out of Grace's little red book. Talking to people Andy had known might tell me how many friends he had, but it wouldn't tell me much else. What else could I jettison – Neil and his hire cars? I put that on hold for a while.

Grace had said Andy was thinking about changing his job, she said he didn't like the way Wilde did business. Neither did Richie Venn, so maybe that was the place to start, digging into his business affairs. Hah! Maybe if I went right up to him and asked he'd show me his books.

I trotted out to the hybrid and perked up when I found it looked just the way it had when I left it. Across the road it was about time for the infants' school to finish up for the day and a crowd of mothers were waiting around with dogs and prams and toddlers; there didn't seem to be a lot of conversation going on except for desultory patches, but maybe there wasn't much worth talking about. I drove back home and painted the bathroom ceiling a quiet dove grey, I never had liked the original zingy apricot. The activity fired up enthusiasm; I emptied out the airing cupboard and painted that.

I can't say all that busyness made me feel homey, but it did make me feel I'd done something with the day. I'd cleaned up and got under the shower when the knocking came at my door. Maybe I should sell tickets. I wrapped up in a bath towel and padded along to see who was there.

Neil?

His eyebrows flipped. 'Leah,' he said. 'Front door was open so I came on up. Nice towel. Not everybody looks that good when they get out of a shower.' I put him down fast, flattery has its place but not around me. He reddened when I told him that. 'Look, I'm sorry,' he said, 'most women like . . . '

'Yeah,' I cut in, 'and a lot of men believe that little myth.' I held open the door. 'You want to come in and wait while I finish off?' He stepped inside. 'Sitting-room's on the left,' I said flatly, 'make yourself at home.'

I pulled on a black knitted dress and hoped he didn't plan on staying to eat, spaghetti was all I had on offer, a well-prepared hostess I'm not!

I gave my hair a quick blow-dry and went to find out how bored he'd got waiting around, I should have guessed he wasn't the type to sit patiently doing nothing. I watched him sorting casually through the contents of my wall-shelves. There wasn't much there to get excited about; books, audio tapes, a dozen or so videos that I meant to watch sometime when life got sufficiently dull, but the way he was working through showed a lot of concentration. It was the kind of thing I'd do myself if I wanted to find out more about somebody. The thought that he might have the same purpose worried me though I wasn't sure why.

I said brightly, 'If you're running a personality check maybe I should go away for a while.'

He turned around his face relaxed, like it didn't matter he'd been caught out. 'The Stones, Beiderbecke and Bach. Catholic tastes.'

'You missed out on Gillespie and Vivaldi, no point trying to find the hidden me without the whole picture. Coffee, tea or cold lager?'

He looked at his watch. 'Pubs are open, we could go for a drink.'

'I'm going to be pretty busy tonight.'

'In that case coffee then, thanks.'

He followed me into the kitchen and watched the glass jug get a quick rinse job. 'So,' I said politely, 'what brings you into my part of town, accident or design?'

'Those hire forms you wanted.' He patted his breast pocket. 'They were in the wrong file, but they're not going to help you find anybody, Leah.'

I quit spooning coffee to look at him. 'Why's that?'

'Because all the cars were picked up by Wilde's hired help.'

'Not guests?'

He shook his head. 'Sorry.' I turned back to the coffee and finished counting.

'Maybe I should talk to the help,' I said.

'If they were talkative he wouldn't hire them.'

'You know his habits that well then?'

'Reputations get around.'

'Don't they just. Fill me in on what else you've heard about Mr Music.'

He shrugged. 'The local wine merchant delivers a lot of booze and there's a fast turnover in maids.'

'Maids? Wilde has maids?' I don't know why that

100

surprised me, he had a butler for God's sake, but when Neil said it, it sounded archaic. I remembered the nice respectful way the music man treated women and thought I could guess what caused the fast turnover.

'People take what they can get in the work line, there's a lot of unemployment,' Neil said. *Too right!* We had a little chat about economics while the coffee slurped and burped its way through the filter. Playing at being Chancellor of the Exchequer is easy.

I piled everything on to a tray and carried it into the living-room. The place looked really cosy when I turned on the gas fire. Neil loosened his jacket and got comfy at one end of the settee, I took the other with my feet tucked under me. 'So,' I said, 'you've come way out of your way to let me look at those hire forms. That's nice, I'm flattered, I'm also surprised.'

He reached in his pocket and gave them to me, and like he'd said, with Wilde's address on every form they weren't any help. Brilliant!

I squinted at him. 'Minders I suppose. That's one of Wilde's business sidelines, isn't it, hiring out bouncers; I'd guess the doorstop at Lakeside is one of his.'

'He makes money where he can.'

'And doesn't worry how. The two who beat up Richie Venn, I'll bet they were Wilde's men too.'

He shifted around and looked irritated. 'I don't know anything about Venn. Look, Leah, I get a lot of business out of Wilde and in the middle of a recession there's not enough trade around for me to want to lose that.'

'That's OK,' I said. 'What's a missing boy on a dollar market.'

His face closed down. 'A lecture on ethics I can do without, maybe I made a mistake dropping by.'

Oh shit! He was right, of course, he'd done me a favour so it wasn't polite to shoot holes in him; I'd have to apologise and I really hate doing that humble kind of stuff.

'Look,' I said, stiff as a new toothbrush, 'that was out of line and I'm sorry, I appreciate what you've done. The truth is I'm not making any headway with this thing and it worries me. I guess I'm a little edgy.' I refolded the hire forms and gave them back. 'Thanks for bringing them.'

His face relaxed. 'It's a pity they won't help, maybe there'll be something else I can do.'

'Maybe.' A picture of Annie popped into my head. I didn't want the same thing to happen to Neil. Thinking that brought me up short: I was still making connections between her death and me asking questions and that wasn't good. I drank what was left of my coffee and set the mug back on the tray. Then I said flatly, 'Remember the little waitress I told you about? She's dead.'

His eyes flickered.

'What happened?'

'Hit and run. She was on her way to a phone box with my telephone number in her pocket.'

'And that makes it your fault?'

'Maybe not, but it doesn't help me sleep nights either. Indirectly I have to accept I'm involved in her death.'

He sat there and looked at me like he was working out something difficult, then made the wrong decision and reached over to my half of the settee. 'Hey,' he said, using that light bantering tone men use when they're trying to make a female feel better about something. 'You talked to me too and look, I'm healthy.' I shrugged his hands away and felt confused.

I'm no easy target where men are concerned but right then having Neil that close was disturbing, maybe it was the nice even tan and cute dimple, maybe it was because it had been a while since Nicholls and I had got together; either way, physically things started ticking like a time bomb and it was another complication I could do without. I took a quick look at my watch and acted surprised. 'Good grief, it's got to that time already! I'm running really late, Neil, it's been good of you to drop by but . . . '

'But it's time I let you get on.' His eyes held on to mine a little bit longer than they should have and I bounced up off the settee before I changed my mind. We walked each

102

other to the door and I let him out. I'm not sure why we shook hands but we did and the heat of him sent a message up through my arm and raised all the hairs. I felt like I was standing on the end of a pier watching the waves come in, feeling the pull and attraction of the water and fighting back an urge to jump.

It wasn't the way I wanted to feel.

Chapter Thirteen

I woke heavy-eyed, with a mind full of buzzing bees. They'd been there all night, keeping me company while I lay awake and stared at the ceiling, not that I could see much of it in the dark. I wasn't exactly making friends, and enemies I could do without. Fat chance of *that*! I'd been going over all the things I seemed to have been doing wrong lately like a regular depressive, and between times my atavistic monkey brain slipped in idiot jingles that drove me frantic. Around seven I crawled out from under the duvet without enthusiasm.

It was a crispy kind of morning, green-apple sharp with an expectant feel to it. Overnight it had rained heavily and the air went into my nostrils with a freshly laundered smell. The weather was really beginning to change now and the trees knew it, bright russet colours taking over from summer green, leaves already falling and turning into brown winter leather.

Another week and the bonfires would start.

I did my customary two circuits round the park, exchanged greetings with a few other regulars, and headed home. Marcie's milk was still on the step so I acted neighbourly again and carried it upstairs, wondering if the new man in her life was still around. Maybe I should just put it down outside her door and sneak on by.

I bent to do that and heard Ben's sharp wail.

As two-year-olds go he's the tough, pugnacious type that doesn't do much crying, but when I thought about it he'd been crying last night too, on and off until around midnight. I straightened up again. Except for one time when he got croup it was about the only concentrated tear-shedding I'd heard him do.

I knocked on the door, thinking if Marcie were in there alone she might need a break. I was all set to ask when the big romantic interest opened up and grabbed the milk without even a thank you. Blue jeans suited him a whole lot better than had Marcie's robe, but today he seemed to have a bit of a lip on and he wasn't giving out any friendly smiles. I said, 'Is Ben OK?'

'He's fine.'

'And Marcie? I haven't seen her all week.'

'Marcie's fine too.'

I tried to peer past his pectorals. 'She around?'

'Busy right now. Uh . . . Thanks for the milk.'

How nice he'd remembered his manners.

'No problem,' I said, 'maybe . . . ' But I was talking to the door he'd snapped shut in my face. Sweet!

I went on upstairs and put him out of my mind. Marcie was old enough to know what she wanted and it was none of my business.

I breakfasted on pasta and buttered mushrooms overlaid with just the right touch of garlic. Being able to eat what I like, when I like, is one of the perks of living solo. Around nine Darius rang and said had I talked to Caroline Spedding. I hadn't, how could I when I'd never even heard of her, but the way he asked made it sound like I should have. I took a cautious approach; I hate admitting I could have missed out on something. I said, 'Huh – er, no, not yet, you think it might do some good?'

'Well, she must have quit the job for some good reason I suppose,' he came back unhelpfully. I stayed quiet and tried to shift some brain cells into overdrive. 'You still there?' he said.

Maybe if I stalled I'd find out what was on his mind without having to ask.

'Umm, well, yes, I should have got around to talking to

105

her by now,' I said, 'and I would have if other things hadn't cropped up and . . . '

'Hah!' He crowed. 'You've never heard of her – go on, admit it.'

That's what happens when you grow up with people, they get so they can spot character weaknesses a mile away.

'So tell me,' I said.

'A Ms Caroline Spedding was once Wilde's PA.'

'Before Andy.'

'Right!'

Shit. I hadn't even thought about who'd done the job before Andy. My but wasn't I a brilliant detective.

I said, 'Thanks, Darius, I appreciate you telling me that. How did you get on to it?'

'Scavenging like I promised which means you owe me. Her name is on a news pic from a year back June.' He read out the caption. *Dean Wilde, accompanied by Promotional Assistant, Caroline Spedding, assesses talent at local rock concert.*

'That's great, Darius, anything else about her?'

'Nope.'

'Got a spare copy?'

'I knew you'd ask that. It's waiting at the front desk. Let me know if you turn anything up.'

'You bet. And thanks,' I said.

The newspaper offices close at twelve on a Saturday, so I didn't dawdle. I drove into town and picked up the print then headed down to the public library and hauled out the local telephone directory. Spedding isn't all that common a name around here, if she'd been Smith, Jones or Ramsden I'd have had a lot more trouble. There were twenty-four listings but three were businesses and could be skipped. I copied them all down and did some cross-checking with the electoral register; by the time I finished it was getting close to the library's two o'clock closing time and I was getting warning looks from the woman behind the counter. I guessed she was the type that likes to shoot the bolts the minute the big hand hits the hour. I said brightly, 'Just one more and then I'm all through,' but that just intensified the stare. It would have really pleased her to know I'd been wasting my time.

You'd think that out of twenty-one Speddings at least one household would have a voter christened Caroline.

I went home, made a couple of sandwiches and contemplated the probable size of my next telephone bill.

When I was through eating I started calling all the Speddings in the book — all those that were home that is, a lot didn't answer. On the ninth pick-up I got lucky, a woman's voice came on and said, 'Spedding,' and I gave her my sales pitch. It was all lies of course like most sales pitches and I felt bad about that. I said, 'Hi, Mrs Spedding, you don't know me but my name's Leah Hunter and I'm trying to trace a girl I once knew. Her name was Caroline Spedding and I know she lived somewhere around your area, I'd really like to get in touch with her again.'

There was a pause while she thought about that and I took it as a positive sign. After a few seconds she said cautiously, 'How long ago did you know her?'

'Oh, a few years ago now, we've kind of lost touch.'

'School?'

I took a chance and hoped Caroline had taken the usual path to landing that kind of job. 'Secretarial college.'

Her voice lightened up. 'Oh, Miss Mott's old place.'

'That's right, we wrecked typewriters together. I'd really like to catch up with her again, find out what she's been doing, but you know how it is sometimes, you get to know people, see them around for a while but forget to exchange addresses.'

'Maybe if you give me your number I could ask her to give you a ring.'

'If you tell me what time she'll be in I'd rather ring her, it'll be more of a surprise.'

'Caroline doesn't live here now, she isn't working in Bramfield.'

'Well, maybe I could have her new address then, or her

phone number. Is she married?'

'No, she isn't, why did you ask that?'

She sounded suspicious again and I wondered if Caroline had warned her not to give out information to strangers. I didn't feel good about what I was doing, but I had to find a way to talk to Wilde's ex-PA, and I didn't want her forewarned about the questions I was going to ask. I said coyly, 'Well, I'll be doing that myself soon, the whole thing, long white dress, bridesmaids, a honeymoon in Tenerife, you know how it is – romance with a capital R; that's why I want to get in touch again, I'd really like to ask her along to the wedding and everything.'

'Tenerife? You know I always wanted to go there . . . ' She sounded wistful and I squirmed a little and wished I'd picked someplace else. 'I'll get the number for you,' she said then, and the phone rattled a little in my ear. After a couple of minutes she came back with an out-of-town number and STD code. I thanked her and we talked a little about how nice it would be in Tenerife in early October, and she said how she hoped I'd be happy. I hung up and felt a real turd. Sometimes lying comes so easy I'm shocked.

I looked at the number I'd written down and fretted. The reference library had closed for the day, likewise the post office, and British Telecom are too damn cagey to give out addresses to go with numbers. I thought about how difficult it is for honest citizens to get simple, everyday bits of information. Then I stopped fretting and rang Tom.

Tom is Bramfield's own Philip Marlowe and he's walked down a lot of streets, mean and otherwise, but that was when he was still a Chief Inspector in CID. Now he picks and chooses. The entrance door to his office over the Quik-Pass Driving School says T. A. Tinsley, Detective Agency, in discreet black lettering. That office of his had been a real disappointment to me the first time I saw it, no whisky bottle, no blonde, and a desk too shiny to park his feet on. Tom himself is somewhere in his late forties, with greying sandy hair, the start of a paunch and honey-coloured eyes that droop a little. We chatted a bit about this and that and then I told him what I needed.

'That mean you're setting up in opposition again then?' he said.

I sighed. 'Tom, I don't know why people jump to these conclusions,' I told him equably. 'I'm just looking for somebody who's gone missing. Nothing else.'

'Shouldn't get into a right lot of trouble doing that then, should you? Give me half an hour or so, I'll have to make a couple of calls.'

Waiting can get tedious. I watched a spider weave patterns on the other side of the window; the web strands caught the sun and looked innocent like all the best-laid traps.

I was still thinking about that when Tom rang back with Caroline Spedding's address.

CHAPTER FOURTEEN

The address Tom had come up with was in Selby, around thirty miles from Bramfield. I'd driven through the place from time to time on trips to the east coast; it's an old town with an abbey dating back to the eleventh century. Local legend has it that in 1069, when Benedict of Auxerre heard 'voices' telling him to sail up the Ouse and build it he did just that, taking along a finger St Germain had carelessly left lying around some place for company. A nice touch!

I guess it was lucky for Benedict that nobody back then knew the connection between disembodied voices and schizophrenia; if they had King William might have thought twice before he handed over such a prime building site.

Of course all that kind of thing helps to make Selby popular with tourists, and when I got there just after four the town centre was still packed with shoppers. Since most of them didn't seem to know which side of the street they wanted to be on I kept down to a sedate speed.

The address I was looking for turned out to be on the east side of the toll-bridge, a square-built two-storeyed house, its cement rendering painted a pale yellowy beige. It stood a quarter mile along a quiet road that ran roughly parallel with the main traffic route to Driffield, and from the front it didn't look all that large, but when I did a little preliminary snooping I found an extension built on at the back that made it big enough to house four flats.

110

Around the front in an itsy wooden porch a brass plate with four push-buttons displayed Caroline's name opposite the number three. I gave her button a good long push and hoped she was home.

It's hard to tell a person's hair colour from a black and white photo and I'd guessed Caroline Spedding's to be midway between brown and blonde. I couldn't have been more wrong, she was rich copper with grey-green eyes and the kind of complexion most women would kill for, it made me wish I'd taken time out to shave my legs or something. She looked at me with that half-wary, half-puzzled look people get when they find a stranger on their doorstep.

'Hi,' I said, 'my name's Leah Hunter and your mother told me where I could find you.' I hoped saying that would suggest I wasn't any threat. It seemed to work, she opened the front door a little wider and took a better look at me.

'Leah Hunter, hmm? I don't remember the name,' she said, 'and I don't remember your face.'

'We haven't met before,' I said. 'I'm looking for someone who's gone missing and I think you might be able to help. Can we talk somewhere?' The wary look grew a little, she edged her foot behind the door.

'So what are you, social worker? DHSS snooper?'

It's amazing how people's minds always move in that direction these days. I shook my head. 'Neither, I'm doing this for a friend.'

She started to look interested. 'Does this missing person have a name?'

'Andy Howe.'

She rocked her head and pursed her lips. 'Don't know that name either.'

'You wouldn't, he was after your time.' I spread my hands and looked at her. I was going to have to take a chance on having another door shut in my face. 'Look,' I confided, 'Andy took on the job of Dean Wilde's PA for a while after you left, and I think something may have happened to him. Nobody will talk to me about Wilde and

111

his business activities and I hoped you would.' Her face froze up and the gap between door and frame lessened. I planted my hand on the wood before it closed any further and said. 'Please!'

We looked at each other for a while and then she pulled the door wide and said. 'You'd better come in.'

'Thanks.' I stepped past her into a cream-painted hall with black and white linoleum tiles on the floor. She snapped the door shut behind us and headed for the stairs. I wished my legs looked that good in ski-pants.

'I hoped I wouldn't have to hear the name Wilde again,' she said as we went up, 'but bad smells are always hard to get rid of. What exactly is it you want to know?'

'Why you left would be a good place to start.'

Caroline looked back with her eyebrows up as she went into her flat. I followed on and squinted around. She was a whole lot more houseproud than me and if I wasn't so dedicated to my sluttish ways I might have felt guilty.

'Telling you about that could take a while,' she said.

'That many reasons, hmm?'

'And then some.' She tidied up pieces of paper pattern from the seat of an easy chair as she went by, commenting, 'I don't know about you but I make a lot of my own clothes, that way I get better quality for less money.' She glanced at me. 'Makes me sound a regular skinflint doesn't it, but I couldn't afford to ring the changes the way I do if I bought ready-made.' She folded up some predominantly ginger-coloured silky stuff and dumped it and the pattern pieces on the table where she'd been sewing. 'Want to come into the kitchen and talk while I brew up?'

I perched on a stool and watched her gather the things she needed. Her cupboards were so neat and the place so tidy it depressed me. I said, 'How long did you work for Wilde?'

She made a face. 'A little over a year. It seemed a dream job, you know, when I first got it, it's funny how wrong a person can be about things, especially men.'

I stopped feeling irritated by all the shiny dust-free zones and felt sympathetic instead. 'Amen to that,' I said, and she laughed.

'So, who's got the job now?'

I shrugged. 'Last I heard there's a new Girl Friday starting next week.'

'Poor cow!' she said with feeling. 'Somebody should warn her.' She opened a biscuit tin, peered inside and moaned, 'Damn it, I'm down to custard creams.' I watched her write *Biscuits* with neat efficiency on a wipe-off memo board and tried to hold on to the sympathetic feeling.

'So why did you quit?'

'How much do you know about Wilde?'

'I've met him, I don't like what I've heard about his business methods, and I don't plan on inviting him home to dinner. That's about it.'

She looked me straight in the eye. 'Look, I left in a hurry and I didn't leave any forwarding address so I'd rather Wilde didn't get to know where I am, and that's the bottom line. I'm taking a chance talking to you at all, you could be on his payroll.'

To my fact-starved ears that sounded really promising. I grabbed my handbag from off the floor and fished around in it. Caroline took my official ID and had a good long look at its little photograph and Inland Revenue stamp before she gave it back. 'Thanks,' she said. 'Time was I trusted everyone, but not any more.' She hitched up on a stool so we were face to face and started pouring tea. Then she stopped. 'Uh-oh. I was going to take it next door.'

'In here's fine by me,' I told her, 'I like kitchens.'

'So do I,' she said. 'I just wish it was a bit bigger. What's yours like?'

'Pretty large and messy.' I got back to the subject. 'What kind of stuff does a promotional assistant do?'

'Promotes things.' She put the teapot down. 'Rock concerts, musicians, record releases – anything marketable. I arranged media interviews, sent out press releases, kept tabs on where all the groups he managed were playing. A PA's just another name for general dogsbody really but I liked it. At first, I mean. It had a certain amount of glamour attached, and I used to get a buzz out of telling people what I did. Then Wilde got involved in other things and I never knew what I was supposed to keep tabs on. He'd blow his top if he thought I was looking at anything he wanted to keep private.'

'What kind of other things are we talking about?' I asked. 'Hiring out bouncers?'

'You know about that? I'm surprised.'

'Andy mentioned it to his mother, I didn't know it was something Wilde wanted to keep quiet.'

'He did when I was around, the agency's operating methods aren't exactly friendly, but I didn't find out until just before I left. Club owners get offered an all-in package based on estimated takings; the deal is to replace their own bouncers with Wilde's, in return for which they're guaranteed a trouble-free club.'

'That so? And what if they say no thanks.'

'Accidents. Bouncers get beaten up, clubs get a little wrecked, owners get pressured into changing their ways.'

'Do you have proof of that?'

'No. One of the beat-up bouncers went out with a friend of mine, so you could say it's all second-hand. I don't think the club owners want to admit what's happening, they're too damned scared.'

'How many clubs are involved?'

She shrugged. 'I don't know, a lot. I suppose it's still spreading.'

'Caroline, what you're telling me about is extortion, I can't believe the police don't know about it.'

'Who's going to tell them? Not the club owners, that's for sure.'

I sat and thought about it. What would Wilde do if someone like Andy threatened to blow the whistle? The answer wasn't something I wanted to contemplate right then. I said, 'Does he know you found out?'

'If you mean did I tell him – no.'

'But you went on working there?'

114

She reddened. 'The money was good, and jobs like that are hard to find. I'm earning only half as much now.'

It was a hard life.

'What else is he into?'

'Raves.'

My ears pricked up again. 'Why would he do that?'

She looked surprised I had to ask. 'It's a fast money maker,' she said flatly, 'and it doesn't go through the books. Part of my job was keeping the financial side of his business up to date, but after the Raves started the rules changed. Wilde didn't want me to see any accounts except those I'd handled before, but sometimes things overlapped, he'd put one of his own groups into a party and that meant I had to handle the fees. The first time I did that he went through the roof, said I should have paid the band and not put it through the books. How am I supposed to know that if he doesn't tell me first?'

'Impossible,' I sympathised.

'Exactly.'

I waited to learn some more but she seemed to have dried up. I tried a change of tack. 'Did you ever get to meet Richie Venn?'

'Richie?' Her face lit up. 'Oh yes, we got on fine, he's a nice guy. You know him?'

'I hear he's moved back down London way.'

There was a flicker in her eyes when she heard that but her voice stayed level. 'Really? I can't say I'm surprised, he and Wilde had a hell of a row over money.'

'I heard something about that. Contractual fraud, wasn't it?'

'That's what Richie said. I know they had a major bust-up and Richie stormed out of the place threatening to take Wilde to court.'

'Nasty. How'd you get to hear about it?' She looked startled. I said, 'According to Richie all that happened a couple of months ago . . . long after you'd left.'

Crimson spread up from her neck and clashed with her hair. 'We kept in touch.'

'Heard from him lately?'

'It's been two or three weeks now, but if he's been busy moving I suppose . . . ' She trailed off.

'He's had his troubles, he got worked over by a couple of bouncers too.'

Her eyes went big and round. A splash of tea went on to the beige ski-pants but Caroline didn't seem to notice. The news had worried her.

'How bad . . . '

I said lightly, 'When I saw him he didn't look pretty, but he'll live. I think that's why he moved. Do you think Wilde would organise something like that?'

'No . . . Yes . . . I don't know. Where's Richie, I know you said London, but where in London?'

'I wish I knew that, Caroline, but like you he didn't leave a forwarding address. A neighbour thought the removal van came from Walthamstow, but I'm not sure she's a reliable witness. When I talked to him last he told me one of the bouncers had planted drugs on him, would that be likely?'

She looked away from me towards the window and thought about it, then she brought her eyes back. 'I'd get to hear things sometimes, from the groups.'

'What kind of things?'

She looked uncomfortable. 'It was just hearsay, I don't think I should be telling you any of this.'

'You're doing fine,' I said, 'and Wilde won't get to know about it, I promise. What kind of things did you hear?'

'That drugs were on sale at the gigs.'

'Raves?'

'Them too. I mean, nobody said Wilde was supplying the stuff, but I suppose he could have been.'

'That was when you quit?'

'Not exactly. I was getting around to doing that but then the accounts got mixed up and precipitated things. He'd left the set I wasn't supposed to deal with on the desk and I didn't know which they were until I looked at them and, well, I suppose I should have closed the folder then and there but I was curious.'

'And you were caught?'

'Not by Wilde, by that bloody cold fish he's in partnership with. I *loathe* that man, he's the pits. When he saw I had the wrong file he said I was a nosy little bitch and started pushing me around.' Her voice cracked. 'I honestly think . . . he would have hit me . . . if Wilde hadn't come in.' She'd gripped her mug like it was a lifeline; remembering what had happened was really upsetting her.

I prompted gently, 'What did Wilde do?'

'Told me to go wait in my office and make sure I shut the door. It really shook me up, standing in there listening to them shout. Then things quietened down and Wilde came in, gave me a month's wages and told me to get the hell out.'

'Could you hear what they argued about?'

'Just odd words, the PA's office is across the hall.'

'So why were you in the study?'

She frowned at me. 'I did a lot of work in there. Wilde didn't normally leave anything private lying around, all that kind of stuff is kept in his upstairs office.'

That was a really useful piece of information, I filed it away and smiled at her approvingly.

'I don't suppose you remember anything about the accounts in the folder?'

'Richie asked me that. I didn't have time to see much at all except that the amounts of money being accounted for were pretty large, and they weren't going through Wilde's bank account. Every so often he'd written "Cash Transfer", and each time the balance carried forward went to nil.'

'So where was the money going?'

'I don't know, but he told me to forget what I'd seen and not tell anybody, and he said I'd be much happier and healthier if I got a job away from Bramfield, because there were people around who might see me as a threat to their peace of mind. Which is why I came here, and I'd appreciate it if you don't tell anyone.'

117

'Not even my own mother,' I said. 'Who's Wilde's partner?'

'Robert Cresswell.'

'Lakeside Country Club?'

'That's right, and if this person you're looking for got on the wrong side of *him* then I think you're right to worry.' She slid down from the stool. 'I've said enough, in fact I might have said too much. I hope you find your friend.'

She was giving me a clear signal that as far as she was concerned the talking had ended, but there was one more thing I still had to ask. I said, 'Caroline, you've been a big help, and I'm really grateful, but there's something else I have to ask about before I go. Wilde holds regular get-togethers in his house, do you know anything about them?'

'All I've heard is that they're mostly a venue for business deals, but I don't know what kind. He always brings in outside caterers and gives the staff a night off. Richie said they weren't the kind of thing you'd take your wife to. That's all I know about them.'

I fished for car keys, then thanked her and told her not to worry I'd already forgotten where she lived. She walked with me to the door and said she hoped I meant that. I did, of course, but it wouldn't stop her having a sleepless night worrying about it.

I drove back along the A63 with my mind on Cresswell. If he'd been that rough with Caroline when he thought she was snooping, he could have done something a whole lot worse to Andy, and I didn't like the direction that idea was taking me. Sweat pricked out on my palms.

I took them off the wheel one at a time and wiped them on my jeans.

CHAPTER FIFTEEN

Sunday morning I drove down the M62 to Hull again, banking on Martin being back in his flat and not still hiding out.

Until yesterday I'd half-believed Andy would turn up again without any help from me; I'd *wanted* to believe that because the alternative Grace had laid out was one I didn't like to contemplate. Talking to Caroline Spedding had upset a lot of my wishful ideas.

I left the hybrid in the university car-park and walked towards the Simpson block, the campus was so quiet I could have been on the moon. I knocked on Martin's door and the sound seemed to travel up and down the stairway and bounce back at me again. The door stayed shut and there wasn't even a shuffle from inside.

Some little time ago I'd acquired a set of picklocks in a neat little case that looked innocently like a manicure kit; I'd got them from a man whose business I didn't enquire into. Using them gave me a real guilt feeling. After a couple of minutes fiddling around and feeling nervous in case someone came along I realised I should get in some more practice. I swore a little and tried again. This time I was lucky. I went inside and shut the door behind me.

The room wasn't the kind of thing you'd find in *Good Housekeeping*, but then again it wasn't a slum. It looked as if Martin had invited some friends in and forgotten to clean up. There was a dumpy settee and two odd chairs, and over in one corner a colour television sat on a low cabinet next to a stack stereo system. The settee and chairs looked out of kilter and there were empty lager cans dotted about in diverse places including the floor. They went well with the empty ale bottles and the plates with bits of Chinese take-away sticking to them. There were still some potato crisps left in the bottom of a plastic tupperware bowl sitting in front of a two-bar electric fire; a few more were scrunched into the rug.

Nice!

I was really glad I didn't have to do the cleaning up.

The kitchen smelled of fry-ups, and Martin, or someone else, had left a bag of chips out of the freezer and they'd gone soggy limp. A little river had run across the scratched work-surface and made a waterfall to a lake on the red vinyl floor. There was grey water in the sink and a pan handle reaching out of it drunkenly. Across from the sink a portable radio was still tuned to Radio One and playing softly.

Martin had left in a hurry again and, for some reason, this time that really worried me. I took a look in the bedroom and saw chaos. Student bedrooms aren't all that large, a bed pushed up against the wall in one corner, a mini writing desk and bendy lamp under the window, a cheap three drawer chest and a built in wardrobe with cupboards over; practical but not the kind of place to look for family jewels.

Obviously someone didn't share my view of things, and Martin, if he came back, would need to do a fast tidy-up before he could climb into bed because the mattress was on the floor, the bedclothes in an untidy pile, and every drawer and cupboard had been ransacked. Somehow I didn't think it had been that way when he left. *If he left.* There was just one last place I hadn't looked and a reluctance to open that final door hung on me like a ball and chain.

Sometimes I can be a real coward with things.

Downstairs a door slammed and feet came on up the

stairs. I froze halfway to the bathroom and listened. The feet stopped outside Martin's door – just before I turned blue from holding my breath they went away again and carried on up to the next floor.

Light-headed from all that carbon dioxide build-up I opened up the bathroom door and took a look inside. It was as messy as the rest of the place, and with the window standing wide open, extremely well ventilated. I stuck my head out. A foot to the left a waste pipe ran down the wall; two feet the other side of that was the platform of a fire escape. For a monkey it would be an easy swing from window to pipe, and from pipe to platform, but Martin was no monkey and if he'd gone out that way he must have been really scared.

Sometimes eye corners are clever at picking up hints of movement. I took a good long look at the wastebins on the corner of the block. A piece of black plastic flapped in the breeze. Maybe I'd been wrong, maybe I was just getting jumpy. I pulled back inside and thought about things. I could stay around and search the flat; that's what Nicholls would do, but from the mess in the bedroom it looked as if someone had already found whatever it was they'd been looking for first try.

Or maybe they hadn't been looking for anything except to scare Martin. I took a last look around, then I got out of there and left the mess for someone else to clean up.

There was still no one around on campus except a lone figure heading toward the administration building, but maybe everyone slept late Sundays. I took my time walking back to the car and tried to work out why someone would go through Martin's flat that way. Maybe he'd been up to something annoying on campus – that made a lot more sense than thinking it was connected with my own interests.

Keys in hand I trotted across the car park. The hybrid now had a companion, an orange-coloured Transit van was parked about six feet away. I don't like the colour orange at the best of times and spattered with rust it looks even worse, I walked on by giving the heap only a cursory glance, my mind on other things. As I fitted in the car key gravel crunched, loud against the silence. Turning was a reflex. The man I saw was around five-nine, not heavily built but not slim either. He'd come around the front of the Transit and was closing the gap between us. Still holding the key in my hand I watched him come.

He looked around thirty-five with thinning pale hair and a round, pink face with a rosebud mouth that was a lot too small for it, badly dressed in soiled denims and a T-shirt that needed a wash even more. Quite apart from the fact that nothing that lived in those kind of clothes could be likeable, he didn't have any life in his eyes and that made him dangerous as well as unlovely.

He stopped to look me up and down. 'You were in the Lund kid's place.' A statement not a question.

'You were behind the rubbish bins.' Exchanging fact for fact.

'Where's he hidin'?'

'Beats me.'

He moved forward and my heart picked up steam, there was just him and me and no one around to come riding to the rescue. Two more quick strides and we were close enough to tango, his breath garlic hot on my face. I wondered what kind of left over garbage he'd eaten for breakfast.

He locked his fingers together and cracked his knuckles, and I counted the big, dull silver rings he wore. One on each finger. I tried stepping back but the car was too close; this was really great! I did a rapid inspection of the stretchy smile that showed his back teeth to such good advantage and hoped it was friendlier than it looked. A pointy snake tongue came out and wetted his lips, his fingers locked and tensed again. He was real good at cracking his knuckles. I said, 'Look, let's calm down a little.'

'I'm calm,' he said, 'you're the one with the sweat, must be guilty conscience, now *me* I don't never have no problems with that crap, which is good, 'cos, like, if I have to do some fucking up it doesn't worry me none.'

I felt behind me and carefully unlocked the car door. 'That's two lots of double negatives,' I said unthinkingly and one hand left the other and caught me a stinging slap across the side of my head. This could get really nasty.

'Look, I don't know . . . ' His other hand moved and this time my teeth rattled. Pain gets me really mad. I jerked his collar and his nose exploded with a grating pop as it connected with the headbutt Jack had said would come in useful one day. He'd been right! I let go of his collar and shoved; he swore nastily and flailed for balance. I ground down hard on his instep. Still staggering he swung a bunched fist that found my left shoulder and banged me back against the car, rattling every bone I had.

It's hard to follow the action when every instinct is to roll into a ball and hide away some place. I wondered how some women managed to put up with this kind of treatment on a regular basis.

Like a slow-motion movie I saw the next punch head for my face. I slid away, took his arm, and slammed him against the car, letting his own momentum do the hard work, then I hauled his arm straight up behind him, yanking until it was just at breaking point. His other fist pounded the car roof, 'Aw, Chrise, bloody fuckin' bitch, aw Chrissake . . . ' I shifted, pulling against the joint, and he moved with me, still screaming: 'Fucking bitch, fucking bitch, aw . . . Chrise.' With the car at my back for leverage and a foot in his butt I shoved hard. He staggered away at an impossible angle. I grabbed at the car door and got inside, it seemed like it would be a really good idea to get out of there before he picked himself up.

I started the engine, got reverse, and put my foot down hard on the accelerator. The shaking didn't start until I got to the motorway roundabout, but when it did I could hear my own teeth join in, and I drove around it twice before I remembered the right exit. I made good time back to Bramfield and headed home, parking on the street and hurrying up to my place as fast as I could get my feet to go.

Then I got down on my knees and hunted for the half-bottle of whisky I'd bought last Christmas, there'd never be a time when I needed it more.

CHAPTER SIXTEEN

I took a good long soak in a hot and scenty bath. This time when the telephone rang I didn't climb out, whoever it was would have to ring back or forget about it. Half an hour later when I climbed out I had a nicely pickled skin and a build-up of righteous anger; I was sick to death of being picked on, what was I, for heaven's sake, a walking red rag?

I dried off, rubbed arnica into my super-bruised shoulder and thought how tomorrow I'd have my own personal rainbow. After that I spent a little time debating whether to use the stuff on my head, if I did I'd end up with greasy hair. I screwed the top back on. Vanity, vanity, all is vanity, saith the Preacher – or something like that. It's a long time since Ecclesiastes was on my reading list.

I pulled on clean undies, a pair of white leggings, and an oversized Lynx sweatshirt, and cooked up some lunch. When I'd licked my plate clean I felt a lot better. I still hadn't decided if Martin's campus problems were linked with Andy, and the sticking point was Lund senior. I didn't think he was the world's best father but somehow I couldn't see him going along with that level of harassment being directed at his own son, regardless of how good or bad the relationship was between them. Of course there was always the possibility it had been done without his knowledge, and if that had happened I thought I'd be doing him a real favour if I took time out to tell him.

I checked Lund's home address in Grace's little red book

and went to fill him in on what someone had done to his son. I didn't expect to get thanked, which was lucky, because I'd have hated to be crushed by disappointment.

People really like to pocket themselves in holes. Lund lived five miles out of town on one of those executive developments that are short on gardens and long on Mercs and BMWs. I parked my nondescript little heap of metal outside number twenty-four and patted it gently so it wouldn't get depressed, then I turned around and took a good look at the house. Dark-red brick and a mock gable overhang at the front, paintwork classy stained oak, windows tallish with leaded panes, and a double garage to give the Merc plenty of room, although right then it was parked outside. Nice! Especially if you were one of the wealthily insecure.

I trotted up to the front door and rang the bell. After a couple of minutes Lund came and looked at me but he didn't ask me in. I said, 'Hi, I thought it might be really nice to have another talk.' He let go the door and came on out with a look that said I was a smell under his hooky nose. 'About Martin,' I added, but his face didn't change. He grabbed me by the arm and started to hustle me back to the road. I could have argued, of course, but in that kind of neighbourhood someone would be bound to pick up the phone and call the police, especially if things got out of hand. 'Look,' I said, 'all I want is to talk, how can that cause you any trouble?'

He shoved me at the car and let go. I put out a hand so I didn't hit metal and jarred the bruise. *Shit!* that hurt. I rubbed at it, 'Get in,' he said.

'You know about Martin's flat? It's been wrecked, Mr Lund. Totalled. I was there this morning. He wasn't.'

All right, so I was exaggerating a little, but I didn't think it mattered if I got the right results.

He backed off a pace and thought about it. The trouble with people who lie is, they think everyone else has the same bad habit. We stood and looked at each other.

'You're lying,' he said, which confirmed my theory.

126

I shrugged. 'Suit yourself.'

I was in the car, starting it up, before curiosity got to him. He came forward again and I wound down the window. 'The Simpson block,' I told him. 'Flat B8. I thought you'd like to know what's going on, the place is really messed up, I hope the guy who did it doesn't catch up with Martin.' I let the clutch out and the car began to roll. He reached in and grabbed the wheel.

'Where is Martin?'

'Who knows? It's just a guess but I'd say he went out the bathroom window in a hurry.'

'You didn't see him?'

'No. But I did see who messed up the flat. One of them anyway.' I lifted my hair so he could see the bruises, then I touched the accelerator and let the car jerk his hand loose. Impolite maybe but I hadn't asked him to trespass. A couple of yards away I stopped and looked back at him. 'He's a nice kid,' I said, 'just like Andy used to be. I hope you find him before your friends do.' I backed up the next-door drive and turned the car around. The skin seemed stretched tighter on his face and the worry he wore looked real, which in a way was comforting.

The problem with neat little executive developments is they have neat little streets and neat little open-plan front lawns where it's impossible to park for any length of time without being noticed. Which is fine from a crime-fighting angle but no help at all when it comes to sitting in a car keeping watch. Part of talking to Lund had included a hopeful supposition that he'd want to unload his anxiety about what was happening to his son on to somebody else, and – foolish me – I'd thought he might do that in person. Like most other people I have to get proved wrong sometimes.

I did a fast and careful trawl of the few streets that made up the development and found there were no secret exits; all traffic fed out on to a minor B road that in turn led on to the A656.

Waiting around for long periods of time is not only

wearisome it's also uncomfortable. I pulled off the side of the B road on to a patch of dirt in front of a five-barred gate that opened into a field of cabbages. Just inside the field a pile of stalks was rotting down and the smell was nothing like Chanel. After a few seconds I wound up the window. The time was four o'clock.

By five I was getting restless. In Lund's place I'd have been on my way to sort things out at least forty-five minutes ago. I let another half hour go by and decided he wasn't the impulsive kind. I blamed it all on Alexander Graham Bell, if he hadn't invented the damned telephone I wouldn't have been sat there overheating. At six o'clock the Merc nosed out on to the road.

It's something I've noticed in the past, the way things always happen at the wrong time. I was fifty or sixty yards away from the hybrid breathing in cabbage-free air and rubbing pins and needles out of my backside.

Sprinting worked wonders.

By the time I'd got my wheels back on to the road Lund was out of sight.

However disparaging I might be about owning a BMW it was nice having one of their engines under the bonnet. Shoving down on the accelerator made the Morris Minor shell do things its designer had never dreamt of.

At the A656 junction Lund was still out of sight. I took a chance and headed back towards Bramfield. A mile further and I saw his car, still a long way in front but going uphill and trapped behind a caravan.

I relaxed, halved the distance, and let two cars pass me by.

A half mile over the hill he turned on to the A655 and drove straight into Bramfield without stopping. I followed him through town until he turned up the alley that led to Bloomers' car-park and thought about how good I was getting at wasting time.

Sunday nights the club opens its doors at eight which made Lund nearly two hours early. Maybe the mountain was coming to Mahomet. I really needed to be two people; how was I supposed to watch both front and back of the damn place at the same time. Life is full of seemingly insoluble problems. I settled for the same spot I'd used before, facing the alley that led in from the main road. Anyone coming to see Lund wouldn't be coming on foot, and access from the back was down cratered derelict streets booby-trapped with broken bottles, which made them places to avoid unless you didn't care too much about whatever it was you drove.

I locked up and crossed the road to the alley. It seemed like a good idea to take a look around and check that no one had got to Bloomers before us, and as far as I could tell no one had, the only car up there was Lund's. I recrossed the road and settled down for another wait, this time I left the window open.

Somewhere near seven a take-away pizza place two doors up opened for business. The car filled with the smell of cooking onions and hot bread, overlaid with Mediterranean herbs and melting cheese, and my stomach filled up with juices that had no work to do. By and by, I gave in and trotted off to get a Margarita and a can of Coke.

It's a real shame the way solving one problem creates another. When the club lights went on at seven forty-five Lund still hadn't had any visitors and I was about ready to burst. I made the superloo fifty yards away with no time at all to spare.

When I got back cars were trickling up the alley. I walked on up and took another look around and tried to guess if they all belonged to customers.

Two more pulled in and parked and I gave up and went back to my look-out point; it was beginning to feel really homey. Hunched down behind the wheel I listened to the radio and waited for closing time so I could get to follow Lund all the way home again. Sometimes I hate myself for being such a pessimist. Around nine I put my feet up on the passenger seat, balled the spare sweatshirt I'd slung on the back seat between my head and the door, and tried to get comfy; right then I felt grateful to the town fathers for slapping an eleven o'clock curfew on Sunday drinking.

The radio DJ was into dreamy music; maybe he had a new love in his life. I thought about changing stations but I was just too damn lazy, and hey – what's wrong with a little romance?

What's wrong with it is I fell asleep and didn't wake up until Bloomers emptied out with enough noise to panic the pigeons.

Something soft plopped on to the top of the car.

I came up straight and scrubbed at the left-overs of sleep with the heels of my hands. Suppose Lund had left already. Suppose somebody I wanted to know about had been and gone while I dreamed dreams about Nicholls and shag-pile rugs. I stopped right there. Had it been Nicholls or had it been Neil?

I got a little hot worrying about that.

By and by, the giggles, squeals and half-hearted scuffles moved on. Cars stopped coming out of the alley and the outside lights went out. At eleven-thirty a pair of taxis took the staff home; Granny Wolf locked up and the foyer lights went out, a couple of minutes later he rolled out of the alley in a Toyota. I crossed my arms on the steering wheel and leaned on them. Anytime now Lund would bring out his Merc.

He didn't of course.

From where I sat his office window was in plain sight and I kept my eyes on its pull-down blind. A couple of times a shadow crossed behind it and I mused about what he was doing up there; maybe he had to stay behind and count the takings.

When it got to midnight I developed a worry. How come I was sitting there so complacently? Judas! I'd been asleep, off watch for an hour. The Prime Minister could be in there and I wouldn't know about it.

I grabbed the dinky little torch the ad said was so handy for reading street maps in the dark and made fast time up the alley. The single light that was still on over the back entrance was coated with dead insects and lit up only a ten-yard radius. The Merc looked lonely again all by itself in the corner.

I hung around indecisively. So what if the car-park was empty, people had feet for God's sake. I trotted over to look at the back door and yes, the idea of putting in a little more practice lock-picking was on my mind until I found there were no locks. Which meant the damn thing had to be either bolted or deadlocked on the inside. How clever! I put my hand out to give it a shove and almost fell into the place.

That's the thing about security systems, they're only as efficient as the people who use them.

I got my balance, went in, and let the door swing shut. Enough light came in through the window to pick out a table and a couple of filing cabinets. I turned on the mini-torch.

The table turned out to be a table but the filing cabinets were stacked boxes of potato crisps. At least if I got locked in I wouldn't starve. The torch beam found a second door and I went over and found security had been lax there too. It worried me.

I soft-footed down a corridor and took a peek in the kitchen and washrooms to check both were hygienic and empty. They were. A few yards further along things became familiar. A faint light came down the stairs leading up to Lund's office.

I started on up and when I reached the third step what little sixth sense I had went into fast overdrive. It was too damn quiet, everything in the place was holding its breath. I shoved the torch in my pocket and crept on up to where light spilled out from the empty outer office.

The raspberry carpet and gold and white desk looked at me expectantly and I looked right back. I half-wished Lund would walk out of his office and break the silence. What was he doing in there? I tiptoed across to his door and couldn't hear a damn thing. Then I listened some more and picked up a soft, persistent buzzing.

I eased the door open. Lund was still sitting at his desk, a red lake had spread across the blotter and when the paper couldn't soak up any more the lake had run across the desk and dripped on the carpet. The sickly sweet smell of blood and death came up at me in a wave and my stomach heaved. I turned back into the outer office and hunkered down until the nausea passed. Going in for the second time was a little easier, at least I knew what to expect. The worst part was the flies, half a dozen of them, feasting.

I made myself stand there and assess what I saw. Lund's right hand still gripped a Stanley knife and it looked like when he'd cut his throat his head and shoulders had fallen forward so he lay part across the desk. The human body holds around eight pints of blood and most of Lund's appeared to have run out.

His left arm reached across the desk, blood from two shallow cuts streaked and stained around his wrist, a fly landed there and the pit of my stomach seemed to drop out. I turned around and went back into the outer office.

After a couple of minutes' deep breathing I rang Nicholls from the secretary's desk. He sounded cosily sleepy until I told him where I was, then he got so aerated it took a couple of minutes to break back in and tell him who else was there with me.

After that he went quiet.

I hung on to the phone and waited for it to explode again but all he did was tell me to stay where I was and not touch anything. He told me that with a kind of fatalistic resignation and I didn't like to tell him I already had.

I sat in the secretary's chair for a while and things were so quiet I could hear the flies buzzing in the other office as they changed positions. I got up and went to sit on the stairs. Something about the suicide scene didn't quite fit together in my mind, but I couldn't think why. I didn't even know what it was that seemed out of order. I leaned my head against the wall and hoped Nicholls didn't take too long; I also hoped he got there before the heavy squad.

He did – but only just, and comforting wasn't on the menu. He was angry as hell.

CHAPTER SEVENTEEN

I didn't see why Nicholls was so mad; like I told him, he should be grateful that I tell him about these things, I could have just left the whole damn mess for the morning cleaners. I told him that too. It didn't seem to impress.

I declined his request to go back upstairs, to my mind twice was enough. Being turned down didn't improve his disposition but taking another look at Lund wouldn't have done much for mine either, so I stuck to my place on the stairs and he went on up without me. By and by, the heavies came and one of them stayed behind and kept me silent company. I wondered briefly why uniforms are always more intimidating than plain clothes.

Nicholls came back and sat at the side of me. I squinted up at the watchdog PC. 'Maybe you could use him on a recruitment poster,' I said chattily, 'he's really good looking.' Nicholls sighed and looked down at his hands. The dark-blue uniform went away and left us alone. 'Sorry,' I said, 'I just hate to be stared at.'

He said huffily, 'Leah, just tell me – what the hell were you doing, snooping round Bloomers?'

I'd known he was going to ask that question eventually, which was why I'd been trying to come up with a good lie ever since I put the phone down. I knew all along the truth would just get him annoyed. It did. He's really predictable when it comes to that sort of thing.

I let him run through a quick résumé of my worst shortcomings. As a responsible and law-abiding citizen I was a failure, and that's a fact.

'Is that it?' I said when he paused for breath. 'Can I go home now?' I started to get up.

He snapped irritably, 'When you've made a statement,' and hauled me back down.

'Well, all right, but can we make it quick then,' I said wearily. 'I'd really like to crawl in under my duvet.'

'So would I,' he said, and I knew he meant mine and not his.

I looked at him. He really needed to watch those mood changes, sometimes it was hard to know where he was coming from. 'Tough!' I told him unkindly, and leaned my head on the wall again. Staying up late when I'm having a good time is one thing, helping Nicholls destroy rain forests is another. I said, 'By the way, I shan't sign it if it isn't on recycled paper.'

He mumbled something I didn't catch, I didn't ask what because I knew it wouldn't be complimentary.

Close on three I got home and dived straight into bed, so tired I fell asleep right away. I didn't set the alarm, I was on holiday, damn it. Hah!

Coming awake again was like crawling up through thick layers of gauze; part of my mind kept trying to burrow back and ignore the knocking but it was too ungentle for anyone but a dead man not to hear. I pulled on a cotton wrap and went to find out who my enemy was.

Nicholls looked a lot worse than me, mostly because I'd had almost four hours sleep and he'd had none. His nice blue eyes were red-circled coal pits.

'I think we found Andy.'

It was the way he said it, flat-voiced and empty that told me Grace had been right all along. I stepped back and let him in and he headed for the kitchen like a zombie and started priming the coffee-machine; it looked like something he needed to do so I waited silently and let him get on with it. He spooned in enough coffee to make a brew that would keep him awake the rest of the day then without looking at me, said, 'If you want to see the end of it get

134

dressed.' I didn't argue. He was working his way round to doing the thing he hates most – admitting when he'd been wrong, and for once I'd rather not have heard it.

I took ten minutes to clean my teeth and rub a flannel over my face. It's funny how domestic things intrude at moments of stress or crisis, like climbing into my last pair of jeans and thinking as I did, that I'd have to get round to some more washing. The triviality of it made me ashamed. God! Andy was dead and here was I worrying about clean jeans. All right, Nicholls hadn't said it out loud yet, but I knew. And someone would have to tell Grace.

I went back out. Nicholls was buttering toast. I fed more bread into the slot and took the coffee over to the table. 'How did you know where to look?' I said. He held the knife still for a minute, then cut through both slices corner to corner.

'Lund left a letter.'

'Where?'

'In the safe luckily, where you couldn't get at it.' I opened up my mouth to ask what safe, and he pre-empted the question. 'In the wall behind the yearly planner,' he said, and started to eat. He likes to think he can read my mind. Sometimes it's harmless fun to let him, like everybody else he needs his illusions.

'And Andy?'

'He's dead.'

'I know,' I said. 'Grace told me that back at the beginning and I didn't believe her. Neither did anybody else.' The toaster snapped. 'You want more toast?'

'Maybe a couple.'

I fetched it over for him, and got a bowl of cereal for myself. 'So. Tell me whose head is going to roll because they fouled up?'

He gave me a bleak look. 'There'll be some tightening up of procedures,' he said.

'Great thinking. That way, next time somebody gets murdered CID might notice.'

'The right questions were asked at the time.'

'No,' I snapped at him, 'No, they damn well weren't and you know it, so let's not waste any whitewash. What got asked were the wrong ones.'

'The only difference it made was in time, it wouldn't have helped Andy any.'

'No,' I said flatly, 'I didn't think it would, but it would certainly have helped Grace. Can you imagine what it's been like for her? No, of course you can't, if you could you wouldn't come up with such crap.'

He said stiffly, 'If you want to complain do it to the right people, I already put backs up helping you out.'

'Huh!'

He shrugged, got up, and started for the door. I grabbed my bag and jacket and went after him, hoping Marcie's toddler didn't wake with all the noise. Outside on the pavement a steady drizzle fell from a monotonously grey sky and everything looked bedraggled. I climbed into Nicholls' car and he started it up and moved down the road without saying anything. Half a mile on he said, 'Nobody's happy, they know they made mistakes.'

'Yes, all right, I'm sorry,' I said. 'I shouldn't have got on to you like that, you did what you could.'

After that the silence felt friendlier.

Nicholls' usual driving method is safe and fast but that morning I could tell just how tired he was by the sedate way we headed out of town along the A638. Little queues built up behind us on tight spots and passed by like a stream of sprinters when the road cleared. It's a shame hedgehogs don't have wheels.

When we turned on to the minor road leading to Wilde's place I made a couple of rash assumptions. The first was that we were heading for his mini-mansion, and the second was that Nicholls now recognised the man's culpability. Both assumptions were killed when he swung left up a lane that wasn't much more than a track between tall hedgerows. After half a mile or so where hedges gave way to wire fencing the track dog-legged uphill between cultivated fields. Three police cars, two police vans and a dark-blue

Volvo stood under a knot of ash trees where a labour-intensive ground search was going on. For the first time it hit me what I was probably going to see.

My stomach bottomed out.

What did a disinterred body look like after close on three months in the ground? I sucked in my bottom lip and bit down on it. Who needed visual proof? I was happy to take Nicholls' word about things.

He stopped on a harvested field with the stubble half ploughed in; ten feet of fencing had been moved to give access and the ground was criss-crossed with tyre tracks. 'I never met Andy you know,' I said conversationally. 'I won't be able to tell if it's him or not.'

'Nobody could,' Nicholls said cryptically. He crossed his arms on the steering wheel and leaned on them.

'This is as far as we go?' I said. The scowl he gave out told me I'd just grown a second head and he didn't like the look of it. I said hastily, 'Hey! That's fine, don't get the wrong idea, this is close enough. Honest.'

We sat there silently and watched the activity.

After a bit, I said, 'What did it say in Lund's note?'

He pushed up from the steering wheel and kept his eyes on the trees, voice weary. 'Usual story of how he drove up here for sex, found Andy wasn't gay, tried rape, then panicked and killed him.'

'After the party?'

'Yes.'

I accepted the answer uneasily, it didn't fit in with what I knew – or what I thought I knew. I said, 'I suppose it *was* Lund's handwriting?'

'Chrr-rist!' He threw his head back and closed his eyes. 'For God's sake let go of it, Leah, it's over, you've done what you set out to do, you've found Andy, we incompetents can do the rest.'

I blinked at him. I said, 'Somebody's got to tell Grace.'

'Somebody already has, around the same time I told you.'

'The whole thing?'

'It seemed kinder than letting her read it in the local rag.'

I said, 'Lund's son . . . '

'Is a resident student at Hull. The local police will get him home.'

'If they can find him you mean, he has troubles of his own.' I told him about the flat without mentioning how I'd got in. Then I let him take a peek at my bruises as evidence of evil intent.

He started the car without saying a thing, but the drive back to town was a little faster than the journey out. I waited patiently while he went up to his office and talked to the Hull police, then we drove back to my place and in the time it took to scramble him some eggs, he fell asleep on the settee. He looked so cosy lying there I hadn't the heart to wake him.

CHAPTER EIGHTEEN

I de-shoed Nicholls and left him snug as a bug under one of
Gran's handmade afghans and went about my business.
When I passed by Marcie's everything was quiet; for a
second or so I thought about knocking and asking how
things were, but doing that could get me tied up, and I
needed to talk to Dora. The way things had turned out I
felt like I'd let her down, although she didn't see it that
way. We talked around what had happened and we both
felt bad about it in our own way. Then Dora put on her
coat and we climbed into the hybrid and went to see
Grace. It wasn't something I wanted to do, I suppose I was
expecting her to have gone to pieces and I wasn't sure how
I'd cope with that. Grief is catching. I could feel my mind
click off, and distance itself, leaving me to drive like a well-
programmed robot.

I suppose Dora was struggling with the same kind of
feelings, because neither of us said more than a couple of
words on the way across town.

Reality is always in between the two extremes painted
by imagination, and most times that's a good thing. When
we got to Grace's she wasn't collapsed in tears but neither
was she untouched by them, She looked as if she'd been
washed over by a tidal wave of emotion so deep I didn't
even want to think about it. Dora walked right in and
wrapped her arms about her. I whispered clumsily, 'Grace,
I'm sorry, so very, very sorry.' She nodded and reached out
a hand that felt a lot colder and thinner than I remembered

it to be. My throat cramped up. *Shit*, things shouldn't happen this way! How come bad things always happened to good people?

Grace disengaged herself and headed for the kitchen, claiming she felt better keeping busy than just sitting around. She ground beans, brewed coffee, buttered scones and all the while talked about Andy, what kind of a baby he'd been, the prizes he'd won swimming, the broken arm when he fell off his bike. Little things about his life that she maybe hadn't thought about in years got brought out and rehearsed so she could keep them close. Dora took it all in her stride but I had to clamp down hard to hang on to my self-control; a fine thing it would be if I ended up being the comforted instead of the comforter.

Inevitably the time came around when Grace wanted to know about the events leading up to that morning. I edited them as best I could, there didn't seem any point in adding agony to what she already knew. Around midday I went home, still wondering why it was that I felt loaded with guilt. Dora stayed behind, and I knew she meant to be there until Andy's brother arrived late that afternoon.

On the way home I stopped by the Mini-mart and did some grocery shopping; lettuce, cheese, tomatoes, French bread, and took it home to share with Nicholls. It cheered me up to know he'd still be around, being solitary right then was the last thing I needed.

I let myself in quiet as a whisper, dumped the groceries on the kitchen table, and went to take a look at my shining armoured knight. The settee was empty. Comfort wasn't on the menu.

I picked up Gran's neatly folded afghan and put it back on the top shelf of my closet. Sometimes I don't know if his tidy ways are a sin or a virtue, in the time it took to fold it he could have written me a note.

I put the lettuce and tomatoes in the salad bin, threw the cheese on a fridge shelf, and heated up some asparagus soup that I ate with chunks of soft bread broken off the long baguette. The afternoon stretched before me with unenticing boredom. In a rare flurry of domesticity I turned out the cupboards and cleaned up. The kitchen still didn't look like Caroline Spedding's but Rome wasn't built in a day either.

Caroline! Yesterday's activity had pushed that second set of accounts right out of my mind, but now that I remembered them it brought me up short. Tax inspectors get intensely curious when such things are mentioned; at the best they smell noisily of a fiddle, but where Wilde and Cresswell were concerned they smelled of something worse. If the story Caroline had told me was true then those hidden accounts probably detailed monies from less than legal sources. The bouncer business sounded like a new line in protection rackets and I could see why a little imaginative accounting might be going on there. Then there were the Rave parties Caroline had told me about and the suggestion of money from drugs. Added together the whole thing smelled suspiciously like a laundering operation. It'd be really interesting to know what else they had on the boil.

I thought how some digging around was called for, but that wasn't a good word choice. It took me right back to the ash trees and that early morning ride with Nicholls.

To hell with domesticity! I slung the vac in the closet and took a good brisk walk. Sometimes when things start to pile up it's the only way to deal with them.

Outdoors, the weather was still in its mean and moody frame of mind but the drizzle had let up. Dust, turned to wet and sticky-black grime on the pavements, made little sucking noises as I walked.

Things boiled in my mind. Nothing I'd done or not done had made any difference to Andy. His grave had been dug before I'd even heard his name, so why was I still swamped out with guilt? Nothing felt right. Lund and Andy. Andy and Martin. Martin and the turned-over flat. I ambled around the back of a bus without thinking and almost got hit by a truck. Shit! that was scary. I took in a few deep breaths and waited for my heart to quit trying to climb out of my chest. Simultaneously I got a quick flash-back to Puggy's unlovely belly button winking in the gap between shirt and jeans.

Bramfield didn't have all that much street crime; bottle fights yes, vandalism yes, push-and-run handbag thieves yes – but Puggy had brought a blade along.

Maybe he'd had rape on his mind and not robbery. I thought back. The look on his face hadn't been lust, that was for sure. It was more like he'd seen a prime steak.

The story he'd handed the police about being out for a stroll didn't hang together. Well, maybe a moron would believe it but not me. Palmer's Run wasn't exactly the kind of locale Puggy'd pick for relaxation; the way I saw it his natural habitat ran to pubs, take-aways, and street corner haggling over the price of a quickie.

Of course there was a slim moon-falling-out-of-the-sky chance I could be misjudging him, he might be a real nature lover who'd gone along to admire the midnight gardens.

How many coincidences was I supposed to swallow just to prove I wasn't paranoid? I'd really like to have someone explain why, when I was just asking questions about Andy Howe, nothing happened, but the minute I poked into who'd been at Wilde's party all hell broke loose.

Lund's suicide had been really convenient. Convenient for Wilde and Cresswell that is. All of a sudden by that one act everybody's problems but Martin's came to an end. No more police questions, no more nosy reporters – and I'd bet a week's wages they thought no more me.

Tough!

I might not be looking for a missing person now, but tomorrow bright and early I'd be doing my damnedest to find out more about Wilde's business interests, I owed that much to Andy. Call it a matter of honour, or call it stupid, it's all dependent on viewpoint.

I circled home.

Marcie was coming down the outside steps with a black eye I could see from fifty yards away. She saw me and began a frantic scrabble in her bag; by the time I got level sun-glasses hid the worst of it.

'Last time this happened the rainbow eye was on me and you dispensed the sympathy,' I said. 'God, you look awful. What happened, can I help?'

'It's nothing, just me being stupid,' she said. 'Would you believe I walked into a door? I mean, it's the kind of impossible thing no one thinks can happen.'

Too right.

'It must have been some door,' I said. 'Where's Ben?'

'Greg's watching him until I get back.'

'He's still there, huh? Good looker, nice biceps.'

Two little spots of red came and showed up how white her cheeks were. 'He's looking for a place of his own. He's a freelancer, like me.'

'Nice. How's Ben doing? I heard him crying a couple of days back, not the croup again I hope?'

'Cutting a back tooth. He's fine now.' She shifted. 'I'd better get to the shop, I don't like to be away too long.'

'I could get whatever you need and bring it up,' I offered. 'I've nothing better to do right now, that way you can relax and put your feet up while I do the legwork.'

She looked like it was tempting but she still said no, adding a bit about how she needed some fresh air. To me it looked like she needed an ice-pack but that was something Greg ought to deal with. I wondered about Greg.

Going up past Marcie's flat I stuck my ear to the door and listened. Once a snoop always a snoop. But everything was quiet. Maybe Marcie really had blacked her own eye the way she said, and I was misjudging the whole situation. I really hoped so.

I went on up to my place, drank half of a carton of orange juice, took a shower, and put my feet up for a while. Just before six I made and ate a sandwich and washed it down with the rest of the juice while I watched the TV news. Around a quarter to seven I drove off for my weekly punch-out with Jack. I hoped he'd show me some new tricks, life was starting to get edgy again.

I'd been in his office, sitting cross-legged in my favourite spot, for a while before he came in. 'Thought I'd find you back here, monkey,' he said, 'been thinking about charging ogling fees, how much you think it's worth?'

'Not a lot. Be better maybe if you taught Sumo.' I grinned up at him. 'Better visual experience, if you know what I mean.'

'You ought'a get your mind off the Y-fronts.'

'Hadn't noticed they wore any,' I said cheerfully, and got up. 'Richie thinks you saved his life, it's lucky you happened along.'

'Yeah, well, things happen that way, Boiled the kettle, have you? Thought so.' He got out the Lapsang. 'Get on with him all right then?'

'I liked him. Could've warned me who he was though.'

His face cracked open. 'Thought it'd be an extra thrill. You get anything useful then?'

'Not really. He's into some tough litigation with Wilde, maybe that's why he got the beating. You think it might have been intended to go too far?'

'Hard to tell. Wouldn't have fancied his chances.'

'It worried him enough to leave town.'

Jack passed me a blue-striped mug. Waves of steam lifted up from smoky-dark tea. 'Gone already, has he then? Can't say it's a surprise, best way to stay healthy from what I've heard.'

'And what's that?'

'What's what?'

'What you've heard.'

'Same as he told you; like how the Brood's down from three, to one. High mortality rate.'

'How'd you know he told me that?'

'He dropped by,' Jack said lazily. 'Said thanks and so long. How's the tea?'

'Fine. He didn' t say anything else?'

'We had a bit of a chat – about you dropping round and that. I told him not to worry, you can look after yourself, but he didn't seem impressed.'

'That's it?'

With casual avoidance he said, 'Think I'll shift a few mats while me tea's cooling down,' and went out. Damn it, he knew me better than to think he could get away with that! I skipped out after him.

'Twice the muscle means twice as fast,' I said heaving a second mat close up to the first.

'Not always, wouldn't be around running this place if it was. Anyway, thought you'd done your job? From what I hear on the grapevine it ended nasty. This morning wasn't it?' He got a third mat lined up and squinted at me. Shit, but I wish I could pick up gossip the way he does, it's really annoying. I heaved on the mat he was standing on but he has real good reflexes. He must have jumped a half-second before I pulled, but he didn't jump off he jumped forward, and the weight of him landing took the mat edge out of my hands.

I went off balance and sat down ungraciously.

Jack grinned. 'Surprise tactics. Always do the unexpected, that's what it's all about.' He heaved the last mat around. 'Tea's going cold,' he said and went back into his office.

Well, that had been a real load of help! I went after him. I was beginning to feel like a poodle.

'You going to tell me about this morning then?' he said. 'If so you'd better make it quick, sounds like the gentle sex have turned up early.'

I'd heard it too; a girlish giggle. Why did women do that? I swallowed most of the Lapsang and swilled the rest around gently. 'Trade. What you know for what I know.'

'I don't seem to remember saying I knew anything. This body, it was who you were looking for was it? Kid that worked for Wilde.'

'Yes, it's a real downer.' I set the near-empty mug down and started playing around with the rim. 'He's probably been up there since the night he went missing.'

'Not something you could have done anything about then, is it?' said Jack logically. 'No point getting on the guilt train. I hear they had a fatality at Bloomers, Sunday night.'

'God!' I said. 'How do you do it!' He tapped the side of his nose and looked smug. I gave in, what the heck, he knew about it already, so I told it him again, including the way Lund's note had led to Andy.

'Going to get on with the painting and decorating now then?'

'Come on, Jack,' I chided, 'you know me better than that. What did Richie say?' The practice room filled up. The giggler gave another high-pitched trill. If she became a permanent fixture I'd need to change nights.

'He said to tell you he'd have liked to help, but he got too drunk to remember.'

'Sh-i-it! That's it?'

'That's it.'

He went out and left me to work up a good spurt of anger. It didn't take long. I watched him get the beginners to work.

So why was I so mad at him?

Why? Because I'd wanted Richie to have come up with something that would give me a handle and I'd jumped to the wrong conclusion again. Jack hadn't promised a thing. It was one of those times when being too clever causes problems. He squinted up at the mirror and came on back.

'Just so disappointment don't turn you sour I heard something you should find interesting. The late Mr Lund did eighteen months bird. Armley it was, nineteen sixty-four. Bet that gives you something to think about. Trust Uncle Jack to come up with the goodies.'

'How'd you find that out?'

He tapped his nose again. 'Aren't you going to ask what for.'

'What for?'

'GBH. Him an' two mates got their fun beating up gays,' he said. 'Funny old world.'

He could say that again!

CHAPTER NINETEEN

The telephone was ringing. I could hear it down at the bottom of the deep cave but I couldn't find it. The darkness felt like cotton-wool and the ringing was persistent. I opened my eyes and crawled out of bed. If it was Nicholls I'd kill him. If it stopped before I got to it I'd drop it out the window.

Two-thirty, damn it; who wanted to ring me at two-thirty in the morning?

Martin did.

He sounded young, and scared enough for his voice to have the stretched quality of a piano string. He didn't say who he was right away, not until he'd checked it was me and no imposter. Imposter? What would an imposter be doing in my bed at this time of a night. Sleeping, that's what. An imposter was in my bed sleeping, and I was in the hall with a draught going up my nightshift. I shook my head and tried to get it out of dream mode.

'You came to see me,' he said doubtfully.

'I came twice, Martin. The second time I was worried about you, your flat had been broken into.'

'Yeh, I can' t go back I'm . . . I've been dossing down . . . different places . . . friends an', aw fuck. FUCK!'

'Martin? You all right? You want me to come and get you?'

'No!

That was plain enough. Plain and panicky. The payphone pips went; he fed it more coins.

I said, 'Martin, tell me the phone number, that way I can ring back.' If he heard he didn't pay any attention, he just went right on with what he had to say. He sounded like he was breaking up.

'I rang home but the police were . . . um . . . so, I . . . rang a friend . . . he said . . . I . . . um . . . my father . . . '

'It's true,' I said gently. 'I'm really sorry, Martin. Let me come and get you, find you a safe place to stay.'

'He k-killed himself?'

'That's how it looked but I'm not too sure. It could have been rigged. Martin, Andy's dead too, and on the surface it looks as if your father killed him.' There was a long and complete silence. I hung on and hoped I hadn't overloaded him. 'I don't believe he did that you know,' I said when the silence had lasted long enough. 'I don't for one minute think your father killed Andy that night, but I'm going to need some help to find out what really happened. It's important to both of us, Martin.'

The pips went. This time he didn't feed the phone. Great! he'd run out of change. I said urgently, 'The number, Martin, read out the number.'

There was a sharp burst of static that drowned out everything; just before the line went dead I thought I heard him say, 'pelican crossing'. How helpful. He was in a phone box by a pelican crossing. Shit! How many were there in a place the size of Hull?

Maybe he hadn't said that, maybe he'd said something else, maybe he'd ring back. I heated up some milk and added a spoon of honey. The phone stayed silent. I rang Nicholls; the way I saw it, ducking out the way he had, he deserved to be awake. He sounded fresher than me. I left him to organise a round-up of pelican crossings in Hull, and went back to bed.

At seven I went for a run, when I got back at seven-thirty the phone was ringing again. I slammed the door behind me and grabbed the receiver. 'Martin . . . ?'

It was Nicholls.

'Wild-goose chase, Leah, he wasn't around. If he rings

back . . . '

'I'll let you know,' I cut in. 'He's scared out of his skin, Dave, I could hear it in his voice. What's happening with the post mortems, anything new come up?'

'How come when I want to ask a question you get six in first?'

'Just luck,' I said, 'so let's have the answers.'

'Yes . . . both PMs are done and no there's nothing new come up. Leah, I . . . '

'Huh! You mean they just confirmed how Lund had a sliced throat and Andy a stove-in head and that's it?'

'That's it. Look, Leah . . . '

'I have to talk to you about Lund – no – Martin. Both. I have a theory . . . '

'When don't you?'

'Is that what you wanted to ask me?' He muttered something nasty; it's so easy to wind him up. 'Go ahead,' I said sweetly, 'if you feel that way have your turn first.' He went silent, but I knew he was alive, I could hear him breathing.

'Right,' he said after a minute. 'Bloomers. I don't want any wriggling around with this, Leah, was that back door open or did you get in some other way?'

'It was open. I fell in, damn it.'

'You didn't see anybody else?'

'I didn't see anybody else, it happened just the way I said. Why?'

'It's a problem. Bye, Leah.'

'Hey! I need to talk.'

'Seven,' he said, and hung up.

Fine. I'd try to be home in time.

I showered, dressed, stripped the bed, loaded the washer, and put on clean sheets, by which time I was hungry from all the activity. Potato waffles, mushrooms and a fried egg dealt with that. I stuffed an apple and a can of Coke into a saggy shoulder-bag fast becoming a dump, shoved my arms into a navy wool jacket, and trotted off to Dora's.

149

She popped out of the front door as I backed down the drive and I recognised the worried look. It's nice to know she cares what happens to me, but sometimes it can be a bit of a fret. I cut the engine and got out. 'Hi, Dora,' I said. 'Grace's son get down all right?'

'Just before five. He says he's going to take her back with him for a holiday but I'm not sure she'll go. He looks a lot like Andy, bulkier across the shoulders but the eyes are the same. Says he wants to see you so he can say thanks.' I felt myself colour. *Thanks?* For what, for pity's sake?

'That's nice,' I said politely, 'but there's no need, I didn't do a thing.'

She looked at me sharply. 'Going anywhere special?'

'Uh. Just round and about. You know.'

'Leah. Grace – the both of us, want you to leave it alone now.'

'Nothing else I can do about Andy,' I said. 'The police are handling it the way they should have in the first place. D'you want anything from town?'

She shook her head and stepped back from the car. 'Come down for a natter when you get five minutes.'

'Soon as I can.' I climbed back in and started the engine, giving her a final wave as I drove away. Part of me felt mean for not being open about what I planned to do, but the other half knew she'd have tried to talk me out of it. Not that the plans I had included anything dangerous; what harm could a few simple questions cause?

I stopped by to see Darius, which was lucky, five minutes later and I would have missed him. He said, 'I tried to get a hold of you yesterday, don't you ever go home?'

'You just tried at the wrong times, I was sort of coming and going all day. You heard about Andy?'

'And Lund. I don't know what the connection is yet but I've got this instinctive newshound feel there is one.' He lifted his eyebrows hopefully. 'Come to give me a head-line?'

'Come to find out if you turned up anything interesting

in the archives.'

He shook his head. 'Nothing even mildly scandalous.'

'Does the *Echo* have access to Profile and Nexus?' His eyebrows went higher. 'Oh, come on,' I said, 'don't try looking surprised, who is it doesn't know about databases these days?'

The answer to that of course is a lot of people, and maybe it's better for their peace of mind that they walk around in happy ignorance. The right kind of knowledge on where to look can unearth a lot about Joe Bloggs that he always thought was secret. The databases I was interested in both held news files. I knew there'd be things in there about Wilde from way back, and I hoped the same would be true for Cresswell.

'Uh-uh, the *Echo* doesn't subscribe,' Darius said. 'No point, we only print local news.' He gave me one of his steady, trustworthy looks.

'But you know a man who can?' I said hopefully.

'Maybe – but why would I want to?'

'Trust me, if there's anything in it you'll be first to know.'

'What do you need?'

'Connections between Wilde and Cresswell. How long's it going to take?'

He snorted. 'Best part of a day – supposing I find anyone who'll give me access. It's an expensive business you know.'

'Any problems tell them to bill me,' I said rashly, and left him to get on with calling in favours while I went to do some snooping of my own.

Inland Revenue, DHSS and sundry council departments live in a sixties glass and concrete labyrinth. It had been a real clever touch the way the planners cut down on foot traffic by siting the place on a corner of the busiest roundabout in town. OAPs had to make it there via a mugger's paradise underpass, the more able-bodied made a hairy dash through fast traffic that about equalled running with the bulls in Pamplona.

I'd been working on a convincing story to tell Pete since last night, Pete being head of department with his own little glass office, and two grades up from me. Most times he's a pussy-cat but he hates having people try to slip things by. The only thing he hates worse is having people avoid paying taxes and that's what I was banking on.

I rode up in the lift, went through reception, and skipped into Pete's office with a smile on my face. Red vein motorways were back in his eyes and I guessed his love life was still running below par. Pete's biggest trouble is he tries too hard. He's thirty-five and already panicking about a lonely old age; which is why he drives a black XR3i to impress. When I went in he took his feet off the desk and looked wary.

'Busy?' I said.

'What happened to the holiday?'

'I'm enjoying it, you wouldn't believe the fun I've been having, but you know me, always an eye open for tax dodgers.' I'd got him, I could tell by the gleam in his pickled eyes. 'And I think I'm on to a beauty,' I added for prime impact.

'This district?'

'Has to be.'

'And you want to go and poke through the files.'

'Well, you could do it if you want, but I'd have to tell you the whole set-up, which would take time, and I know you're busy.' He steepled his fingers and rocked his head a bit.

'Whereas you could go right to it.'

'No trouble.'

'Whose dealing with the file?'

'Files,' I corrected. 'One is or should be Trish's, the other I think will be Arnold's.' His ears pricked up. Arnold is something of a golden boy, which is why it was so nice to think he'd let something slip past him.

'Not another Cluedo game of your own you've got involved in,' he said suspiciously.

'Pete,' I said, 'once was enough, from now on anything I

get into is accidental. I promise this fiddle involves a lot of money. Mega-bucks. It'll earn you a gold star.'

'I want to know what you come up with.'

'Of course,' I said sweetly. 'But remember whose investigation it is when next Monday comes around and I'm back at work. Will you clear it?'

He went out and had a little chat with Arnold and Trish. Trish looked over and waved at me and gave a nod; Arnold seemed to take a little more convincing.

By and by, Pete came back and gave me the go-ahead, complaining all the while about why it couldn't have waited until next week. 'Easy,' I said. 'I'm just too conscientious, I'd have spoiled the rest of my holiday worrying.'

A worryaholic like himself could understand that.

I busybodied off among the files and gave Arnold a little wave as I went by.

He looked really choked.

CHAPTER TWENTY

Say 'tax file' to a lot of people and right away their eyes glaze over. I can understand that, say 'furniture polish' to me and you'd get the same reaction. It's lucky we all have different boredom levels. I dug and delved into the affairs of Wilde and Cresswell with happy abandon; after a while Trish wandered in and asked how it was going, and wandered away again when I told her fine. By noon I had a list of declared sources of income for both men, substantial enough to make me ask if all those profits were real or part of a laundering process. Singly, Wilde had made himself into a company called Wilde Enterprises, under which umbrella sheltered Wildnites Entertainment Agency, and DW Records (Hull); none of them were limited companies. DW wasn't a record label I was familiar with, its main business seemed to lie in exports, with only around twenty per cent of business coming from home sales. Coupled with Cresswell's profits from Lakeside and Bloomers the final figures made me wonder if the current recession was just imaginary. Some people are born to make money I guess. Until they get caught.

I tidied up neatly and stopped by Trish's desk to tell her everything was fine, I didn't do the same for Arnold, it wouldn't hurt to let him sweat a little.

Pete was on his feet before I got level with his office, I guess he thought I'd probably just walk on by if he didn't show himself. He was right. I gave him a wave and fled, taking the stairs instead of hanging around for the lift, and driving fast out of the car-park just in case he was panting along behind. I picked up a sandwich from an off-licence and ate it as I headed north along the bypass, swinging off when I got to the A650 which took me into Bradford and Wildnites Entertainment Agency.

The south side of Bradford isn't all that impressive with its rows of aged terrace houses, derelict land sites, and run-down housing estates, but the town itself is something else, a rambling, busy shopping centre down at the bottom of a hollow with a steep climb out whichever road you take. I swooped down into the one-way traffic system and eased my way around on to Thornton Lane and the six-storey office block that housed Wildnites. I cruised around the car-park looking for an empty space without finding one. Great.

A girl in a fringed plum-colour skirt and sequinned bra came trotting out of a side door and got into a Mini. I backed up and waited. She reached over to the back seat, found a black sweater, pulled it on and started pinning up her hair. I sighed. An ancient Escort came out of the far corner and a newcomer Montego tried to beat me there. He didn't make it. Over by the door the Mini backed out and the Montego's gears crunched, a blue Porsche swept in through the exit and beat him to it by a hair. Mr Montego was having a bad day. I started to get out and the Porsche driver did the same. I ducked back in and crouched down on the driving seat thinking how I owed the Mini driver a vote of thanks. If she hadn't stopped to do her hair Cresswell would have walked right in on me.

I angled the rear-view mirror and pretended to be invisible.

Fifteen minutes went by and boredom set in. All I had to look at was a brick wall in front and parked cars behind. Some music would be nice; it would also be like waving a flag. I fished around in the glove compartment and found half a Snickers bar; eating it filled in a little more time. Up on top of the wall a shiny grey-black starling mugged a sparrow for a piece of bread; crime's on the upturn everywhere these days.

A couple of minutes later Cresswell came out with two men I'd never seen before, one the type you'd pass in a crowd and not notice, the other with hair like a firethorn. Both were in jeans and lightweight anoraks and carried Adidas sports bags.

They got into the Porsche with Cresswell, and when it left the car-park I followed it sedately back around the one-way system to the Interchange. *How nice*, I thought as he dumped them by the station entrance, he's been giving them a lift. He didn't bother with any prolonged goodbyes, just put his foot down and went out into the A650 traffic stream back to Bramfield. I filtered back into the town centre lane and played ring-a-ring o' roses back to Wild-nites.

The entertainment agency occupied the west corner of the building on the ground floor, accessed via a heavy glass door with a diagonal red push-handle. I leaned on it and got near dazzled by zingy red carpeting with eye teasing black overcheck; the theme got picked up again by the chair seats on which half a dozen people were waiting around. One, with long black hair tied in a pony-tail and an air of boredom, looked like he might not be averse to some social chatter. I flopped on to the seat next to him. 'Hi,' I said brightly. 'You waiting for an interview?' He blinked like he'd just come down from another planet. I gave it another go. 'I mean, is this a first visit or are you on the books?'

That did better, it got, 'I'm on the books,' delivered in a flat monotone. He went back to staring at the wall: hung with posters, photographs, handbills and press reviews the way it was, I guess it had a lot going for it.

'Musician?'

'Yeh.'

'Metal?'

'Rock.'

This was getting me nowhere. I stuck a hand out. 'Zee Carson, I'm doing a round up of northern agencies for the

New Musical Express. Maybe you'd like to give me your own views on Wildnites? Do they find you plenty of work?'

His attention zapped from wall to me, he held my hand like it belonged to Cleopatra, the bored look went like magic; there's nothing like the smell of publicity for concentrating minds. I took back my hand before it melted and fished out pen and notebook, flicking pages fast so he couldn't see the shopping lists. 'What do you reckon then,' I said, 'are Wildnites OK?'

He waved an expansive hand. 'They're not bad, you know, considering, like, how many clubs are going down, you know, around here like, I mean it's the same all round, shops shutting, an' everything, it's all going down, like, if you know what I mean?'

'Same all over,' I agreed. 'Manchester, now – uh-huh, it's bad around there. Grim.'

'That so? Me and the fellas thought we might have a try around there, thanks for putting us right.'

I swallowed down hard. *Shit*, the place might be really jumping and I'd put him off.

'Well, you know I wouldn't want to discourage you,' I said, 'talent always finds work even in times like these.' He glowed a little.

'Mad Lads,' he said. I looked at him, 'That's what we play as, like, Mad Lads. Thought you'd want to get it down, you know, for doing your write-up. There's just the three of us like, in the group, but we've got a couple of singles out.'

I wrote Mad Lads and underlined it. 'Really!' I enthused. 'Now that' s *interesting*, I mean, really interesting, the readers'll love it. What label?'

'Well, it's . . . er . . . you know, not one of the big boys, well, I mean it's doing it what counts and, like, if you get lucky one of the top labels picks it up and you're away. You know. I mean that's how it goes. Yeh?'

'Definitely, yes, that's the way in. So what label did you say?'

'DW.'

'Right, that's Dean Wilde's own company.'

He perked up some more. 'You've heard of it then?'

'Oh yes, it's known, around . . . in the business. Talent spotting, that's the way I see it. DW picks up new names and by and by a big record house pulls them out. So where do you do the actual recording, Hull?'

'That's right, you know the set-up there then.'

'Not really,' I said cautiously. 'I know he does a lot of exporting. Big market on the Continent.'

'Yeh. Well, we're hoping, aren't we. What happens is, like, DW press a few thou what they think'll sell, an' we get a couple of hundred to sell local, off the top. Gigs an' things.'

'What about royalties?'

'Well, we got to earn expenses back first like, lot of groups don't, DW's money down a drain then, isn't it?'

'Right. So, how do you do for gigs? Dean Wilde owns a few clubs of his own, doesn't he?'

'Haven't heard that, no, but he's got a mate owns a couple we've played at. Mostly it's bookings round working-men's clubs, they're the ones give the most work. Played a few holiday camps back in summer, them was all right, looked after us well.'

'Great!' I wrote Holiday Camps and underlined it. 'So this friend of Wilde's, Bob Cresswell is it? Owns Bloomers over at Bramfield?'

'Yeh, that's right, other's here in Bradford, Pelican Crossing, Queens Road; you can't miss it, not if you're looking for it. Tell you what, we got a gig there Thursday night.' He fished in his pocket and gave me a pink ticket. It said:

PELICAN CROSSING

Mad Lads

admit one guest

'Give 'em that an' say you're with Ned, shouldn't have no trouble getting in then.'

I thought about all the pelican crossings Hull police

must have driven around before the birds woke up that day. Ho-hum, if nobody else told them they'd been wasting their time I certainly wouldn't.

I sighed.

'You're Ned?'

'Yeh, that's me. I'll look out for you then.'

Nothing could keep me away.

'Can't promise,' I lied. 'Do my best but Thursday could be a bit difficult. How about Rave parties, Ned, do you get asked to do that type of gig? I've heard Wilde puts on some good all-nighters.'

'You going to write all this up?'

'Whatever my editor let's through.'

'Yeh, well, don't make it sound like it came from me.'

'I won't,' I said hastily. 'I'll put it in another piece altogether.'

'Yeh, well, right then, if you know it already can't do any harm, can it? Yeh, we played a couple of Raves, they're not, you know, uncontrolled, I mean Wilde won't have that, they've got to be kept really tight, like no alcohol, no outside dealers making trouble . . . I mean he's got his own muscle so it happens like he wants.'

'Bouncing bouncers.'

'Yeh! Right!'

'No outside dealers.' I looked at Mad Lad Ned and wondered how far I could take it. 'But a Rave wouldn't be a Rave without a little pill or two. Maybe he has that organised too.'

His eyes flicked over to the wall and back again. 'We just play,' he said, 'an' we don't ask questions. How long you been with *NME*?'

'Oh, a while now.' Fifteen minutes at least, a pity the paper didn't know what a good reporter they didn't have. 'I freelance, special articles, in-depth research, new groups to watch – that's where I plan to slot in the Mad Lads.' I was really getting carried away, it was a shame the office door opened and spoiled our tête-à-tête.

Middle-aged women in tweed skirts and green-framed

159

glasses always look so respectable. This one cooed, 'Ned, love, it's your turn. Sorry you've had to wait so long, chuck, not upset with us are you?'

'No,' said Ned, getting up off his chair. 'Course not, I like hooves on me bum.' He shook hands and said he hoped I'd make it on Thursday. The long fringe on the sleeve of his leather jacket bounced up and down. He sounded sincere and I felt really bad about the game I'd played with him. Maybe I could write the *NME* a fan letter saying how good the Mad Lads were.

Maybe Darius knew somebody who wrote a column about the music business. Maybe I should stop telling lies.

Ned was putting on a lot of dog and the woman's eyes swivelled back to me. He gave me a wave. What could I do but give him one back. The woman came on over; she looked about forty-five and a lot more formidable than the cooing voice suggested. I bounced on to my feet.

'Hi,' I said offering my hand again. 'I'm Zee Carson, and I'm doing an article on northern agencies for the *New Musical Express*, and it was really exciting to find Ned in here, we've had rave reports about the Mad Lads, I'd say they were a group to watch. He's been telling me they've cut two singles. I bet you're really glad to have them on your books.'

'We look after our artistes,' she said. 'Plenty of work and no messing.'

'HAH!' came from my left. The woman didn't even blink.

'Anyone not happy here is free to move on ... unlike some agencies we never hold anybody to a contract if it isn't mutually rewarding.' The rebuke over, she got back to me. 'If you want an interview it'll have to be an appointment, love, we're absolutely chock-a-block today, well, you can see that for yourself, can't you. I can slot you in for half an hour Friday, half nine?'

I told her Friday I'd be in Birmingham but maybe I'd give her a ring next time I came up this way. We shook hands again and I waited for her to disappear; she did the same for me. Obviously she didn't want me to find out where the 'hah!' came from. I retreated, anything more would probably be gilding the lily in any case.

I went back out to the car and headed for home.

Nicholls always gets things wrong, I don't know how he does it. With a couple of hours to fill in I'd skipped the Tuesday work-out and got busy painting the hall a warm white; at exactly seven the doorbell rang.

Maybe my watch had stopped, since when did he ever come on time?

I finished the last ten inches of skirting board, put the lid on the paint can, and went to let him in. Of course if I'd expected him to turn up looking like a dream-date in his best suit I'd have spent my time prettying up instead. His hands were empty.

'You forgot the take-away,' I said.

He looked at my messy state.

'I thought we'd eat out.'

Great! I wondered which hot-dog stand.

'Maybe you could clean the paint brush for me while I change.' I looked at him dubiously. 'No, better not, you'd only blame me if you got your suit messed up.' I dumped everything on a newspaper in a corner of the kitchen and went to get cleaned up.

At seven-thirty I went looking for him, dressed up for anything Bramfield had on offer in a skinny mulberry dress with matching high heels and a black silk jacket. His eyes took them all off again.

I love it when he looks that appreciative.

CHAPTER TWENTY-ONE

We dined at Bailey's. Note I said dined and not ate. I was glad I hadn't worn just any old thing. It wasn't the first time I'd eaten there, but it was the first time with Nicholls, and I was trying to work out why he'd gone to all that trouble, the place is five or six miles out of town on a hilly stretch of road between Bramfield and Kirkburton, and its culinary reputation has been made solely by word of mouth. No point even thinking about a table for Friday, Saturday or Sunday unless you want to book two months ahead. Even mid-week is dicey. I finished the last drop of asparagus soup and wondered why we were here and not at the Burger King or the Raj Poot.

The empty bowl got whisked away and I watched the waiter's receding butt appreciatively.

Bailey's waiters are really cute; tight black pants and shiny shoes, white frilly shirts and black bow ties, the whole thing tied together with a bright red cummerbund and not a spreading waist among them. I gave my attention back to Nicholls and the way his eyes had fixed on me with speculative intent.

Maybe it was his birthday.

I sipped wine. The dimple at the side of his mouth winked at me. If he played his cards right he might even get a present . . . Later.

'So,' he said. 'What do you want to tell me about Lund and Martin that I don't already know?'

He's really great at spoiling a good mood.

The waiter came back; he had nice brown eyes and a sexy mouth, definitely Byronic. I got his attention and gave him my best come-on look. He spilled some gravy on to Nicholls' napkin. Satisfied, I dropped my eyes demurely, he hovered a little behind Nicholls' chair but he'd had all he was going to get.

I got on with feeding the inner woman.

Nicholls sighed. It was loud enough for my mother to hear in Wales so I guessed it was done for effect; such things are best ignored.

After a while I set my fork down and looked across the table. 'You know why Lund couldn't have taken Andy on that last ride?' I demanded. 'Because Martin was there too and that's why he's hiding.'

'You don't know that.'

'I talked with Martin, remember.'

'You know,' he wagged his fork at me. 'One day you're going to get yourself arrested for obstructing police inquries.'

'What inquiries?' I said nastily. 'I didn't notice there were any going on.'

'Maybe you should drop by every morning so you can read the work schedule.'

'Are you interested in what I'm saying or not?'

'There's more?'

'Be like that,' I snapped, and went back to eating.

'All right,' he said when the silence had got as thick as meringue. 'Tell me the rest of it.'

'Not unless you really want to hear.'

'I really want to hear.'

A sixtyish couple at the next table squinted across, obviously thinking we were in a lovers' quarrel. I said, 'Don't shout, you've got people watching.'

He rolled his eyes up. 'God!' Nobody answered.

I said sweetly, 'Drop a little word into CID ears with my compliments, something they could have found out for themselves if they'd asked the right questions. Lund did eighteen months in Armley for GBH. He liked to

163

beat up homosexuals.'

Some of the blue went out of Nicholls' eyes. 'When?'

'Nineteen sixty-four. Does that kind of a leopard ever get to change its spots?'

He shook his head and stared at me.

Our plates disappeared. Two profiterole mountains took their place, dripping in chocolate sauce and swathed in sugar angel hair.

'You'd better be sure about this,' he said.

Jack, I thought, this is the one time I really need that spy-network to be right. I crossed my fingers.

'I'm sure.'

Nicholls nodded and got on with eating. Sometimes food seems to be a great consolation to him. I waited until we reached the coffee stage before I told him sweetly that Lund hadn't killed himself either.

He set his cup down very carefully and reminded me about the suicide note. I tore a page out of my little notebook, signed it at the bottom and gave it to him. He's not dumb, he knew what I meant. He scrunched it up and put it in the ashtray.

'The note had Lund's prints on it, not anybody else's,'

'I bet. Just like the knife that cut his throat was in his right hand. Nobody else's prints on that either.'

'There wouldn't be, would there.'

I shrugged. When I'd found Lund in his office something had seemed out of kilter, something wrong about the whole scene, and it had taken me a long time to work out what that was.

'So how many left-handed men slice their throats open from left to right?' I said flatly, having finally worked out what I'd subconsciously picked up on as wrong when I'd first seen the Stanley knife in Lund's right hand – although it had taken until last night to work its way through to conscious recognition and I was really annoyed with my laggard brain. The first time I'd met up with the nightclub manager at Bloomers he'd been nervous, his left hand busy pen tapping, and when the tapping stopped he'd set the pen down at the left of his blotter.

'I tried to tell you this morning,' I said when Nicholls kept on looking at me, 'but you didn't want to hear it right then.'

'How long have you been sitting on it,' he said sounding angry with either me or someone else.

'Since last night. Damn it, Nicholls, it took that long for the penny to drop. Look, if he'd had a wife, or Martin had been home you'd have picked up on it sooner.'

'Would we?' he said bitterly. 'It's a bloody shambles.' He pushed back from the table, snapped: 'Telephone,' and stalked off. When he came back neither of us brought Lund up again; I'd said what I had to say and he'd done his listening. We drove home amicably. I felt warm and re-laxed the way I always did after a good meal and the right kind of wine. I let my head droop on his shoulder and he nuzzled his chin over and grinned. It was definitely going to be a cocoa night. He parked neatly outside my door and we had some fun working through a few of the prelimi-naries. By and by, I said I could think of a much comfier place to be doing all this.

He untangled himself carefully and said he had to catch the red-eye to London.

'Uh-huh.' I eased back over to my side of the car, 'I wondered why we weren't eating burgers.'

'It's my birthday,' he said.

'Uh-huh.'

'Honest.'

'Right, I believe you,' I agreed. 'And I had a present, all wrapped up and waiting.'

For a second I thought he was going to weaken. Hah!

'I'll collect it Friday,' he said.

'Uh-huh. I hope it keeps,' I told him frigidly, and got out.

'Leah . . . '

I went on up the front steps.

'Leah . . . ? I'll be back Friday morning; we'll fix some-thing up then.'

Like his teeth maybe!

I thought how ramming that nice, sexy smile right down his throat would dissipate a lot of frustration.

'Have a good trip,' I said, and shut the door on him.

Passing Marcie's place I listened in again. Canned laughter came from the TV, other than that things were quiet. Maybe Greg was a nice guy after all . . . like Attila. I went on up to my attic and started a strong coffee brew to dilute the effect of all that good wine I'd drunk. I didn't need a warm happy glow to play solitaire. Soaking in a hot bath while the coffee dripped through I tried to remember what else I'd intended to do that night, but it slipped away in dozy warmth.

The telephone rang.

Ignore it.

It kept on.

Unwillingly I left the tub and staggered to the phone. Darius said, 'Did I get you out of bed?'

'Uh, no. The bath.'

'Progress report. I found a man who can,' he said.

'Can what, for God's sake?' I hunkered down, back against the wall and shook my head. The fog lifted. 'You found something on Wilde and Cresswell?'

'Nope. I'm just letting you know I can get into the databases, but there are conditions.'

'What conditions?'

'If there's a meaty story my helpful friend wants it ahead of the other dailies. I told him you'd go along with that.'

'Darius, the minute anything happens I'm on the phone.'

'That's good enough,' he said. 'I'll get back to you.'

'Uh . . . look, Darius, I might not be home much the next couple of days, maybe I should do the calling?'

'Whatever.'

'Still got the same number?'

'Can't afford to move.'

'Poverty like yours makes me cry. Night, Darius.'

I hung up, turned off the coffee-machine, and took a mug of the stuff to bed with me – caffeine being a necessity if I wanted to do any serious thinking. I dumped the towel, stacked the pillows and crawled naked under the duvet to drink and think. Next thing I knew it was eight in the morning, the coffee was cold, and I felt as lethargic as a log.

I closed my eyes and wished the world away. Such wishes are useless against the urgent need to pee.

CHAPTER TWENTY-TWO

Coming back from a heavy-footed run I met up with Greg; I can't say he looked overjoyed but I thought I ought to try and make friends, especially if we were going to be close neighbours for a while. I slowed right down.

'Hi, there, nice morning.'

'Hadn't noticed,' he said without even breaking step to say it. Nice guy! I went on in and took up my milk; Marcie's was already gone but that didn't stop me knocking on her door. It took a while for her to come and say uncertainly: 'Leah . . . ?'

'How about coming up for coffee and a gossip, it's a while since we got together.'

She pulled her robe up round her neck and gripped it. 'Uh, well, I'm not dressed yet and Ben's asleep, maybe another time.'

'Fine. I thought with Greg being out . . . '

'He's just gone down to the shop, that's all, he'll be back anytime.' She'd got the cotton material clenched so tight her knuckles were bleached. What was going on here?

'He can come too, I'll brew extra.'

Her eyes shifted from me to her feet. 'I . . . um . . . don't think he's . . . '

Nothing else came. I felt awkward, standing there hugging a bottle of milk like we were strangers. I plunged right in. 'Look, Marcie, I don't know what's going on but anytime you need me I'm right at the top of the stairs.'

She flushed brightly and shut the door.

I took a couple of seconds worrying time. That edgy female wasn't the Marcie I'd swapped friendly chit-chat with for the last two years. Downstairs the front door banged. I sped up the next flight of stairs on my toes and crept in home like a thief. Great! Now he'd got me intimidated too.

I took a quick shower, fixed breakfast, and fished out Andy's diary, propping it up before me while I ate. The problem with coded jottings is that it takes a cypher expert to understand them. I felt like a dyslexic trying to make sense of Shakespeare as I flicked pages. I chewed around on ifs and maybes for a while and then gave up – if Andy's diary entries concerned Wilde's dodgy business deals then the music man had nothing to worry about, I couldn't make head or tail of them.

Maybe I should give the diary to Nicholls . . . when he got back.

As I stacked breakfast pots and felt hard done by, I brooded on how lucky my sometimes lover was to have back-up files, books full of mug shots, and tame snitches all to hand.

What I needed right then . . . *really* needed . . . was a snitch of my own; somebody with inside knowledge of the local crime scene, somebody who kept an ear to the ground and . . .

Sid!

It was comforting to know that when push came to shove I knew the right people. I grabbed a jacket and took the car down to Charlie's Car Repairs. Charlie's yard is hidden away off Market Street, and back before horseless carriages killed off four-footed trade the place had been an ostler's. The old stables had fallen down years ago and Charlie picked the whole lot up cheap. He's built himself a nice little business doing repairs and rebuilding bangers. There were three of his tarted-up remakes flaunting FOR SALE stickers over by the far wall when I drove in, outwardly two were Ford, the other a Vauxhall, but where Charlie's bargain bangers are concerned only a fool goes by appearances.

I parked neatly and got out.

Charlie was on his haunches tinkering with an engine block. He squinted up suspiciously. Like most people he works at paying less tax than he should which is how I got to know him.

'Relax, Charlie,' I said, 'I'm on holiday.'

'Nice you can afford the break, me, I have to keep working.' He glanced at the hybrid and got up. 'Giving trouble then?'

'Sweet as honey.'

He picked up an oily rag and wiped his fingers.

'What's up then?'

'I want to talk to Sid.'

He looked at his hands. They weren't any cleaner. 'What you after this time then?' He gave me a squinty look.

'I'd go direct, except I don't know how,' I reminded him.

'Not a lot of people do, security conscious, that's what Sid is, love. You got yourself into some bother then?'

'Come on, Charlie, don't give me the run around, I need to talk to Sid.'

'Business or pleasure?'

'Shit, Charlie, need is need.'

'Yeh, well, depends if it's trade, Sid don't do much charity work.'

'So what's he selling?'

'Depends what you need, love. He'll want to know.'

I watched him rub a black streak into his nose and wondered about the caginess. It was a side of Charlie's character I hadn't seen before and there had to be some good reason for it. Maybe Sid was keeping a low profile.

'I'm insulted, Charlie,' I said and stuck a wrist out. 'Smell that perfume . . . not Gorgonzola is it?'

He sniffed appreciatively. 'Aftershave,' he said. 'Bought some last week for me girlfriend. Wouldn't catch no mice though.' Charlie's a lot brighter than he looks.

'So tell it to Sid,' I said.

He moved off to his lean-to office. 'Want a cuppa? Got a

170

bit of Earl Grey.'

'Nice,' I said. 'I'll make it, shall I?'

He looked at his hands and grinned. 'Bit of muck never hurt anybody, but suit yerself.'

Charlie's office is about as opulent as a dog kennel and just as spacious, with roughly the same kind of smell. I filled up the kettle and found two mugs, ears active as he got busy with the phone. From the sound of things, Sid seemed to be playing a little coy.

'Suit yerself,' Charlie grumped, 'you don't want to take my word, 's up to you.' He listened for a bit. 'Course I'm bleedin' sure. Straight up she is, allus has been.' I felt a little glow; testimonials are always nice. Another pause. 'Don't leave her much time.' There was an explosion of noise. Charlie shifted the receiver from his ear. 'Yeh, all right then. Eleven. I'll tell her.' He hung up and turned round. 'Better forget the tea, me old love. Crown and Feathers, twenty minutes. Know where it is?'

I did a quick run through Bramfield's pubs and shook my head.

'Denby Dale an' turn up Penistone. Half a mile up t'hill, right-hand side. Been havin' his toes trod on a bit so he'll not wait.'

'Who by?'

'Yeh, well, that's half his trouble, doesn't know for sure, does he? Wouldn't be so flamin' cagey if he did.'

I said, 'Thanks, Charlie, shame about the cuppa.'

'It'll keep.' He walked me back to the car and gave the wing a rub with his rag. 'Don't want to change it yet then?'

'Uh-uh.'

He grinned.

'Character car, that's what you've got.'

I started the motor and lowered the window.

'Getting back to Sid's toes,' I said. 'What kind of treading?'

'Nothing he won't handle. Off you go then, have a nice chat.'

I gave him a little wave as I went.

171

Mid-morning traffic is usually light, but not that day. I came off the roundabout on to the A636 and half a mile along met a tail-back. I crawled a couple of miles in second gear and hoped Charlie was wrong when he said Sid wouldn't wait; another half mile and I saw the problem: the high cab of a tractor with a muck-spreader hooked on to its back. Every so often a gap in oncoming traffic let a car or truck pull round and zip away into the distance. Just before my turn came the damn thing made a right turn down a farm lane. I cursed tractors in general and that one in particular; I now had eight minutes to cover ten miles on a twisty two-lane road. What fun!

By the time I turned up the steep hill to Penistone I was getting a foot cramp from all the fancy braking I'd been doing.

The Crown and Feathers fronted on to the road, brick-built and hung with ivy. Parking was around the back and out of sight. When I bumped round the corner there were three cars on the weed-cracked tarmac. Sid's Jaguar wasn't one of them.

I pulled into a slot, turned the engine off, and felt disappointed. Five minutes, damn it. He could have waited that long. I locked up and went into the bar.

Sid was in the window corner with half an inch of whisky left in his glass. I got a cold Pils and went over.

'Park it,' he said, and patted the scratched red vinyl seat next to him. 'Don't know why it is women like to be late. Came alone I hope?'

'Who would I bring?'

'You tell me, pet, you tell me.'

Late fifties, neat and dapper, his green Argyll sweater had exactly the right degree of bagginess; cashmere of course, not lambswool, I could tell that without even seeing the label. I lifted my glass in salute.

'Cheers.'

'So,' he said. 'What's it about then, what have I got that you want?'

'Information about a man called Dean Wilde. I'd be

172

really interested to know about his business dealings, especially any that don't happen to be legitimate.'

'So would a lot of people. What's the interest?'

'I think something he's mixed up in got a friend of mine
killed. I don't like to think of him getting away with it.'

'That I can understand, but why come to me?'

'Instinct, Sid. Charlie never said what line of business
you were in, but my guess is you're pretty well versed in
who's doing what to whom on the shady side of life.'

'Flattery,' he said. 'Never could resist it. I'll ask around a
bit. That do?'

Disappointment fell on me. I'd played this whole scene
over in my mind before I got here, but it hadn't gone quite
this way. I took a long draught of Pilsner and let a couple
of minutes pass while I stared at the table.

He tilted his head on one side. 'So what was you expecting, instant miracles?'

I shrugged. 'Maybe so. Sid, I'm sick to my stomach
thinking how Wilde's set things up so he'll get away with
it. I hoped you'd help me get a handle on him. He's got
everybody thinking he's Mr Innocent.'

'And you're the lone voice crying in the wilderness.'

I squinted at him. Biblical quotes were not what I expected from Sid. 'Something like that,' I said.

'I know the feeling. Like the man said, we all have our
problems. Me, you, the Pope.'

'Uh-huh. And I'm sure my friend Andy appreciates that;
being dead probably lets him be that philosophical. Me, I
don't see things the same way.'

He tilted his head back and looked at the ceiling. 'Got to
think of the money side too. A lot of people do business
with your Mr Wilde.'

'Like you,' I said.

'I do some.'

Maybe what he was trying to tell me was that his own
financial dealings with Wilde put us on opposite sides;
which made this get-together about the biggest mistake I'd
ever made. The idea wasn't pleasant. The first time I saw

Sid I'd thought what a great insurance salesman he'd make with his good shark's teeth and nice smile. I'd also thought that in his line of business he'd got no right to look that honest. I finished the Pils and started to move out.

He swung his eyes back down to me.

'Changed your mind then?'

I shrugged. 'Seemed like you weren't all that interested in my little problems. I promised Charlie I wouldn't push.'

'So do me a favour and sit still while I think. This friend of yours . . . is he the kid I hear got dug up, Monday morning?'

'Yes.'

'Not nice that kind of thing, not nice at all, specially when it happens to a friend. So what's the bottom line then, you had a look round Wilde's place on the q.t.?'

'Uh-uh. Not possible. Rottweiler, guards, the lot. Except for party nights it's like Fort Knox, and I'm not on his guest list.'

'Could be healthier that way. What is it you think he's into?'

'A neat twist in extortion. New bouncers for old.'

Sid's eyes iced up, 'Is that so? Now that's interesting. Think Wilde's behind that bit of arm-bending do you?'

I sat quite still; if I was wrong about Sid, if we were on opposite sides, I was in deep shit. We looked at each other, weighing up options, and I couldn't read his face.

'I didn't think it would be news, Sid,' I said. 'I hear some club owners round and about Bramfield have been under pressure for a while now.'

'Too right,' said Sid. 'Had one of my own boys hospitalised, didn't I. What's news is Wilde being in it. If he's the one been rattling my chain I'm not happy.'

'I guess that gives us a common cause then.'

'Maybe.' He looked at me, his eyes not warming up any. 'I need to ask around. I'll be in touch.'

'Fine, do that. Maybe better not hold my breath though, huh?'

He showed me his good teeth again.

I drove back to Bramfield a lot more sedately than I'd left it, and thought how nice not to leave rubber on every corner. It being on my way I called in at the *Echo*; Darius was out someplace so I left a message and took a walk to the baker's, picking up fresh bread-rolls for a soup and salad lunch. Around one-thirty the phone rang. I left my gourmet snack and went to answer it, expecting to hear Darius, but hoping it was Martin.

It wasn't either; some days being wrong turns into a habit. Neil said, 'I thought a quiet dinner for two at Bertolini's, just you, me and a candle, tell me it sounds good.'

'It sounds good,' I said obediently. 'But . . . '

'Pick you up at seven,' he said, and hung up.

Shit, he'd been too fast for me. I got back to a dialling tone and started to punch in his number.

Bertolini's, huh? Maybe I wasn't that busy after all.

I put the phone down and went to finish up the canned soup.

CHAPTER TWENTY-THREE

Everybody has faults, and somewhere along the way Neil had to have picked up a few too, but whatever they were a lack of punctuality wasn't among them. I was glad I wasn't having one of my tardy days. Right on seven he rang the front doorbell. I wondered if maybe he'd been sitting out there counting the seconds off.

When I skipped downstairs the high heels on my shoes made clackity noises and let everybody know I was coming. Marcie's door opened a crack and I could hear Ben crying, then it slammed shut with enough force behind it to shake the banister rail. I went back up two steps and banged on the wood.

'Marcie? Marcie, everything all right in there?' Greg did all the answering and he sounded really wound up, 'She's fine, mind your own damn business, Leah.'

I pounded again. 'Marcie?'

'*Piss off!*'

'When I hear from Marcie.'

There was a little thud. *Judas*, what was happening in there? I started to feel panicky. 'Marcie!' The downstairs doorbell rang again. 'Greg,' I yelled, 'you've got thirty seconds before I get the police.'

I counted out loud; a second before time Marcie said 'It's all right, Leah, I'm fine, honestly.' She didn't sound it. Her voice sounded thick, like she was talking through a mouth full of treacle.

I said tightly, 'How about opening the door, Marcie. I'd

really like to see that for myself.'

'Um . . . no, I can't right now, Leah, I'll talk to you tomorrow, huh . . . I fell off a stool and Greg's in a panic. I'm getting really clumsy.'

'You hurt?'

'An Elastoplast and I'll be fine. Ben's only crying because I scared him a bit.'

I bet!

'Listen, I'll be home around ten,' I said, loud enough for Greg to get the message too. 'You want me after that just yell.'

'Have a nice time,' she said. A floorboard creaked. With my ear jammed up against the wood panel I could hear her shuffling away. *Shuffling?* Since when did Marcie shuffle?

It was ten minutes after seven when I went out the front door, and the street-lights had come on. Neil stood with his arms crossed, leaning on the railings. He shoved upright when he saw it was me and peaked his eyebrows. 'That much excitement every night?'

'Judas, no.' I shook my head and went on down the front steps. 'Marcie on the middle floor's picked up with this loud-mouthed yuppy, Greg. I think he's giving her a hard time.'

He held open the car door and I lowered myself in, wondering why expensive cars smelled like every penny they cost.

'He's violent?'

'I hadn't noticed her wearing a black eye until he showed up. Some men seem to get off on that kind of thing.'

He walked around and got in on his side.

'I could see to it he broke a few bones,' he said off-handedly. I squinted sideways in the half-light and he wasn't smiling.

'Hey,' I said lightly. 'I thought you were a disco dancer not a mafia heavy.' He turned the key, swung away from the kerb, and didn't mention it again.

Bertolini's is not only pricey but one hundred per cent

Italian; not just in the dishes it serves but in its staff. Ask for steak and chips and you get bowed all the way to the door. Lit up at night with its outside fairy lights and glassed-in, candle-lit terrace tables, it's hard to believe the hill rising half a mile behind it is just a grassed-over slag-heap.

The waiter pulled out my chair and swished at its seat with his little white cloth, I waited for dust to rise but nothing happened. He got me neatly lined up with the table and hovered, obviously longing to translate the menu. I smiled at him sweetly and batted my eyelashes; the dark, liquid eyes filled with pleasure, clearly I'd made his day.

Neil said, 'Shall I order for both or would your feminist side find it unthinkable?'

'When in Rome . . .' I said, feeling lazy. 'Just remember we split the bill.'

While he studied the menu I studied him. That little comment about breaking bones didn't fit in with the image I had. Coming from Sid it wouldn't have raised a blink, and even Jack had his wild side . . . but Neil?

He finished ordering. The waiter bowed the menu away and with a quick sleight of hand gave him a long wine list to read instead. Watching covertly I got the feeling I was standing on the edge of a pier again, the sense of smouldering sexuality grew every time I saw him, it oozed across the table like leaking electricity and made me aware of what dangerous stuff I was playing with. The waiter went away looking satisfied. Neil gave all his attention back to me.

I felt myself begin to pink up, and self-consciously dropped my eyes to rummage around in my bag like I'd lost something valuable. Damn it, this was worse than I'd felt on my first date.

'What have you got in there?' he said interestedly when I'd lifted the same things out a couple of times.

'Uh. Nothing.' I fished around for a good lie. 'There was this old school photograph I turned up, you know how these bits of junk hang around. I meant to bring it along but I've left it around somewhere.'

He nodded. 'I've never got into nostalgia.'

'Just as well it's lost then.' I gave everything a final mix and snapped the fastener. He smiled. The waiter brought a bottle of wine and went through the tasting ritual. Neil managed not to grimace so I guessed it wasn't too much like vinegar. When he'd filled mine and gone away I tried it for myself; rich, full-bodied, and fruity. I tried a little more but it hadn't changed. I started to worry about the bill.

'Relax,' Neil said. 'I'm celebrating, tonight's on me.'

'Uh-uh,' I shook my head. 'Rules of engagement, I like to stay debt free. Fifty-fifty.'

He shrugged. 'I heard what happened over the weekend, it must have knocked you back a bit.'

'Some.'

'Better it's over though.'

'I don't know it is over.'

He narrowed his eyes, looking at me quizzically. 'Want to explain that?'

'It's a matter of not feeling comfortable when things come together too pat.' The waiter came heading towards us, doing a clever balancing trick. I watched him come, swaying between tables, both hands in the air. 'Look, I'd rather not discuss it,' I said, 'it won't help any, so let's just enjoy eating together.'

'Whatever you like,' Neil said, but there was a note in his voice that said he wasn't all that happy to be put down. The waiter shed his load. Two plates of roasted capsicums, skinned, sliced thinly, and soaked in seasoned olive oil, with a basket of small, fresh Italian bread-rolls to soak up the juices. I ate, mopped, and felt contrite. It wasn't Neil's fault that things hadn't worked out the way I'd hoped.

'Neil, I'm sorry,' I said. 'Maybe we can talk later, right now I'm feeling unhappy about the whole thing. It isn't over but it isn't going well.'

'And you hoped for an evening without any reminders. What can I say except things usually get better. Maybe now you've done what you set out to do you should step away from it – leave it to the professionals.'

'I keep hearing people say that all over the place,' I said politely. 'The only comfort is that so far the professionals aren't doing any better.'

He filled up my glass, 'Good wine relaxes, drink up.'

'Good wine also anaesthetises,' I said, but I took another drink anyway and found he was partly right; some of the snarl-ups in my brain cells loosened. I leaned back and sighed.

'Better?'

'Better.'

A richly sauced Fettucine Alfredo replaced our empty plates. The side salad alone would have fed me well.

We ate and talked and kept away from the subject of Andy. By the time we were served a Cassata a la Siciliana my stomach was groaning and a doggie bag would have been appreciated.

I couldn't remember how many glasses of wine I'd had but I could feel my head buzzing happily with the stuff, and what with that and the electricity oozing over from Neil every time he looked at me, I was feeling pretty charged up. Espresso coffee came as a relief, I really needed to get back down to ground level before Neil drove me home. In the candlelight his eyes looked black and deeply intense, and his face was full of exciting shadows that changed him chameleon-like into all manner of men. I found myself leaning forward, drinking him in, wondering if all that sexuality had been turned on for me or if it was there all the time. I drank a second cup of coffee fast and signalled for a third. After the fourth I went to the ladies' room, and when I came back he'd paid the bill. We haggled a bit about whether I should pay half but I can be really stubborn about such things and eventually I wore him down.

Moving out together through the restaurant I was intensely aware of him; he held open the door and rested his hand briefly on the small of my back, little shivers ran through my bones, when we walked across the car-park I could still feel it there. This whole thing was getting too dangerous. I sneaked a look at his face, wondering if he was thinking the same thing, but it was impassive and ghost-like in the artificial light.

Neither of us said much as he drove me back to Palmer's Run, just desultory snippets of conversation about nothing much in particular. I was grappling with the problem of asking him in; it seemed churlish not to offer coffee but I was wary. I didn't want to start anything up with Neil, didn't want to get sexually involved with him. I'd made up my own rules for a long time now, and chief among them was never to have more than one man in my life at any time. It was a good rule.

I stared straight ahead, afraid to look at him in case I found he was looking at me. I swear the air crackled between us. *Shit!* What was I supposed to do?

He pulled up at the kerb and reached for my hand, his fingers sending a high voltage current surging through its skin; my mouth went dry. The sexual heat between us when we kissed would have roasted an ox. By the time I got my brain back into working condition things had got really steamy. Disengaging wasn't easy, he knew all the tricks.

When I finally pried myself loose most of what I wore badly needed adjusting, and I was panting like a peke. I told him I needed to go inside, which was fine until he found I didn't intend him to go with me.

I scrambled out and stepped back to a safe distance. 'Neil,' I said unsteadily, 'you're a real sweet man, but I need some thinking time. Give me a call.'

As I let myself in the front door he took off in a squeal of tyres and engine noise. I guessed that like me he was in a hurry to get to a cold shower.

CHAPTER TWENTY-FOUR

The hall light was off, leaving it full of grey darkness, and I was glad about that. There are two hundred and six bones in the human body and all of mine were shaking. I sat on the bottom step and waited for the earthquake to subside. Light sneaked out from under the door of the ground-floor flat, but the place was quiet. Sometimes I wonder what the couple who live there do with themselves, except that lights go on and off you'd never know they were around. I took some good, deep breaths and got a hold of myself before I headed upstairs.

Stopping outside Marcie's and gluing my ear to the door was getting to be a habit; like last night the TV was on but apart from that things were quiet, and I was glad, facing down Greg wasn't something I felt equipped to do right then.

I climbed the rest of the stairs, really pleased to get home.

I took a bath, pulled on an oversized T-shirt and made some cocoa, during and around which I tried not to think about Neil. Such strategies are always useless.

The telephone stayed coyly silent, and that was another irritation. I curled up on the settee to watch the last half-hour of *Newsnight*, then telephoned Darius at home. I listened to the ringing tone for a full minute before I gave up and went to bed.

It wasn't the most restful night I'd ever spent. Disturbingly dark images floated through my sleep, not erotic exactly although some of them trod that territory. When I finally jerked awake the impression that stayed behind was less one of pleasure than of apprehension. Something threatened me, and I didn't like the feeling.

It was a quarter after six and except for the orangey glow of street-lights still dark. I swung my legs out from under the duvet into air chill enough to make me think about turning the heating back on. Another few years and I'd be a real hot-house plant. I did a few stretches and some limbering up exercises to get my circulation going, pulled on sweats and an extra T-shirt, and went out to shake off a few toxins. The damp streets were still asleep; only idiots get up before they must. A couple of cars and a post van went by, somewhere out of sight an electric milk float whined and rattled and the sky began to change colour, chill grey chasing out cold black. When it caught up with me I headed home; I'd been gone an hour and I hadn't expected early visitors.

Another example of how life gets out of hand.

Neil more or less unfolded out of the Porsche and waited for me. I drew level, did little sideways running steps, and eyed him warily.

'I tried the bell,' he said.

'I wasn't home.'

'No kidding.'

'So,' I panted. 'What gets you up so early?'

'I got out of hand last night.'

'Right!'

'I came to say sorry.'

'Hey, it takes two to get in a tangle, I got a bit over-heated myself. Don't worry about it.'

He reached in the car and came up with red roses, a big bunch of them. He looked faintly embarrassed.

'A peace offering . . . no strings.'

I quit jumping around and took them. There were around two dozen, all fresh and closed up tight. 'Judas! It's seven-thirty in the morning,' I said, 'how'd you manage that?'

'I went by the wholesale market.'

'Clever, thanks, I really appreciate it.'

I tried to show some enthusiasm, he'd gone to a lot of trouble, but I didn't feel comfortable about it.

He leaned against the car, body language saying the next move was up to me. I hate it when I'm made to feel awkward. I said, 'Huh . . . look, Neil, I'd ask you up but I need to shower and get cleaned up, and . . . uh . . . that takes a little time.'

'How about lunch?'

I picked around in my head; Darius had to be tracked down, that was for sure, but I'd nothing else to do that was pressing enough to make me say no, not unless I was really desperate for an excuse. I looked down at the roses; if I didn't want to make peace I shouldn't have taken them. I grinned. 'Greasy Joe's?'

'Fox and Grapes.'

'Bar snack?'

'Whatever. One.'

'One. And, uh, thanks for these,' I wiggled the roses and went on up the front steps and into the house, by the time I turned around to close the door the Porsche was moving fast down the street.

Being unaccustomed to such lavish gestures and not being in the habit of buying flowers for myself, I was going to have a problem finding vases. I stood the whole lot in a bucket of water and went to scrub off some sweat.

At eight-thirty I telephoned the *Echo* and asked for Darius. He hadn't got in yet. I pecked in his home number. No reply.

Maybe he'd got lucky and had a heavy night.

I scratched around under the sink and came up with two classy jam jars and a cracked pottery jug.

Shit, they were no good at all.

I trotted down to Dora's and borrowed a fluted monster in heavy crystal that weighed a ton; sometimes unexpected gifts can be a curse. When I got home Greg was taking in the milk. I gave him a tight smile and asked about Marcie.

184

Obviously smiling wasn't on the day's agenda, he viewed me with a chill eye and rapped out, 'Marcie's fine and I'm looking after her. What we don't need is nosy-parker neighbours butting in.'

'That's OK then,' I snapped back, 'because what Marcie has are concerned friends and you know what, smiley face? Any trouble you give her is going to bounce right back on you!'

I shoved on past and went upstairs. There are some people I just can't take and Greg led the field.

I turned on the radio, moved the roses from the bucket and caught up on the latest news in fornicating cabinet ministers, money crises, and bombs at King's Cross.

Finding the world hasn't changed overnight can be so reassuring!

I was on my way out when Darius rang. He said, 'Leah, er, look, sorry I've been out, I um, er, just got your message. Said I'd get in touch yesterday, didn't I?'

Darius being shifty was Darius telling lies.

'It's nice I don't have to identify your corpse,' I said.

'What! Huh! No! I got tied up with other things.'

'So,' I said, 'what's new?'

'Um, Wilde and Cresswell? Didn't find a thing.'

'Darius, stop wriggling and give.'

'Nothing, really, I'll keep trying.'

'OK. Scrub the arrangement then. No story. I've got other sources.'

I always could lie better than him.

There was a little silence. 'Well, OK, if that's um . . . I mean . . . well, you know, I did my best.' He didn't sound happy. 'Anyway, um . . . I talked to a few people and it all seems pretty straightforward, and I – er, picked up on what went on between Lund and Andy, can't print it yet but it seems cut and dried.'

'Clichés, Darius.'

'What!'

'Six in that last sentence. Who did you talk to?'

Silence.

'OK, I'll rephrase it. Who talked to you?'

I thought I could hear his fingers tapping on the blotter. I caught a whiff of noise that sounded like he'd sighed.

'Oh, for God's sake! I thought we were friends,' I said crossly, and put the phone down.

A couple of seconds later it rang again. I grabbed at it. 'Darius, if you're not going to tell me what you've found out don't bother apologising.'

'Darius who?' said Nicholls interestedly.

'Uh? Oh, er, Darius? A friend from way, way back. He's picked up on this really interesting gossip about an old school chum and he won't tell.'

'Really niggles I bet.'

'You know me.'

'Don't I though. Um . . . there's a Darius Dixon on the local paper, wouldn't be him, would it?'

'We-ll.'

'Thought so.'

Smug ape!

'Missed the bomb then?' I asked sweetly. 'Yes, of course you did, wrong day wasn't it. Time really flies when I'm having a good time. Don't rush back.'

His voice went flat and distant. 'What bomb?'

Uh-oh, maybe I'd picked the wrong thing to joke about. 'I just heard it on the radio, King's Cross, wasn't it?'

'That's the reason you mentioned it?'

'Why else? Judas! Nicholls, sometimes you get paranoid, what do you think I'm doing up here, shipping Semtex?' He went quiet.

Great. So what was I supposed to have done this time? I counted seconds and wondered who was paying for the call. There was a bit of under-breath mumbling as if he was talking to someone. By and by, he came back and said grumpily, 'I'm getting the late train, try staying out of everybody's hair until I get there. All right?'

'Shit, Nicholls,' I snapped, and we both hung up together.

If he hadn't been so stroppy I'd have remembered to tell

him about the Pelican Crossing.

Lunch with Neil turned out to be not the world's best idea. I could still feel attraction pulling like a magnet, but now that I sensed danger too the pleasure had gone. He reminded me too much of Will, and I didn't want to go through all that painful kind of garbage again.

Besides which there was Nicholls, who could make unburnt toast and didn't need anybody to do his ironing.

He wasn't too bad in the sack either.

I felt myself go all rosy thinking about that. If he wasn't around I'd really miss the fights.

'So,' I said brightly. 'Has the party-happy Mr Wilde booked any more cars yet?'

He forked about in his food without picking anything up. 'Why the interest?'

'He's an interesting man.'

'And in the clear about Andy.'

I shrugged. 'That's for the police to decide, not me, I've other fish to fry.'

'Such as?'

'Uh-uh.' I shook my head.

'If you want me to tell you titbits about Wilde I've got to know why.'

'Look, Neil, I told you already, people I talk to end up in all kinds of trouble.'

'The waitress was a hit-and-run, nasty but nothing to do with you. Who else has had trouble?'

'Lund.'

'Suicide.'

'Maybe.'

He scanned my face with care, 'When Wilde makes a booking I'll think about it, but a little trust would be nice.'

'I trust you. I think I'll go for apple pie, how about you? And forget about Wilde, I'm back at work on Monday, I won't have any time left for running around.' He looked irritated but that's the effect I have on people.

He tried fishing around for a while after that, but I'd done what I wanted to do, which was concentrate his mind on something other than getting me into bed. We finished the meal and split the bill, then he said he'd ring me and we went our separate ways.

I did a little shopping and messed around until eight o'clock when I put on my Zee Carson persona and drove to Bradford. Mad Lad Ned had said I couldn't miss the Pelican Crossing if I was looking for it, but he was wrong, it took me two trawls, and when I finally found it I half-wished it had stayed invisible.

CHAPTER TWENTY-FIVE

The entrance to the club was at the side of an old ware-house building and if I hadn't been cruising at snail's pace I'd have missed it again on the third trawl. There wasn't any name outside to tell me I'd found the right place, but a flashing red man chased a flashing green one over an open door. A couple of males in puffa jackets and baseball caps went in. I drove snail speed past. At the back of the building the headlights picked out a high-walled car-park with a sign that read: *Top Fun Toys Ltd.* Two standard lamps on metal posts spread dim light on a tarmac-covered square. Directly under one lamp a white Bedford van had MAD LADS painted on its side. Three cars bunched up on its right. Two more stood under the second light. The rest of the space was empty.

I tucked in on the left of the Bedford and took a really careful look around; outside of the puddles of light, shadows piled up thick enough to hide an elephant. It'd be a great place for a quiet murder.

Such thoughts weren't welcome, they hung in my mind like a bogeyman under the bed and when I moved across the empty space darkness seemed to move with me. I didn't loiter.

Imagination is a curse.

I trotted back to the flashing men, went down six feet of corridor, and met up with a bouncer. He looked a really sweet man, with neat little piggy eyes and a Neanderthal-style forehead; the scent he gave off had the same kind of male smell as a mean bull, and I guessed he didn't go much for niceties like deodorant sticks. I stepped back a little.

He said, 'You gotta pass?'

I showed him my freebie ticket.

'Huh! Where'd you get it then?'

'Mad Lad Ned said it'd be all right.'

'Ned,' he intoned, stretching his mind a little. 'Yeh, yeh, I know Ned. All right is Ned.' He gave back my ticket and let me in.

I went down a metal staircase to a basement the size of two tennis courts. Sound castrated both ears and left them bubbling. Foolish me, I'd thought Acid House was all finished. Smoke sagged under the low ceiling. I sniffed and thought, how nice, I could raddle my lungs without paying a penny extra.

Except for some dim illumination where perimeter tables were bunched up three deep, all the lighting came from pulsing strobes. At floor level the place was so dark I couldn't see what I was treading on. A couple of times something crunched. I headed for the bar and tried not to breathe in too deep. Up on stage a stoned-looking group thwacked out a harsh deranged throb that seemed to be inciting fifty or sixty violently frenetic people to shake the dance-floor apart.

The barman had cotton-wool in his ears.

I leaned on the bar, pointed to a can of Pils, and worried about how long it'd take to go deaf. He took the wads out and leaned over. 'Cold and alone?'

I said yes and hoped he meant the beer.

'What time are the Mad Lads on?' I yelled.

'After this lot,' he bawled back. 'That who you come for then?'

'Right. When do this lot go off?'

''Nother ten minutes.'

'The noise this bad every night?'

'Yeh. Deadly, in'it?' He grinned and shoved his ear pads back in. I went and parked my butt at an empty table, it'd been good fun screaming at each other that way.

By the time the noise and strobes stopped and the over-head lights came on my brain was just about anaesthetised.

Sweating bodies flowed off the floor to the bar. A richly ripe mingle of aftershaves, musky scents and body odours drifted in my direction. I moved tables and took a good look around. Across the room people who'd been knowl-edgeable enough to miss the early Acid session were drifting down the metal staircase and heading for the bar scrum. In the back right corner the gents' was doing heavy trade and a queue had backed up for the ladies'.

Ned wandered on stage in a sleeveless T-shirt and looked around. I waved. He gave me three fast nods and a thumbs up and went off again. A couple of minutes later he came back with a mate and dragged on a drum kit.

I peered back at the ladies' queue; it had got longer, but trade at the gents' had dropped right off. A thickset man in a DJ came out from a door near the stage and shoved a way through the bar crowd. After a couple of minutes the crowd started thinning a bit faster and I guessed the bar-man had got some help.

A couple of lights dimmed down; another little crowd assaulted the bar; Ned and his mate shuffled back carrying a synthesiser. Somebody else came on and did mysterious things with a bunch of wires. Ned's mate played a little chord. The stage lights went down and a loudspeaker crackled.

A pushy-looking stud started hooking out the spare chair. I rolled my eyes and developed an off-putting twitch. Some people are easy to discourage.

There was a lot of activity going on under the stairs, somebody tucked away in the shadows there seemed to be doing as much trade as the bar, but with a different kind of merchandise. More lights dimmed; two purple spotlights crossed on stage. The centre light went out and I couldn't see what went on under the stairs any more. The bar queue was down to four. DJ came out from under the flap, went on stage and blew down the microphone. *Wheeee-thwa-c-ck*. I was surprised it still worked.

'Ladies and gentlemen, the turn you've been waiting for all night. A big hand please for the Mad Lads!' He pounded his hands together.

I helped him clap, everybody else seemed too busy.

Ned leaned over the mike. 'I hope you're all going to be nice to us here tonight, because there's a foxy lady from *New Musical Express* to see how good we are. How about a hand for Zee Carson.' The Mad Lads clapped; DJ joined in, the barman tried to help things along. I kept my head down and wondered if the club crowd was always this demonstrative. Things looked up when they started to play, obviously music was appreciated more than pep talks. The dance-floor filled up again but this time it didn't seem in danger of being demolished.

Someone new came out through the side door; recognition bloomed, hair that colour was hard to forget. Wherever the journey from the Interchange had taken him, it hadn't kept him away for long. He collected the bar takings and came back. It'd be really interesting to know what went on behind that door. I was about to take a look when he came out again and cut through the dancers, heading for the dark spot under the stairs; after a bit he surfaced with another little bag. The door shut behind him.

Whatever had been traded in the dark, the profits went to the house. Even more interesting.

I got another Pils and a bitter for the barman.

'Thanks for giving me a hand back there,' I said. He looked mystified. 'Zee Carson, *New Musical Express*, you helped out with the applause. I never got a five-handed clap before.'

He shrugged. 'Thursday nights they wouldn't clap Madonna, don't take it personal.'

'Quite a rush you had back there, must have been nice to get some help. Is it always like that?'

'Nah, steady trade most nights, What d'you reckon then?' nodding at the stage. 'Not bad?'

'Good music, neat act. I think they should have a good

write-up.'

'Yeh? Be good that, yeh . . . good.'

'Who was the redhead?' I said. 'He the manager?'

'Nah, he's the one in the monkey suit. Mick's a spare, like, comes and goes.'

'Get any trouble with pushers?'

'Don't get in.'

'Right,' I said. 'House trade.' He gave me a look. 'Hey, don't worry, better to have quality control.'

'Yeh, that's the way the boss sees it.'

'Monkey suit?'

'Nah. Big boss. Don't come round often.'

'Right, Cresswell, I know him well.'

'That a fact?

'I was over at his place a couple of weeks ago, Nice.'

'Yeh?' He looked impressed.

'Classy, You like him?'

'He pays the wages.'

I nodded sagely. 'I get the picture. Hard man when he wants to be. Not given you any trouble though, huh?'

'I keep my head down. You know.'

'I know. Believe me I know. Same in my business.'

'No kidding?'

'Cut-throat. Different with Mick and Cresswell though, eh? I hear most times they're real close.'

'I gotta start closing up,' he said unchattily.

I checked the bar clock; ten forty-five. 'That soon: what time does the show close?'

'Eleven.'

'I'd better go catch the rest of the act then.' I raised my glass. 'Don't forget the name – Zee Carson, maybe I'll give you a mention.' I turned away.

'Hey,' he leaned across the bar. 'Look, no offence, all right? Mick wouldn't want to be mentioned, he keeps a real low profile times he's around.' He patted my upper arm. 'You're a nice piece, I wouldn't want you walking into trouble.'

'Thanks,' I said. 'I'll remember that.'

Back at my table for one I meditated on why Mick the red was so coy, and eyed the door. If I wanted to snoop it was now or never; the Mad Lads were still giving their all, but two more numbers maximum and they'd be through for the night. I drifted down the room and loitered for a while, heart keeping pace with the drums. When no one seemed to be looking I ducked through the door.

A stumpy corridor with three rooms off. Stockroom and lavatory on one side, office on the other, door open just enough to let me hear voices but not enough to catch what was said. I shoved close to the wall and moved sideways until I could make out the words. There were just two voices, both sounding angry as hell.

' . . . end it, the change-over's on Friday.'

My skin prickled; it wasn't a voice I could mistake, I'd just been telling the barman how great its owner and Mick got on together. It looked like I might have hit the jackpot after all.

'Look! *We* run the risks, it's our sodding right to see the end.' That voice was soft and nasal, with an accent he'd tried to iron out; it sounded a lot more dangerous than Cresswell's and I wouldn't want to tangle with its owner.

'Except you dropped it in chicken-shit, Mick, deep chicken-shit.' That was Cresswell again.

'Ah, well, and wouldn't you be the expert there, since you've cocked up yourself just lately.'

'Button it, Mick, not my cock-up and not Wilde's. The sodding bagman fouled up, and you can tell Keneally he near as enough pulled the network down.'

Who the hell was Keneally?

'Aah, that's your side of it all right, but what's his if I ask him? Wouldn't want me to do that would you, wouldn't like him to know you're putting the word out.'

'Keneally wants you home Friday, take it up with him, far as I'm concerned you're out.' Cresswell's voice got louder, and the door handle gave a little jump.

I moved fast across the corridor to the john, when I got in there I closed the door and slid the bolt. The office door banged shut. I waited a while then looked out; the corridor was empty. I eased out quietly and went back to the club room. The Mad Lads were through and the place was emptying fast. I queue-jumped a little and kept looking over my shoulder until I got out into the night air. The chill of it cooled me down. There wasn't anything moving when I got to the car-park, but the dark lakes of shadow still hung around uninvitingly and bogeyman thoughts came back. I set up a tuneless whistle the way I used to do when I was around ten and had to go down gran's cellar to bring up some firewood. Of course, I *knew* there wasn't anyone hiding down there but I whistled anyway.

Halfway to the hybrid I stopped. There might be nothing out there moving but I knew I didn't have the car-park to myself. Someone else was sharing the space. I stopped moving and wished I had dog ears to swivel around. I didn't know what had started up the feeling of another presence, I hadn't consciously heard any sound, but something had caused a muscles' bunch-up around my shoulders. I listened. Nothing.

I stepped out for the car again, cursing my inventive imagination. Something stirred to my left and a bent-over shape rushed me. At me or past, I wasn't sure which, but when I spun to face him I got an out-thrust arm that sent me staggering into the car's back-end.

I cracked an elbow and scraped a shin, and I didn't bother chasing him, from now on I left all that stuff to Rockford and Magnum. I unlocked the hybrid, climbed into the driving seat, and went home to bed. The glimpse I'd had was that he was young and carrying something that looked very like a car stereo. It was really wicked to hope it had been Cresswell's.

It was also comforting to know that for once I hadn't been the target.

Chapter Twenty-Six

I woke up with energy levels I'd almost forgotten about. The air was sharp and autumny, carrying a spicy, tangy smell. I felt hyped, as if I was on the edge of something exciting and it would have helped a lot to know what. The milkman, all bundled up, sneezing and sluggish, was still two streets away, and Marcie's place was quiet again, I found myself hoping she'd dumped Greg.

I tripped happily back upstairs, showered, cooked breakfast and caught up on the washing-up, then still riding an energy wave squashed a pile of clothes in the washer and wondered what my reward would be for so much virtue.

I didn't expect it to be instantaneous.

At quarter past eight Charlie rang: 'Got a message from Sid, Leah love. Drop down in sometime. OK?' There was a bit of muttering at his end. 'Better make it round two then,' he amended.

'Charlie, tell me now,'

'Don't trust BT, love, dicky-birds have ears.' He hung up. That's one of Charlie's strong points, he never argues. The outside doorbell rang, I trotted down and let Nicholls in. Supper calls I was used to, breakfast visits were different: I hoped he wasn't on a bad news trip like the last time he dropped in early. I stuck my head out and looked behind him. Down at the bottom of the street the milkman was getting slower every step, I guessed he'd be really glad to get home to bed.

I shut the door and looked Nicholls up and down. 'What's the matter,' I said snidely, 'couldn't you sleep?'

'Early Friday morning, that's what I said, so how come you forgot?'

We stood in the hall and scowled a little, sharing one of those thrilling moments of mutual grump. After a while I realised he looked quite good, blue eyes shooting sparks, nice shoulders, lean hips, flat belly . . .

'Better come up,' I said before I got carried away, 'I don't want the neighbours talking.' As we passed by Marcie's, Ben started crying. I dawdled a little.

Nicholls said, 'Snooping on the neighbours now?'

'She has problems,' I said curtly, and went on up. He headed straight for the kitchen and homed in on the filter machine, it's nice we have so much in common. I peeked in the fridge. No milk. Great! I could take another trip downstairs; I squinted at Nicholls, he's the one who likes to ruin his coffee, maybe he should get the milk. He was busy with the bread.

'You want anything to eat,' I said kindly, 'feel free.' He grinned, sometimes he takes that kind of thing for granted. I left the flat door open and trotted downstairs. The milkman had just made it to the steps. He sneezed like a volcano. 'Nasty cold you've got there,' I said, 'You should be home.'

'Ay, it's a right bugger,' he gasped, 'got it in bloody Spain. Teemed every soddin' day. Wife's in bed wi't' same bug.' He shuffled back to his cart.

'So where's the lad – the one that helps out?'

He climbed back on board. 'Gone off on flaming holiday, lucky sod,' he said and rattled off. Feeling so healthy made me guilty.

I took Marcie's milk up with me. Ben was still crying. I knocked with polite restraint. Nothing happened. I knocked a little harder. Greg came, looking really unchuffed to see me. I said, 'Ben OK?'

'Ben's fine.' He grabbed the milk.

'Doesn't sound it.'

'Mind your own bloody business.' There was a minor crash and the crying picked up a bit. Greg shot back inside and slammed the door; he didn't slam it hard enough though, it hit my upturned foot and swung open. Ben was coming out of the kitchen dressed in a grubby T-shirt and damn all else except a nose-run down to his chin. Bottles in one hand, Greg swung Marcie's son off his feet with the other and threw him back into the kitchen. Ben started screaming. I dumped my milk on the landing and went in.

'Hey,' I yelled, 'what the hell are you, some kind of psychopath?'

He unloaded the milk then stood in the hall and waited for me, the humanoid equivalent of a pit-bull. Some people's faces are transformed when they smile, but the movement did nothing for Greg, his face stayed as mean and unpleasant as ever, I couldn't believe I'd ever thought him a hunk. I stopped just out of arm's reach.

'You going to pick him up?'

He motioned at the flat door. 'Out,' he said.

'Not until you show me Ben's OK. Where's Marcie?' I raised my voice. 'Marcie? You around somewhere?' Some kind of noise came out of the bedroom.

'Out!' he said again.

'Uh-uh. You let me see Ben's OK and Marcie's OK, or I get the police.'

'You can walk out the door or I throw you out the door. Your choice.'

'I'm taking a look in the bedroom,' I said.

'Try it.' He raised his hands invitingly.

'Going to slap me around a little? Gives you a buzz, does it? Big he-man, picks on kids and women.' Ben's screaming had dropped to a whimper and I didn't like that, I wanted to get in there and see what had happened but I didn't know if I could handle Greg; he looked like there was nothing he'd like better than to bounce me off a few walls.

He moved towards me and I watched him come. He was too damn big, in a confined space like that I wasn't going to be able to take him. I took a good breath and yelled for

198

a little help. 'Nicholls,' I bawled, 'get down here, I need some muscle, dammit!' Greg's grin widened, he thought I was trying a bluff.

I stepped around and watched his eyes, and wished the hall was a little more roomy. I let out a scream I was proud of. He didn't like that, the smile went and he came forward and swung at me open-handed. I ducked, twisted, rammed an elbow under his ribs, and listened to my hero running down the stairs.

Squinting at the door was a big mistake, I should have kept my eyes on Greg. I saw the next blow just before it landed and missed the worst of it, but it still knocked me off balance. I crashed into Marcie's hallstand. Nicholls looked angry enough to bust and he didn't shilly-shally, just came on in on a run, head down and ready to do damage.

While they slugged it out I edged into the kitchen. Ben had curled into a ball and was sucking his thumb, convulsing every couple of seconds into a sob that hurt me just to see it. I grabbed the fleecy rug from his push-chair and wrapped him round; he looked at me with big worried eyes while I told him what a clever, brave boy he was, and mopped his face with tissues. We were getting on great until Nicholls came flying in backwards and set off the crying again.

Martial arts are fine but times are when copper-bottomed pans are better. Marcie's rang out like a bell and cooled Greg's temper; he'd have a hell of a headache when he woke up. For some reason that didn't worry me. Nicholls was griping how I should have rung for back-up.

'You had back-up,' I said sweetly. 'How come you weren't doing so good on your own?' Ben clung round my neck, he'd stopped crying again and was looking at Greg with interest. 'Bad man,' he said. He's a boy of few words but he usually gets them right.

Nicholls said, 'Where's the damn phone?'

'In the living-room.' I went in there with Ben; worry came back on his face. I patted Nicholls' arm. 'Nice man,' I

199

said. The look didn't change, I guessed Ben was going to take a lot of convincing. I set him down in an easy chair and went to find Marcie. Going into the bedroom was hard, I really didn't want to see what Greg had done to her, she had to be really hurt to hear Ben crying like that and not come out.

The first thing I saw were her eyes, wild-staring at the door and full of God knows what: panic, fear, pain, and something that went a whole lot deeper. He'd taped her mouth and tied her to the bed. I started shaking, sick, angry tears flooded my face. 'Oh shit, Marcie, shit, I'm so sorry.' I tugged off the tape and got busy with the knots. She put out her tongue and licked her lips.

'I really know how to pick 'em,' she said weakly.

'He won't get to do it again.'

Judas I'd kill him if he tried!

Rage burned in me like acid; I couldn't remember having felt this mad before. Nicholls came in and saw and said a few things I won't repeat, then he got busy on another knot. Marcie had pulled on them so hard they'd cut through her skin. Between us we got her untied. I pushed her hair back. 'Huh . . . maybe I'd better tell your mum what's been happening? D'you want me to do that?'

'I guess so.' She started to shiver. I tucked the duvet round her and felt useless.

'Ben's OK,' I said. 'Honest; you don't have to worry.' She started to cry. I got down on the bed and put my arms round her, Nicholls stood around awkwardly, wanting to ask questions. I liked him for the way he held back.

I didn't get back to my place until almost eleven. The flat door was still wide open; I hoped some opportunistic thief hadn't been around taking advantage. Not that it would have been my fault, Nicholls had been last out.

When I reminded him of that he looked a little embarrassed.

The filter machine had done a great job on the coffee; it was now a neat, black concentrate that probably scoured the drains really well as it went through. I left him to make a fresh brew while I went down to Marcie's place and did some tidying up. By then Greg had been banged up in a cell, for ever, I hoped. The last I'd seen of Marcie she'd been tucked up in a hospital bed with enough dope to let her sleep for a day. She'd looked really lost and damaged and I got a peck of guilt at not having butted in soon enough. I'd worried about what her mother would be like, the fluttery panicking kind, or one of the you've-brought-it-all-on-yourself-ers.

She wasn't either; she'd come in calm as anything, cuddled Ben and comforted Marcie, and I'd been envious enough to bust.

I righted all the things that had been overturned, stripped the bed and shoved all the linen in the washer. The pan had a dent in it; maybe I'd get her a new one as a coming-home gift. That stopped me short. Maybe she wouldn't want to come back. If I'd been violated that way in my own home, how would I feel?

'Shit!'

I locked up and went back to Nicholls, I needed a little comforting myself. He'd been busy. Soup, sandwiches and coffee. 'Hey,' I said. 'That's nice!' He looked pleased. The left side of his jaw looked purpley red and sore. I went over and eyed it critically.

'Looks worse than it feels,' he said bravely.

'Great,' I told him smartly, 'I won't need to cut your sandwich up small.' It doesn't pay to let men know you're worried.

I sneaked covert glances at Nicholls while I ate. He still looked good; the bruised and rumpled look really suited him. We took the rest of the coffee into the living-room and got a little comfier. Nicholls sat primly in the corner of the settee and eyed the roses in Dora's big vase, I grinned a little. Competition is good for the soul. 'Nice flowers,' he said when he got tired of hearing the clock tick.

'Aren't they though.'

'Birthday or something?'

'Uh-uh. Friendship gift. Some men go for that kind of

gesture, nice, don't you think?'

'Sucks,' he said.

I was pleased it bothered him. I slid down on to the rug and turned on the early news. 'So,' I said. 'What were you doing in the big city?'

'Conferring.'

'Vice, drugs, illegal immigrants ... ' I remembered something. 'Bombs at King's Cross? Why so stroppy when I mentioned that?'

'It had been under discussion.'

'How so? Think they're heading north?'

'None of your business, Leah.'

I didn't disagree with that, the truth is I get a lot of fun poking into things that aren't my business. I was about to tell him so when the photofit popped up on TV, an eye-witness description of the King's Cross bomber, nicely enhanced by a police artist and shown in glorious techni-colour. I stared at the red hair stupidly and hotted up.

'That's him,' I said.

Nicholls got the wrong idea. 'It's only a photofit,' he informed me, kindly answering a non-existent question. 'Nobody knows if it's close.'

'It's close,' I said, feeling like I'd just walked away from a quick and nasty end. 'It's Mick the red, and I was this far away from him last night.' I measured a gap a little more than arm's length. 'Somebody called Keneally thinks he messed things up and he's being sent back home.'

Nicholls turned off the TV and grabbed a hold of me. 'What the *hell* have you got into this time?'

'How the hell would I know?' I snapped, 'I was going to tell you Tuesday but you damn well drove off!'

'Tuesday!' He let go and looked at me as if I'd stolen his lollipop. 'Keep going.'

'OK,' I said, 'but you won't like it, a little lateral think-ing on your part and you'd have found him yourself.' I enjoyed saying that, sometimes the truth can be really hurtful.

202

CHAPTER TWENTY-SEVEN

Getting to Charlie's on time took something of an effort, Nicholls being the stickler for detail that he is, he had me rehash everything until I was sick of hearing myself talk. I parked at the side of the workshop and went to find Charlie. He gave me a beady little sideways look and winked.

'What you been up to then, blooming with health like that? Don't know what you're on but I wouldn't mind a bit.'

'Charlie,' I said, 'I've had enough hassle today to last me a week. What's Sid got to say?'

'Better ask him, he's inside.' He got back to his engine plumbing and left the office to me. Sid sat in Charlie's chair, feet on the desk, cigar going nicely.

'Been helping the police with their inquiries have you?' he said. I looked at him. Judas! didn't I have any secrets? He grinned. 'A friend of mine saw him go in, around eight-thirty?'

'It didn't concern you,' I said, 'a neighbour had problems, it took a little help to sort it out.'

'Yeh, I heard about that too.'

'Sid, I don't appreciate being spied on.'

'Thought it'd be provident . . . considering.'

'Considering what?'

'Considering what you've been stepping in, doggy doos is nice in comparison. You ready for a ride?'

'Where to?'

'Thought you'd like a talk with the girls.'

'What girls?'

'Some of the frail sisterhood.'

'You're a pimp?' I frowned a little.

'Don't have to look at me like that,' Sid complained. 'They get their own trade, life is life an' they like the work. You coming or not?'

I followed him out. He'd parked around the back away from snoopy eyes, a cautious man is Sid. He drove smartly round the back streets and joined the ring-road traffic south, ending up outside a detached Edwardian house with bay windows and creepered walls on the fringe of town; it looked the respectable kind of place where a dentist or doctor would set up shop, but according to the plate outside it housed a photographic model agency, an escort service and a massage parlour instead.

'How nice,' I said edgily, 'and it's all yours.'

'They got a pension scheme, free clinic, free dental checks, and they don't have to do a thing they don't want. Ask 'em if you like. It's a lot better than a park bench.'

'I bet. Good socially responsible management like that you'll get to heaven for sure.'

'Not on the cards,' he said. 'Never fell for all that apple-pie-in-the-sky line of thinking; me, I'd rather plan on staying alive. Come on in.'

I took a quick peek around, not wanting word to get back to big sister Em that I might be contemplating a career change. I trotted down the hall after Sid; nice décor, nothing seedy, good plain wool carpet, or maybe that was just top dressing. A neat little door-plate read Staff Room. 'Have a sit in here,' Sid said. 'Put your feet up if you like, everybody else does.' I went on in. Wow! He was right about the working conditions. Nice thick carpet, lots of easy chairs, TV, stereo, subtle colour scheme; maybe I was in the wrong line of work.

'Not bad,' I said.

'Anytime you like a change,' he offered, 'just drop a word. I'll get the girls.' He left me to poke around, and by and by came back with six nice people. Delia looked around thirty, Sharon twentyish; the other four, Beccy, Ruth, Sandra and Jo fitted in between. Sid did the introductions and we eyed each other up.

Sharon said, 'Sid says you're a private eye, what's it like then, dead exciting?'

'Uh-uh. Sid's exaggerating what I do, it's just I like snooping around where I shouldn't.' I squinted at Sid.

'Park your bum, for God's sake,' he said, 'and stop being modest.' I sat down obediently; so did everybody else. We looked at each other. He said, 'Get on with it then, Bec, let's hear about the waitress.'

I said, 'Annie?'

'Little redhead?' asked Beccy. I nodded. 'Suppose so then.' She jerked her head at Sid. 'He told you what we were doing there? No? Thought not. Well, we . . . us six, we . . . er, sort of get booked up for parties and stuff,' she took a look at Sid who was looking at the ceiling. 'Any-- way, we got some business at Dean Wilde's place that night his PA went missing, the one with his photo in the paper.'

Jo said, 'She brought this tray upstairs and took it in the wrong room, went in the office with a confab going on and got shoved out in a right state, poor kid.' *Poor kid?* I'd have bet Jo was younger.

Beccy said, 'Me and Jo were hanging over the rail, watching for who was coming up, and there's this noise, so we looked round and this feller's pushing her out the door. 'Open your mouth and you're dead,' he says. Then he saw us watching and went back in.

'So we helped her pick the broken pots up,' Jo came in, 'right mess he'd made . . . and we took her for a sit down . . . '

'You'll like this bit,' Sid said. 'Curl your hair.'

' . . . so course we asked what'd been going on. She said she'd seen five or six men messing with guns, and they'd started swearing blue hell when she walked in, Then this ginger-nut shoved her out. That's it.'

'Except,' said Beccy, 'we saw her talking to that young feller, and a bit after that he came upstairs, but I'd just got a client, so I don't know if he went in the office or not.'

'What about the client,' I said, 'did he see?'

She shrugged. 'Shouldn't think so.'

'Who was it?' said Sid.

'Didn't ask.'

'Never do,' said Delia. 'Pricks don't have names.'

'What about the men,' I said. 'Did Annie mention any names or say what they looked like?' They eyed each other and shook their heads.

'The one you just called a ginger-nut . . . did he have hair like Annie's?'

'Brighter, more orange marmalade.'

'What about his voice?'

'Softish . . . nasty softish, funny sort of accent, Liverpool but not Liverpool if you know what I mean.'

Delia said, 'There's another shindig on tonight. Want to come?'

'At Wilde's?'

'He's done it short notice,' Sid said. 'Rang yesterday, lucky we weren't too busy. I'd have said no except I remembered you wanting a look round. Go in with the girls an' you'll have a chance.'

'He knows me.'

'Give me half an hour and your mother wouldn't know you,' Delia said.

'Uh-huh. Can I take a little time here?'

'Sure – all you like.'

'How'd you get there? Taxi?'

'Limo. Sid does us proud party nights, don't you, boss?' She hipped over and rumpled his hair. He slapped her backside. I guess it was meant to be friendly.

'Limo stays there at the house,' said Sid, 'driver gets to sit in the kitchen. Any trouble, they all come home. Business rules.'

'You'd be all right,' said Delia. 'We'd look after you real well, we go up the back stairs, nobody sees us but kitchen staff. Wilde lays on drinks and a cold buffet so we go in early, sevenish, don't start flashing any leg 'til after eight.'

'What about getting into the office?'

'Sid tells me you're good with locks.'

'Uh-huh,' I said. 'Well, I hate to bring out the old chestnut but I haven't a thing to wear. You got a dress to fit me?'

Delia waved her hands like she was raising the sick. 'Everybody up – you too, ducky.'

I got up obediently and she sized us all up. 'It'll have to be Ruth,' she decided. 'Closest size. What colour will it be tonight then, Ruthie?'

Ruth shrugged. 'Blue.'

'Stand up close then, the two of you, so I can get a look. Mmm, what d'you think, Sid, 'bout the same size?'

'Near enough.'

'Ruthie'll need another blue dress then, can't do a stripper in the car.' Delia held out her hand and rubbed thumb and fingers together.

Sid looked at me. 'How about it, still want in? Don't have to if you don't want.' I stood there and did some fast thinking. Half an hour wasn't time to snoop through anything, but that didn't really matter, I knew everything I needed to know now, the only thing missing was proof.

'Depends,' I said slowly, 'on whether somebody could get hold of the right bugging equipment.' He grinned and gave Delia fifty pounds.

'Remember to get a discount,' he said. 'An' have a cup of tea with the change.'

The room felt real empty when they'd all gone.

He said, 'You and me have got the same minds; I like that. What d'you want? . . . High-powered crystal an' pick-up in the car . . . that what you're thinking of?'

'On to tape.'

'Nice. So what makes you think I'd know the right people?'

'Sid, I think you know all the *wrong* people, that's why I'm asking.'

'Wouldn't want to have you saying that in the wrong ears.'

'Scout's honour.'

'Infiltrated them as well, have you? I'll have to leave you for a bit.' He got up and went out. While he was gone I started worrying about how unhealthy I'd look on a slab in the morgue. To get caught in Wilde's office would be a lot more than risky, Annie proved that. But I didn't intend to hang around in there; just plant a bug and get out again.

I wondered how long Wilde had been laundering money, and how long he'd been raising funds for arms. A record company like his could import and export all kinds of things freely through customs; without opening up a crate who could say if it held records, drugs or guns.

I shivered, remembering Mick the red's explosive habits. The IRA didn't like people who spoiled their plans. I got up and turned the gas fire on, suddenly icy. Shit, but I'd have to be fast tonight.

I got home around four with adrenalin already flowing. The flat was empty but this time Nicholls had remembered to leave me a sweet little note. *'Back around ten. Stay home!!! Dave.'* How nice. I rang his office: he was in Bradford. No ... they didn't know when he'd be back. When I mentioned the Pelican everything went quiet. I said, 'Thanks,' and hung up.

I made coffee, fixed a sandwich, and psyched myself up. At five-thirty I took a shower, pulled on some sexy underwear and eased into a pair of black fishnet stockings I'd bought on the way home. The mirror misted a little when I showed it the new me. I shoved a pair of black high heels into a bag, climbed into jeans and a sweatshirt, and went to learn more about life as a hooker. While I waited for Delia to make me over I rang Nicholls again. He still wasn't back. Maybe having him where I needed him twice in one day was too much to ask.

By and by, Delia came and turned me into a stranger; mop-head blonde wig, beauty spot, half-inch of pancake, glitter-shadow and spiky lashes and, shit, she was right, I could have passed my mother on the street. I got zipped into a midnight-blue dress that fitted like a banana skin, stood side by side with Ruth and looked in the mirror.

Twin sisters had nothing on us.

When the limo dumped us at Wilde's back door I had a real stomach-ache and a heart doing flip-flops. Everybody climbed out except Ruth, she'd get her turn a little later.

I got hustled through the kitchen and up the back stairs, thinking how a little Dutch courage would have been really handy. Halfway down the upper hallway we stopped. I looked at the oak door and hoped it wasn't booby-trapped. 'There'll not be anybody in there,' said Beccy. How nice to be so certain! I tugged the picklocks out of the diddy, pink silk bag Ruth had loaned me and got to work. Time went by. I swapped tools and tried again. It took a couple more minutes before the lock clicked back and let me in. Bug in hand I looked for a place to put the damn thing. Forget the chairs, they'd get moved around, forget the filing cabinets, it'd stick out against the metal casing like a sore thumb; and the desk was a definite no-no.

I got down on my knees and stuck the mini electronic spy up under the radiator shelf, then I got out of there fast. I just hoped no one had any chewing gum to get rid of in the same place.

Locking up was worse than getting in, by the time I'd finished I was sweating a little and the girls weren't in much better shape. Wilde's buffet supper came as a real life-saver.

I drank a couple of glasses of white wine and ate half a plate of canapés. All that excitement had really hyped me up, and staying around to party would have been fun if it hadn't been for what came next on the menu. I said my goodbyes and skipped euphorically downstairs, I guessed by then Ruth would be really glad to change places.

Sid's limo driver was built like Rambo, and it was a great comfort to have him walk me out to the car. Ruth got out from under the rug and dusted herself down looking glad not to be curled up on the floor any longer. I gave her a little time to get back in the house with Rambo before I peeled off the fancy-dress; somehow jeans and running shoes made me feel a whole lot more secure. I hunkered down with a neat stack of gadgetry and waited.

Hanging around is never any fun. Time dropped down to snail speed. Maybe the bug had dropped off. Maybe it wouldn't work. Maybe there wouldn't be a meeting in there tonight; *maybe I should think of something else.*

Just before eight the tape came alive, I grabbed the headphones and listened in. Bottles clinked on glasses. Somebody asked how somebody else's kids were. A couple of football freaks got on to World Cup prospects.

Great.

Then a voice said, 'Is Duffy away?'

'Couple of hours. We'll be better off with Hogan, Mick's too much a solo artist, he's risky.' *Wilde's voice.*

I grinned happily. It was so nice to hear him cook his goose. I waited for somebody to talk guns, but arms buying wasn't on that night's agenda, instead they talked plans and statistics. I froze up, so casually did they estimate how many dead, how many injured, what the backlash would be, how many friends might be lost overseas, as if they were working out some penny-ante business deal. Nicholls should be here listening to this not me. Shit, I felt useless, an amateur playing with professionals; stripped of pretence I didn't want to do that any more. Amateurs dabble, amateurs have too much self-pride and mess things up, amateurs can't tell a mangy tom from a tiger.

Shit!

I fed Nicholls' number into the car phone and near dropped it in relief when he picked up. I said, 'Don't talk, just listen,' and held the headphones up against the mouthpiece. I gave him a good couple of minutes listening time before I took them away. 'Heard enough?'

He said, 'Where are you?'

'In a limo behind Wilde's place, it's party night again. I bugged his office.'

He went quiet. After a bit he said, 'How many men?'

'Five voices. Wilde and Cresswell are in there.'

'Leah, just this once, stay put and don't move.'

'Listen,' I said, 'Inside there are six hookers and the limo driver; they sneaked me into the place and I'd appreciate it if you pretended not to see them, OK? You owe them a favour not a booking.'

'Where are they?'

'The women are upstairs, the driver's in the kitchen, so are three catering staff and a couple of Wilde's men. The dog's tied up someplace.'

'Any men in the grounds?'

'Probably. You want me to go and see?' I held the receiver out from my ear. 'OK,' I said, 'you'd rather I stayed put, why didn't you just say that instead of wasting time shouting.'

'Leah,' he snapped. 'Sometimes I could screw you rigid!'

'Likewise,' I replied, then put the phone down and waited for the cavalry to come over the hill.

CHAPTER TWENTY-EIGHT

I got home around three in the morning; it took that long to download the theories and facts I'd been carrying around in my head. If it hadn't been for Nicholls I'd still have been locked up somewhere, detained under some obscure sub-section of the Prevention of Terrorism Act so I couldn't open my big mouth and tell the world what an exciting time I'd been having. It was nice he'd been able to pull that much weight with the heavy squad. I was so bushed I just crawled under the duvet and slept until ten.

I took my time under the shower. Two whole days holiday left . . . however would I fill in the time! I ate scrambled eggs and a stack of toast washed down with three cups of coffee and looked around for something to do; not having anyone else's problems to solve left a big hole in the day. I moved some things from the washer to the drier and thought about how I'd like to ring Caroline and say she and Richie could stop worrying about Wilde now, but a promise is a promise, especially when it's made under the Official Secrets Act.

Darius rang up at eleven asking if I knew anything about a police raid on Wilde's place last night. 'Uh-uh,' I said. 'Can't tell you a thing about that, sounds like it could be interesting though, how about letting me know what you find out?' I don't think he believed me but he didn't try to quibble, he knows my stubborn nature.

I walked into town, bought a big bunch of flowers, and went to see Marcie. She was wearing one of the cute old-lady nighties hospitals like so much and sitting up in bed. She looked half-embarrassed when I walked in. I dumped the flowers in her lap and pulled up a chair. 'Hi,' I said, 'how're you feeling? I thought you'd be up and around.'

'I was, only I – um – passed out, so they put me back to bed.' She looked at the flowers and played with the ribbon. 'God, I have a lousy taste in men,' she said, 'you've got to admit that; if you hadn't butted in it'd probably be my epitaph.'

'Look,' I said, 'it wasn't your fault, men like that don't walk around with a sign round their necks, the first time I saw him he looked a real hunk.'

'You thought so?'

'I thought so. Do you want me to pick up any stuff . . . nightie, towels, clothes to go home in?'

'It'd be nice, sure you wouldn't mind?'

'Marcie, anything you want you've got.'

She pulled at the winceyette. 'This is odious.'

I said, 'Look, Greg's stuff is still in there, how about I dump the whole lot off at the police station? Save having to do it when you get home.' She coloured. 'You *are* coming home?'

'I . . . it's not . . . I mean, after what's happened I don't know if I'll feel at home there any more, you know?'

I knew.

'I'll clear out his junk,' I said, 'that'll make it easier.' I stayed around a little longer and chit-chatted about trivialities, then the dinner trolley trundled in and I went home.

Nicholls was parked in his car. I couldn't think why he looked so relieved when I showed up. 'I thought you were staying home,' he said.

'You mean I can't go and see Marcie now, is that it?'

'Ah! How is she?'

'Not good. I wish you'd kicked his balls off. I'm going to clear out his stuff, maybe you could drop it off for me.'

'Where?'

I opened my attic door and looked at him, sometimes he's none too bright. 'His cell. I was going to take it around myself but since you work in the damn place . . . '

'All right . . . I'll get rid of it.'

I hung up my jacket; the paint tins in the hall closet looked glum, like forgotten party guests. Damn! I'd never get this place redone.

Nicholls was squatting by the fridge.

I said, 'You haven't eaten yet.' It was a statement, not a question.

He poked around in the breadbin and came out with a crust. 'This'll be fine.'

'There's a bit of mouldy cheese in the fridge, why don't you have that too?' I got a pack of stir-fry and some quick-boil rice. That little-boy-lost act of his was a real pain sometimes.

'So,' I said, 'why the worry? Don't tell me they've all escaped and you thought I'd been kidnapped. How many did you net?'

'You know I can't . . . '

'Talk about that,' I finished. 'Yes. I know, you never can. Nice you got the tape though.'

He scowled. 'All right, you did well,' he said in that grudging tone people use when they hate to admit a thing. 'Is that what you wanted to hear?'

'No,' I snapped, 'it isn't. What I want is to hear that there's been some butt-kicking going on. I want to hear CID are running intelligence tests before they take on new hands. I want to have someone tell Grace that Lund didn't kill Andy and then to apologise for all the shit they handed her. That's what I want, OK.'

He pinked up prettily. 'It's in hand.'

'It'd better be,' I said darkly, 'and before it hits the papers.' I looked at him. 'Did you get Mick the red?'

He shook his head.

'How about Martin? Anybody looking?'

'Yes. Anything else?'

'You could get the coffee started.'

He got busy. I dished up. 'So,' I said, 'things are kind of hectic, huh?'

'So-so. Stir-fry's good.'

'I'm still waiting to hear why you dropped by. It wasn't just the free lunch or you wouldn't be acting so guilty.'

'I have a personal interest in your state of health,' he said. 'I worry when you don't answer the phone.'

'How sweet,' I said, 'maybe I should carry a bleeper, or get an ear tag so you can track me around.'

'Do that,' he snapped.

By and by we stopped sulking at each other, finished up the coffee, and went down to Marcie's place. I wasn't too careful about the way I shoved Greg's rubbish into a bin-liner, the way I saw it he was lucky it didn't arrive in shreds. When I'd finished the chore I packed some things for Marcie and rode into town with Nicholls. He wanted to hang around and take me home but that kind of thing is claustrophobic.

Marcie's mother was up in the ward with Ben, he'd climbed into Marcie's lap and looked happy there. I put the suitcase by her locker and said I'd call by tomorrow. Marcie's mother jumped up and gave me a hug. I could feel myself get red and embarrassed, I never know what to do about things like that.

I did some shopping and walked back home again. This time it was Neil's car parked outside my door. He got out and watched me walk the last few yards. I grinned at him and said, 'Hi, how come you're slumming again?'

'I thought about going for a drive.'

'Where?'

'Mystery tour.'

'I don't think I can do that,' I said, 'I need to dump this stuff and I'm expecting someone round tonight.'

He opened the passenger door and put a hand casually in his pocket. 'Get in,' he said pleasantly.

'Uh – no, I can't do that Neil, I told you I have someone coming round, if I'm not here he'll raise a rumpus. Some other time . . . tomorrow maybe?'

'Today.'

Ever so slowly his hand came out of the pocket. I stared

at the gun in disbelief.

'Stop fooling around, Neil, somebody might think it's real.'

'They'd be right,' he said. 'Get in.'

I backed off. 'Uh-uh.' The gun levelled at my belly-button. Perspiration spurted in my armpits. 'OK,' I said, 'as practical jokes go you've got a winner. Now will you put that thing away.'

He tapped the long metal nose. 'This is a silencer. I can fire and leave you on the pavement and the neighbours won't hear a thing. Is that what you want or shall you get in the car?'

I moved my hands helplessly. 'Neil, I don't understand, what is this?' His finger tightened, 'OK, OK, I'll get in.' He slammed the door on me and then walked round the front, watching all the while. Shit, what was wrong with him?

For a couple of seconds after he got in he just sat there staring out, then he put the gun in his pocket and accelerated hard enough to slam me back into the cushions. I dumped the carrier bag off my lap and fastened the seat-belt.

'It'd be a real help to know what this is all about,' I said.

'It's about not taking advice, you walked on to a battle-field and now you get hurt.' We swung on to the bypass and he took his eyes off the road for a second. 'You shouldn't have taken a hand in it.'

I shook my head. He was a stranger; I'd known him most of my life and now I didn't know him at all. 'We're on opposite sides? I don't believe this.'

'Growing up in Bramfield doesn't make me British. My father came from Belfast. So did my grandfather, come to that, but the old fool changed sides.' He smiled at me. 'No one else knows about that, and you won't be telling.'

And how did he know that? The answer stared back at me with big hollow eyes. I wasn't supposed to live long enough to pass on the news. I paid attention to the road. Traffic was light, there wouldn't be any jams to slow us down. We passed a couple of lorries. 'So,' I said, trying to sound worry free. 'Tell me more about your father. Everyone believed your mother was a single girl.'

'So she was. They would have married if he'd lived long enough.' He looked sideways again. 'He was shot in the back by a Paisleyite.'

'She told you that?'

'Every day until she died.'

We took the M62 turn-off and headed east. Traffic was heavier now, straddling all three lanes, but it wouldn't be a help. Neil hung in the fast track and kept to the speed limit. It looked like he had every angle covered.

I examined a couple of options but they both fell down without a fight. Central-locking put a stop to leaping out, which was probably good, because if I did that I wouldn't survive the fall, and the second option would probably be just as fatal; it meant grabbing the wheel so we did some fancy swerves, but that way I'd probably not just kill the two of us, there'd be a big enough pile-up to kill twenty or more and I'd never get into heaven at all.

The palms of my hands were sweating. I rubbed them down the side of my jeans. 'It won't help any,' I said, 'but I'm sorry about your father.' He didn't answer.

I went back to looking out the window.

'People will start looking for me,' I said, 'the friend I was expecting to drop by tonight is Detective Sergeant Nicholls. If I'm not around he'll know something's happened.'

'He won't know what,' Neil said, 'and he won't know where to look. He'll probably think you forgot all about him, it wouldn't be the first time you weren't home when he called, would it? A strong-minded, independent woman like yourself pleases herself.'

'A lot of people could have seen me get in your car.'

'They could,' he agreed. 'Not likely though, is it? I didn't see anyone around.' He ran his hand up my thigh and left it there. I stiffened. 'We could have had a lot of pleasure, you and I, if you'd left things alone.' I shoved his hand away.

'Leaving things alone wasn't an option, I had to find out what happened to Andy.'

'And now you know.'

'I don't know who killed him.'

He smiled, a thin tight movement of his lips and my scalp prickled. Neil had done it. Oh shit, and I'd told him about Annie. If I hadn't blabbed she'd be alive.

Culpability made my eyes sting.

His eyes slid round calculatingly. 'Playing guessing games again?'

'Not any more, I just got all the answers. Why did you kill Annie, because she saw the guns?'

'Yes.'

'Andy too?'

'I didn't enjoy it.'

'I bet you didn't,' I said bitterly. I sat quietly for a while, trying not to let him see I was shaking. 'What are you going to do with me?'

Silly question.

He shook his head. 'If it's any comfort I'll try to make it quick, I don't like hurting women.'

'Shit, Neil, I thought we were friends?'

His forehead puckered, he rubbed at it irritably and didn't answer. When I got out of this, *if* I got out of this . . .

How the hell was I *going* to get out of this?

'How'd you get away last night?' I said conversationally.

'I wasn't there, I had other business to attend to.' He smiled again. 'In case you were wondering, Mick is safe home in Derry, I put him on the plane myself.'

'So you're the bagman,' I said. 'Cresswell thinks you screwed up.'

'That so?'

'Judas! Why did you get into this shit, Neil? Damn it you're as English as I am.'

'No I'm not. You've never been to Derry have you, Leah?'

'No.'

'I have. Twice every year since I was six; two weeks with

my mother's family, two weeks with my father's, that's long enough to learn the cause is just.'

'The killing isn't.'

He glanced at me flatly. 'It's a war, Leah, not a sodding game.' He changed lanes smoothly, moving the Porsche towards the A63 and South Cave, turning off when we got there on to minor roads, cutting speed for a run of bends. Panic nibbled; nobody can outrun a gun.

I dried off my palms again and concentrated.

What would Magnum do? . . . Who the hell cared what Magnum'd do, I wasn't some American hero, I was me, Leah Hunter, about to join the ghost squad.

I watched the road. A left turn, two swinging bends, slow down for a T-junction, Howdendyke right, Deddyke left. He turned the wheel anticlockwise and I tried to forget phonetics; what's in a name?

A dip down, a swinging curve right, the finger of a jetty reaching out into the Humber and the derrick of a crane, part hidden by an ageing corrugated building, liver-spotted with rust. A dozen seagulls took time out on the roof but apart from them the place was deserted. The road ran on, paralleling the river, but we bumped down a dirt track past the back of the warehouse and stopped close up to a side door. The revolver came back in Neil's hand. He waved it a little.

'Out.'

'Who's arguing?' I said.

I stepped in through a narrow door and found myself among crates and stacked pallets, most of the crates empty, a narrow path between them making the leg of a T with a wider aisle.

He gave me a push and slammed the door, and I knew this was where he meant me to die.

CHAPTER TWENTY-NINE

For a couple of minutes my brain froze up. He prodded and I went forward obediently, detached, viewing it all from a great height, watching this idiot woman ambling along on a gentle death walk. I knew I should do something about it but getting back in control wasn't all that easy; it'd happened to me before, that feeling of dissociation. I'd been ten and hanging on to a scrappy bit of scrub part way down an old quarry. Letting go and being dead had both meant the same thing. I'd been shit scared then too.

God! it was so sick-making walking along like that, such compliance made me angry enough to spit. I connected up again, moving along nicely and boiling up with rage. I was in a broad aisle with crates and boxes on either side, some stacked more than head-height. Down by the bottom wall a fork-lift truck stood like a skeletal moon machine and I wondered how the damn things worked; one thing was for sure, next time I saw Charlie I'd get to know the neat trick of hot-wiring an engine.

I kept up the same pace, thinking how thirty seconds' distraction might buy enough time to slide between stacks and play cat and mouse. A gap came up on the right. I staggered a little, put both hands to my head, walked on, swayed gently, and crumpled at his feet.

Every gamble carries a risk, he could have shot me then and there; what I banked on was him wanting the added kick of having me know it was going to happen.

220

He nudged me with his foot. 'Get up. It won't work, I've seen all the dodges before.' He nudged a bit harder. Judas! if he kicked I'd have to give up. Instead he swore, bent down and began to roll me over; I buried both hands in his hair and twisted savagely. He went off balance. From the way he cursed I think I near broke his neck. Before he hit the floor I was up and through the gap. I sped across the next aisle and hunkered behind a pile of crates, then I stopped breathing and listened. A minute went by before I heard his feet shifting as he tried to work out which way I'd gone.

Then his voice came, friendly as a snake's. 'Leah, don't make it hard. I didn't want any of this to happen, you know that. Give up now, there's only one way out and I have the key.' He was right on the other side of the crate stack. I stayed quiet. Fear built up, the urge to run was hard to fight. He moved away and I relaxed. 'I know just where you are, Leah, it's only a matter of time now.'

A difference in the sound of his feet . . . he was moving along a gap of his own, when he came out the other end he'd see me. My palms were wet again, sticky with sweat.

I edged quietly back the way I'd come. I heard his feet in the aisle I was heading for. Shit, he'd changed his direction. I turned tack and sprinted diagonally over the next aisle looking for a way through. Most of the stuff on this side was stacked in a solid wall and I couldn't find a gap.

'I can hear you, Leah . . . don't run away from me . . . just stay still and let's talk . . . ' He was crooning, caressing the words the way he would if he were making love. 'I have to kill you now, Leah . . . it's part of the game.'

I ran on and heard him come out behind me. No more need to be quiet then. I put on a frantic spurt, and dived for a gap. Something hot and hard hit me in the left side. Just under my ribcage, pain flared like a rocket and I fell on my face, banging into the boxes. Somehow I got myself up, sobbing as I moved, teeth grinding with the pain of it. My shirt and pants were warmly wet, I felt it trickle down over my thigh, tickle the side of my knee. The game was over.

221

Game? What game? Oh shit . . . how much blood was I losing? I felt dizzy and didn't know if it was blood loss or fright that caused it. The pain was part of me, spreading and heating up, and I couldn't run any more. I had to find a place to make a stand. Neil came after me lazily, knowing I couldn't move fast, couldn't climb, couldn't fight, he didn't need to hurry, finishing me off would be easy peasy. I turned down a narrow walkway and almost fell, the jolt setting up fresh waves of pain, but the hand I put out for balance found itself a weapon.

I stared dully at the crowbar laid across a half-opened crate; when I lifted it, it weighed a ton. I didn't have the energy. Little grey spots danced around my eyes. I bit my teeth together and took the metal bar's weight on my shoulder. All the while I kept hearing strange, gasping noises, then realised they came from me.

The crates here were stacked two deep and two high, the tops eighteen inches above my head; here and there a crate was missing. I could hear Neil on the other side of them, not level with me yet but getting closer, whistling as he came.

Two missing crates made a square cave. Three empty pallets made its floor.

Hunter's last stand.

I passed the gap and gave him a longer blood trail to follow; no sense letting him know where I was waiting. Three crates down I doubled back.

I stood weakly in my chosen battlefield, the urge to slide down and sleep was almost irresistible. Holding the crowbar ready increased the pain. I got the curled end, with its two sharp, flat teeth, uppermost. I'd have to use it two-handed, fast enough to take him by surprise and hard enough to only need one try.

I didn't know if I could do that.

The whistling came close.

I took the bar in both hands. A chill seeped through me. I wanted to whimper like some hurt animal but if I did I'd be dead. I leaned back against the crates, trying to take in some extra oxygen, I had to aim high, I couldn't be squeamish.

My ears made whistling, squeaking noises, my knees shook. *I didn't want to do this.* I lifted the bar, elbows bent, tipping it back a little. I was playing cricket with my brother, Neil's head was the ball. *Hit it square, send it for a six.* I stepped into the swing just the way I remembered, his face pulped and vanished and we both screamed together.

I don't remember much after that, but I must have got the door key from Neil's pocket, and the keys to the Porsche, because I rang for help from his car phone before I passed out on the front seat. What I didn't do was take his gun away, but it didn't matter; the sharp butterfly of bone behind his nose had pushed up into his brain. I don't feel proud of that, I just feel sorry that the Neil I'd known and liked all those years had never really been there at all.

When I woke up in hospital Nicholls was holding my hand and that was really nice. I grinned at him as best I could and went to sleep again.